Enjoy the a...
Greg Smith
Dec. 2013

HOLY LOTTO

A Novel By

Greg Smith

*Thanks Judy,
Enjoy + Have
a Merry Christmas
Greg*

Enjoy the Adventure!
Jim Smith
Dec. 2013

Our goal in life should be to get to Heaven.

Dedicated to my brother Derek

    A few days before my book was to be readied for e-book release, my brother passed away suddenly. It was a devastating shock to us all. He had always been my mentor, my teacher, my protector, my friend, my teammate and at times my most ardent competitor. I will miss him dearly.
    Bro enjoyed reading books by some very famous suspense writers and before his passing he got to read this book in its nearly completed form. Though my genre is somewhat different from his norm, he said he really enjoyed it and wandered where I was in getting it published. Though he will not get to see it down here, I feel he will be reading the finished product on his e-reader in heaven.
    God Bless you Bro. I know that unlike in the story, your spirit will not come to visit us, because you are at peace with where you are, even though a lot of us miss you dearly down here.

This novel is a fictitious work. Most of the places do not exist, some do. I even had the pleasure of visiting some of them. To my knowledge, no characters or incidents exist.

Createspace, Version 3

Copyright © 2012 Greg Smith All Rights and terms reserved.

No part of this book may be reproduced or retransmitted in any form or by any means without the written permission of the author.

eBook optimization and format: eBook-Dynamics.com

cover design: eBook-Dynamics.com

Acknowledgements

I would be amiss if I didn't thank my wife Linda for allowing me the time to chase my dreams in life.

To Bobbi Madry, who taught me how to put my ideas on paper in such a way that someone would want to read them.

To the people and bowlers of Toledo, Ohio, for allowing me to use their fine city as a backdrop for my story. I do actually have family there and visit from time to time.

Holy Lotto

01 † 07 † 10 † 26 † 42 † 45

Chapter One

But for the mechanical tick, tick, tick of the antique clock on the mahogany clad wall, the entire courtroom sat in breathless silence. Eyes darted anxiously between Judge Hardman and the defendant Clinton Hess. Ears strained to hear the words they wanted to hear. Hearts feared and prayed they wouldn't hear the words they might. It seemed even the heating system knew better than to interrupt the judge's deliberations or the silent vigil most of us found ourselves in, because it never made a sound.

Crowded as it was, nearly everyone had come to witness the dirtbag, Hess, receive the death penalty...or at the very least a life sentence for murdering Derek Sims and raping his wife, Kelly. At this very moment, however, the State's so-called bullet-proof case teetered in extreme peril. A tagging error, which to me and probably every other non-lawyer seemed totally insignificant, had Judge Charles Hardman seriously contemplating the unthinkable, the defense's motion of a mistrial.

The grounds under which the motion had been made didn't seem to make any sense. Unfortunately, I'd learned during nearly two excruciating weeks of coming to this courtroom that the insidious rules of law seldom did, unless it was just Hardman's personal interpretations or manipulations of them that didn't.

Though meek in stature, the slight pale man, graying, wrinkled and old, ruled over his courtroom with the zest of a youthful tyrant. Physically, he couldn't have stood more than five foot five. The way he sat high behind his bench clad in a shiny black robe, you'd have thought he had to be over six feet tall.

None of us who had come regularly to this seeming fiasco thus far knew who he thought he was kidding. We had all watched in humor as he used some sort of make shift ladder at the beginning and end of every session to get into or out of his towering pedestal.

Right now, though, none of us were laughing. He held a death grip on our universe. We sat petrified, scared to death by the words he might say, praying to God we'd hear the words he should say.

Hardman's extreme behavior during the trial thus far was why we were so concerned. He had not only taken great pains to insure that the accused, Hess, was deemed innocent until proven guilty, but seemed to have gone so far as to treat the victim and witnesses almost like liars, even when proven otherwise. As such, he seemed to be every convict's wet dream and a perfect example of what was wrong with American justice today.

Hess was guilty, plain and simple. The question of guilt was non-existent. Except for a confession, the evidence was not only overwhelming, but incontrovertible. Eight days of laborious courtroom drama had produced motive, Hess's prints and DNA both at the crime scene and on the recovered murder weapon. Furthermore, there was the added bonus that Kelly Sims, being blind, had identified Hess's voice from a police line-up.

Up until just minutes earlier, we had simply been waiting for the jurors to be sent away to deliberate on Hess's fate. At this point however, the question wasn't whether they would render a conviction. It was whether they would even be given the chance.

At today's inception, the common belief was the calling of witnesses would likely conclude by day's end. The State's case was expected to wrap up this morning with the testimony of one final witness.

By District Attorney Brad Anderson's calculations, the Defense's side of the trial would take less than a day. He believed that Clinton Hess had no chance of proving any degree of innocence. The preponderance of evidence was just too incriminating and substantial to be rebutted or contradicted to any degree. Leaving a day for Final Arguments and Judge's Instructions, the jury could be in deliberations as early as tomorrow's end.

To us spectators, we figured the best Hess could hope for was to elude the death penalty. Character witnesses weren't exactly standing in line to tell what a good upstanding bastard he was. What friends he had tended to stay away from courtrooms and police like the plague.

During prior testimony by police officers and other Crime Scene Analysts, an aluminum bat had been entered into evidence with Hess's prints and Derek's hair and blood on it. The Coroner had taken the stand to confirm it to be the murder weapon. He also concluded that due to the damage done to his inner ear by the wielded bat that nobody so severely wounded could have been able to protect himself or anyone else during the ensuing melee.

Patrick Reader, a thirteen year old youth from our church, was the real hero, if any could be considered in such a case. It was because of him that police had picked up Hess after Derek's death. Upon procuring

Hess's prints via a soda can, they were able to easily match his prints to those found at the crime scene.

Warrants and ignorance took care of the rest. Hess was too stupid to get rid of the bat he'd used in the murder. The police found it tucked neatly away in the trunk of his vehicle wrapped in an old t-shirt. Though it had been wiped off, traces of Derek's blood were recovered by examiners using some kind of sophisticated equipment.

Patrick testified on the stand that Clinton Hess had approached him along with some of his friends with drugs only a couple of days prior to the murder. He had reported the incident directly to Derek, his youth group leader at church. He went on to tell how Derek had become enraged and had Patrick go with him to locate this man. At that point, Patrick pointed out to the court that the man he'd identified to Derek as the drug dealer was Clinton Hess.

"After I pointed him out, Mr. Sims told me to go wait in his car. I started to leave, but I wanted to see what he was going to do. I found a place to watch from and waited. Mr. Sims walked up to that guy," stopping to point at Hess again, "as if he was just going to walk past him. But when Mr. Sims got close though, he grabbed the guy and threw him up against the nearby building where he searched him for weapons. Mr. Sims found a gun hidden inside the guy's outer shirt. He pocketed the weapon before screaming at the guy and banging him against the building a couple more times. I couldn't make out what was being said from where I was, but I could tell Mr. Sims was really mad. And that guy," he stopped and pointed again, "he looked like he was going to cry or something as Mr. Sims kept him pinned against the wall."

Patrick then said, "Before Mr. Sims let go of the guy, he hit him in the gut, then belted him a good one in the mouth. After that, Mr. Sims spun the guy around and kicked him in the butt. As the guy scurried away, I heard Mr. Sims shout that he better never ever see him around here again. He said something else too, but I couldn't make out what it was."

Anderson then asked, "Patrick, what happened to the gun?"

"I never saw it again. I'd been watching from the corner of a nearby building. There was a scraggly bush there that I stood behind. When the guy ran away, I ran to wait in the car like Mr. Sims told me to do. I don't think he ever knew I watched the whole thing."

"Is there anything else?" Anderson asked.

"Yeah, one thing. Mr. Sims was the nicest guy I ever met and Mrs. Sims, well...she is a really nice lady and used to make us cookies and..." He paused.

"Yes?" Anderson asked, wondering if Patrick was finished.

"They were just trying to give kids like me a better chance to make it. Why did that man have to go and kill Mr. Sims?"

"MMMMotion to strike, Your Honor!" Jajuan Coker, Hess's slick tongued Defense Attorney was caught off guard and couldn't get out of his seat fast enough. I thought he was going to swallow his tongue the way he stammered to get the words out.

It would have been funny to watch if not for the seriousness of the situation. Though the judge upheld the objection, the boy's words clearly made it to the jurors' ears. Their faces relayed the message that his words would not be forgotten.

Chapter Two

As for me, I certainly understood Patrick Readers' frustration. I had tangled with Judge Hardman myself and was on a short leash with him and doing my best to control my contemptible outrage at his impassive attitude towards the victim during the whole ordeal. He'd already kicked me out of the courtroom once and reprimanded me twice. In no uncertain terms, he'd let me know after the expulsion two days ago during Coker's cross-examination of Kelly that there would be no further warnings.

Kelly, herself, had already spent two exasperating days on the witness stand either answering or attempting to answer questions asked by the prosecution. During their questioning it seemed like every time a question was asked or Kelly began to respond, Coker found a new way to object.

I had to admit Coker was creative, but it was puzzling how Hardman seemed content to let Coker have his way most of the time. Hardman would force Anderson to ask every question six different ways before he was satisfied with it. Then, every time Kelly began an answer, Coker would take issue with her words in some way.

I didn't know why the judge had such a hard on for the prosecution, but it was especially showing during Kelly's testimony for some reason. It seemed totally unprofessional as far as I was concerned and a lot of people commented about it outside the courtroom. Noting that some of those who were appalled were law students made me feel fairly certain it wasn't just my closeness to Kelly speaking.

Fortunately, Prosecuting Attorney Anderson had prepped Kelly well for the difficult testimony she was subjected to and like the trooper she was, she never got overly frazzled. Even so, the first day took forever as she tried answering Anderson's questions amid Coker's continual objections. I even began wondering if Anderson could ask Kelly her name without hearing an objection.

During the second day, Anderson changed his strategy somewhat to combat Coker's tactics. Instead of asking a lot of questions, he simply allowed Kelly to tell the court in her own words what had happened

Friday evening, March 14th of this year with only a little direction now and then. After the expected initial objections from Coker to get the question stated in just such a way that Hardman couldn't find a reason uphold the objection, Kelly finally began telling her story.

"We had gone to Cavetto's. It is...excuse me, was our favorite place for Italian food in the city. As always, it was busy and we had to wait, but that was alright. We didn't mind. We returned home at about 9:20 pm. A few minutes later, someone rang the doorbell. We were both in the bedroom changing into our lounging clothes. Derek went to answer the door while I finished changing. A moment later, I heard a thud and a muffled cry of pain from Derek."

"Was it normal for your husband to open the door without knowing who was there?" Anderson asked.

"We live in a fairly quiet neighborhood. Friends are always stopping by. So yes, it wasn't uncommon."

"So, your husband had innocently opened the door only to be knocked senseless by an intruder?" Anderson remarked.

"Objection! Sounds more like a statement than a question. Besides, it calls for speculation by the witness." Coker demanded.

"Sustained. Find another way to ask your question, Counselor." Hardman ordered.

"Yes Your Honor. Go on with your story Mrs. Sims." Anderson said, reverting to his original game plan.

"Hearing Derek's muffled cry, I hurried to investigate. When I entered the room, someone grabbed me, hit me in the face with his fist and threw me against the wall. Then he proceeded to beat and kick Derek. Every time I got up to try to help him, they would stop long enough to hit me and throw me against the wall again."

"Was there more than one person in the room?"

"Objection. Calls for speculation. The witness is blind. Five people could have been watching or participating. She cannot possibly say for certain how many people were in the room." Coker demanded.

"Sustained."

Rolling his eyes, Anderson said. "Go on Mrs. Sims."

"At first I wasn't sure how many people were involved, but after a couple of times of trying to get to Derek to help him, I realized it was just one man because whoever it was would have to stop his hitting and kicking long enough to hit me and throw me back against the wall. And then when he left the house afterward, I only heard one set of feet leave. So yes, he was alone."

"Did that person say anything during the attack?"

"He kept calling me a bitch and a slut."

"What else did he do?"

"Up to that point, he just kept yelling at us. It didn't make any sense. He didn't ask for money, he just screamed like a madman. Then, every time I got up to help, he would throw me across the room again and yell for me to stay there if I knew what was good for me. Then he'd go back to hitting Derek either with his feet or the bat."

"Do you remember anything else?"

"He shouted at Derek that he was going to F his black bitch real good one last time just for him."

"Did he say F or did he use the F-word?"

"He's an animal. Of course he used the F-word."

At that point, Coker naturally jumped up and objected, to which Hardman quickly upheld his objection before instructing the jury to disregard Kelly's words. Hardman then reprimanded Kelly for editorializing.

Shaking his head in disbelief, Anderson asked. "About how many times did this person throw you against the wall before he wrapped your wrists with duct tape?"

"Objection. There is no way she can say what her hands were bound with." Coker chided in, sounding disgusted.

Before Hardman could rebuke him, Anderson said. "I'll withdraw the question. Mrs. Sims, what happened next?"

"After eight, maybe ten times of trying to get to Derek, the monster hit me again. But that time, instead of pushing me against the wall, he grabbed my hands when I fell on the floor and wrapped my wrists together with some kind of tape. Then, he picked me up and shoved me back against the wall again."

"And every time he swore at you and your husband?"

"Yes. I couldn't understand how anyone could be so hateful to someone they'd never met before. Derek hadn't told me about any confrontation with a drug dealer."

"Then what happened?"

"It took me longer to get up with my hands taped together as they were, but I knew Derek desperately needed my help. When I got to my feet I ran at them again. That was when the man threw me on the floor. After securing my hands to something above my head using more tape, the animal raped me in front of Derek. All the while he was raping me, he taunted Derek with what he was doing to me. Then, shortly after that, he killed Derek. I will never forget the voice of the low life piece of trash who murdered my husband as long as I live."

Coker had objected vehemently during all the other State's attempts at voice identification. The judge had upheld all of them, seeming to treat expert testimony and precedent with contempt. This time was different. For some reason, Coker didn't object. Little did we know why.

Chapter Three

After Anderson finished his questioning of Kelly, the Defense took its turn. I knew Coker would try poking holes in Kelly's testimony. For the life of me, I couldn't imagine how he could. To me, it was all so cut and dry. As for her character, she was the nicest person I'd ever known. And I'd known her forever. She was also the victim. I didn't expect him to try anything underhanded. Obviously, I didn't know Coker.

When Coker stood up from his table, he slowly looked around the courtroom. Dressed in his expensive three piece navy suit, he was saying look at me. I'm about to begin. At six foot tall, he was athletically built and handsome. His shaven black head shone in the court's lighting. He probably had his pick of women outside the courtroom, presuming he wasn't married. I hadn't noticed, cared, or bothered looking to see if he wore a wedding ring.

When he finally spoke, I was perplexed by the questions that spewed from his mouth. After several seemingly mindless questions, his tactics changed and became vividly clear. He seemed to actually be trying to win the case by placing the blame of Derek's death on Kelly. I couldn't believe it.

About the tenth question in, he asked. "Just how is it, Mrs. Sims, that you were able to pick Clinton Hess's voice out of a line up?"

"As I testified earlier, I will never forget that voice as long as I live."

"Surely Mrs. Sims, you don't expect the court to believe that you can dissimulate one voice over another after hearing it just one time?"

"I'm blind, not deaf. My hearing is as acute as your eye sight. Besides, I heard him say more than just one thing one time. The experts didn't seem surprised by it during their testimony." Kelly responded.

"I ask the court to strike the witness's last comment and instruct the witness to answer the questions that are asked and not elaborate." Coker demanded.

"So noted. The jury will disregard the witness's last statement. Mrs. Sims, only answer the question that is asked. Do not expound on your answers." Hardman ordered.

Kelly apologized even though none of us thought she should have. The look on her face said she didn't really think so either.

"Isn't it more likely that you supposedly recognized this voice because you knew Clinton Hess outside the marriage?" Coker demanded, curling two fingers in the air from both hands to mimic quotation marks before and after the word supposedly.

My jaw dropped at hearing the accusation. I sure as heck didn't see that one coming. With one offhanded question, he was trying to explain away the rape charges, Hess's prints and the DNA evidence at their home. What a bastard! I sat gripping the bench in front of me as fury burned through my veins.

Dad put his arm around me. "Maybe we should wait outside, Son."

I heard his words, but I couldn't have left if I'd wanted to. If I'd have let go of the bench right then, I would have gone after Coker.

"What? No Sir. You are no gentleman and an idiot for asking such a question. I had never met the bastard who killed my husband!" Kelly sniped back.

"Your Honor!" Coker demanded.

"Good for you Kelly." I wanted to shout.

"I know. No adlibbing, but the answer remains that I had never met that piece of trash." Kelly stated before the judge could reprimand her further.

Instead of saying anything, Hardman cleared his throat to show his disdain. He then informed the jury to disregard her remark concerning the gentleman and idiot.

I snickered to myself. Yeah, you can always forget to hear what you just heard. How stupid is that?

Then Coker asked Kelly the unthinkable. "Isn't it possible that the semen found in you after your husband's death was from an encounter with Clinton Hess earlier in the day and that someone else in fact, possibly even you killed your husband?"

My knuckles were turning white, gripping the seat in front of me. If I ever met that S.O.B. outside of court, he would regret ever asking that question.

I could tell Kelly couldn't believe her ears. She just sat there trying not to cry, wanting to be strong through this for Derek. After a moment, she composed herself enough to answer. "M...My husband is the only man I ever slept or had sex with. And I had never met Clinton Hess in my life." She answered quite sternly.

"Or...couldn't it be true Mrs. Sims that because you are black and your husband was white that you yearned for companionship of your own kind? That you had been carrying on an elicit affair with Clinton Hess and that you really are and I quote from your own testimony just a black bitch like you say you were being called?"

That was it. I jumped to my feet with my mouth already in gear. "What the hell, Hardman? Are you going to let that bastard question her like that? She's the victim in this not that piece of shit!" I yelled, pointing at Hess.

Judge Hardman slammed his gavel to the bench and shouted. "Bailiff remove that man from the courtroom."

"Christ Anderson, aren't you even going raise an objection? You sure as hell wouldn't let him call your wife or daughter a bitch!"

People around me tried to quiet me, but my mouth had already said plenty. The gavel dropped again and two big burley police officers grabbed me and half escorted, half carried me to a locked room on another floor where I sat for the remainder of the day, fuming at the questions that my mind invented that Coker hopefully never asked.

An hour after court was dismissed for the day, Hardman had me brought to his chambers in cuffs. He admonished me severely for twenty minutes before finishing with, "If I so much as see your lips move, you will be seeing the inside of a jail cell for a month. Am I clear?"

"Perfect! Screw the innocent and free all the frigging murderers." I mumbled to myself.

"What was that?" He scowled.

"Perfectly, Your Honor." I said, nodding my head.

As I walked to my car, I called Dad on my cell to see what I'd missed. He wouldn't tell me anything about the remainder of Kelly's cross other than it was over. He was afraid I might go off again. He was probably right.

When Brad Anderson called me later that evening, I figured he was going to ream me out again. But he didn't. Instead he asked, "How are you doing, Mr. Maxwell? Those were horrific questions that Coker asked."

"You think?"

He chuckled. "Yeah, I think. I just wanted you to know that even though I certainly understand your frustrations today, my staff and I had prepared Kelly for just such tactics by Coker. He's a real piece of work, but he's effective."

"That's not what I'd call it."

"Probably not. I'll have to admit, your outburst gave Kelly a much needed moment to compose herself today. It worked in our favor this time, but please...please keep control of yourself in court from here on out. If need be, wait outside for Kelly's sake. We really do have this quite under control."

"I'll try. How did it go after I was ejected?"

"Kelly was a real trooper. Coker's misdirection hit a brick wall because of her answers. By the way, did anyone tell you Kelly's response to Coker's question?"

"No. Dad wouldn't talk to me about it."

Anderson chuckled at hearing what I said before going on. "After you were ejected, Kelly said and I quote, 'I haven't seen people by the color of their skin for nearly forty years. In many ways my blindness has not only been a blessing, but it has opened my eyes to see what you will never see.'

"To Coker's dismay, he asked. 'And what is that?'

'For one thing, I can tell that you are a black man by the way you lazily enunciate certain words and by the way you pose your questions. Like Clinton Hess, you see the world tarnished by the color of your skin instead of embracing it.'

'Your Honor!' Coker demanded, pleading to the judge for help to get away from the mistake he'd made.'

"For the first time during the trial, Hardman rebuked him, saying 'You're the one who asked the question, Counselor.'

"Seeing that Hardman was on her side for a change, Kelly continued, 'Besides, if he's all the bigger you black men are, I'm glad I married a white man.'

"The courtroom erupted in laughter at Coker and Hess. Even Hardman had to chuckle before pounding his gavel on the bench to bring order back to the courtroom. Once he succeeded, Coker's line of questioning tanked."

Chapter Four

In comparison to the day prior's fireworks, yesterday's courtroom drama had been innocuously boring. What testimony was given had been technical in nature, time consuming and with not much in the way of substance. It did, however, lay the groundwork for today's expected finale for the prosecution and quite possibly all testimony.

Up to this point in the trial, Patrick Reader's testimony had given Hess motive. Bringing his own duct tape and weapon to the crime constituted premeditation. Forcing Derek to watch the rape of his wife before killing him was just plain vicious. By all that was right Hess certainly deserved and would likely receive the death penalty.

The level of drama picked up significantly first thing as Marcus White walked to the witness stand. White was the Forensic Specialist who had collected the most incriminating evidence of all; the duct tape with Hess's DNA and prints along with Derek's blood and hair on it. Unfortunately, his testimony came to a screeching halt within minutes of being sworn in. Mostly but not totally because of Hardman, White's evidence led to nowhere good.

From his position behind the lectern, Anderson led White through initial questioning to inform the jury who he was, what he was and what his job had been concerning this particular case. After confirming for the court that he had been called to the crime scene in question, White was asked to tell what he had found during his examination of the area and specifically the body.

Kelly squeezed my hand at hearing Derek being referred to as the body. I could tell it was tearing her apart. It was me too.

Referring to his notes periodically, he answered Anderson's question.

"Responding to a call from dispatch, I arrived at 4245 Treadwell at 9:58 PM. I was directed to the murder scene, which was in the living room located just inside the front door. The body of Mr. Sims, a Caucasian male in his mid to late fifty's was lying on the floor covered in blood. The officer in charge, Sergeant Ames, informed me that the victim's wife was en route to St. Luke's accompanied by a female officer and that someone from our unit would meet her at the hospital to retrieve DNA evidence."

"Upon preliminary observations, the deceased suffered multiple abrasions about his head and upper body consistent with having been beaten severely by someone wielding a blunt object. No weapons were found at the crime scene. His hands had been wrapped in duct tape behind his back."

White went on to explain how he had carefully cut the tape from Derek's wrists and taken it along with other evidence back to his office to be tested for finger prints and anything else that could prove useful to the case.

"Did you perform these tasks yourself or did someone else analyze the evidence for you?" Anderson asked.

"Yes and no. Although Toledo has its own crime lab to test for finger prints and trace, we depend on the Lucas County Coroner's office to do our DNA testing. We don't have the capability to do that work in our lab." White answered.

Asking for permission from the judge to approach the witness and receiving it, Anderson walked to and handed the evidence container he held in his hand to White. "Is this part of the evidence you collected from the crime scene?"

White took the brown paper bag from Anderson and inspected it. "It has my ticket and signature on it. Yes." He answered.

"Can you tell the court what is in the bag and its importance to this case?"

Looking at the tag, White answered. "According to the tag, it contains the duct tape that restrained the victim's wrists on the night of March 14 of this year. Upon testing it, we found finger prints from the accused, Clinton Hess. When we sent it to the coroner's office, they found DNA consistent with both the victim, Mr. Sims, and the accused."

"Counselor, would you mind showing the court your supposed evidence." Hardman said. His voice showing disdain for criminal science within his courtroom.

Anderson nodded for White to remove the tape from the bag.

White took a pair of tweezers from his jacket pocket so as not to contaminate the evidence. After carefully opening the exhibit bag, however, a steely look came over his face. He paused a moment and coughed to clear his choked up throat before speaking. "There seems to be a problem. This must be the wrong container."

Upon hearing White's answer, Anderson's eyes flew wide open. In disbelief he stood in shock.

I had no idea what was going through his mind, but I sure as hell knew what was going through mine, nothing repeatable.

In an attempt to move things along, White held up the contents, which turned out to be a broken shard of glass, along with its tag to show Anderson that what was in the bag was in fact another exhibit belonging to the same case, but not the duct tape that the outside tag said it should have been.

Anderson finally collected himself and quickly asked for a side bar. While there, I overheard Anderson explain the situation to the judge and ask for a recess to get the proper evidence to court. He also asked for the jury to be removed from the courtroom until the matter could be resolved.

Hardman merely scoffed. I heard him say something to the effect, "This is my courtroom and I'll make those decisions, not you young man."

As soon as the two counselors returned to their tables, Coker stood and petitioned the court. "We demand a mistrial."

Instantly, the courtroom went into shock. Judge Hardman mashed his gavel to the bench, demanding silence. With not so much as a moment to consider the motion or Anderson's objection, Hardman said he'd wait to review the entire contents of the evidence container before making any ruling.

He then asked Anderson how long it would take to get all the evidence to the courtroom. Anderson answered that it would take at least thirty minutes. Taking a quick look at the clock, Hardman recessed the courtroom for an early lunch, but not before instructing the jury not to discuss any details concerning the case amongst themselves.

That certainly didn't keep any of us from doing so. Hardman had been so pro-Defense the whole blessed trial and now with his contemptible attitude concerning the scientific evidence, we re-entered the courtroom after a nervous lunch on pins and needles.

A large cardboard box, presumably the entire evidence container, was already sitting atop Anderson's desk; guarded by the same two officers who had hauled me out of court a few days earlier.

Once Hardman entered the courtroom and the jurors were seated, against Anderson's second objection, the contents were emptied onto a table. The items were then inspected thoroughly and checked against the investigation's list and the exhibit list one by one. About half way through the inspection, the bag that should have contained the glass shard was found. Upon opening it, they found that it held the gray duct tape that should have been in the other bag. Someone had either goofed or there had been a deliberate switch-er-roo.

Upon that discovery, Coker again sprang out of his chair like a cat pouncing on a mouse. "The Defense demands a mistrial."

I couldn't figure out what the big deal was. Hell, there was plenty of other corroborating evidence to substantiate Hess's guilt if neither piece were used. Besides, it was all still there. As far as I was concerned, the State's case already seemed to be a slam dunk.

Not knowing the law probably makes me ignorant, I suppose, but I certainly know right from wrong. And I knew one thing for sure. Wherever this circus was going was anywhere but right.

Chapter Five

And then, there we sat in quiet horror watching Hardman high atop his make believe pedestal, twitching his eyebrows and twirling the gavel like a baton in his left hand. Between heartbeats we prayed justice wouldn't be lost. All quite aware that the fate of the entire proceedings rested solely on whatever decision he was about to make.

The way Hess sat there smirking at us made me wish there was a way to forego the proceedings altogether so I could deal with him myself.

Except for the ticking of the old clock that plodded along like a lone soldier marching time forward regardless of what was happening around him, we could have been inside a morgue for all the noise that echoed absently throughout the so-called halls of justice. The deafening silence was broken several times as Hardman stopped twirling his gavel long enough to write something down on his legal pad. With each sudden pause, a gasp for air would erupt as hearts skipped a beat then raced to catch up once his baton twirling began again.

Perched on the edge of our seats as we were, each monotonous tick that reverberated throughout the air became another dagger deepening the wound in our hearts, prolonging our agony. After several more minutes, the ticks seemed to grow fainter and farther apart as the anger started boiling the blood in my veins. As the sound of the ticks faded so did any hope of justice for Derek's death. Before long, the sound of the clock faded altogether. My mind withdrew entirely to relive the night of the attack of more than six months earlier.

As the TV in my house suddenly played in front of my eyes, my cell phone rang and I heard myself answer it. Knowing from the ring tone that it was either Derek or Kelly calling, I laughed and started to say something stupid. Kelly's frantic screams let me know instantly that something was horribly wrong.

Jumping to my feet, I ran for the garage and my truck. I dialed 911 on my cell as I impatiently waited for the door to open far enough to get under before putting the hammer down on the accelerator. When the dispatcher answered, I yelled, "Get someone to 4245 Treadwell.

Something awful has happened there... No, I don't know what! I'm not there yet. I'll be there in a few minutes. Just get somebody there, now!"

In another second, I relived the three minute drive down Heatherdowns as fast as the truck would go, blowing through two red lights in the process. A moment later, I was again sliding to a stop in their front yard.

From behind me, two squad cars slid to a stop behind me. I heard their shouts of "Stop!" as I jumped out of my truck and ran full speed into the house, not paying them any attention.

Inside I found Kelly sitting on the floor holding Derek's lifeless battered body. Both were covered in blood. I fell to my knees, gathering them both up in my arms. Tears ran down my face as the horrific picture unfurled itself one more time in my mind.

Hardman's words ended my trance and the silence, snapping me back to present reality. I'd missed the first words out of his mouth. "The motion of a mistrial is granted" were ones that I didn't miss.

Instantly, Kelly jumped to her feet. "What? He killed my husband. The evidence is all there. If you let him go, I hope he visits you at your home, you poor excuse for a judge." She screamed.

Her mother was beside her, clutching Kelly in her arms, trying to comfort her.

Hardman slammed his gavel to the bench. Whether it was to quiet the courtroom or hold Kelly in contempt, it was already too late. In the two seconds since his decision was voiced, the entire courtroom erupted in mass chaos. More than thirty other people stood and shouted derogatory remarks at him. I was among them.

Even the juror's faces looked like they wanted to shout something, but none had. Or if they had, I hadn't seen them.

As Hardman rapped his gavel on the bench again and again, I reached forward and grabbed Anderson's shoulder.

"How can he do that?" I shouted, to be heard over the jeers.

"Hardman is being an arrogant bastard. We tried to get this trial moved out of his court because he's such a hypocrite. Now he's paying us back. His decision is completely absurd. There's not a higher court anywhere who would concur with his assessment that the chain of evidence was broken and therefore constitutes double jeopardy. He has completely overstepped the law and destroyed the states case." Anderson answered in a huff.

"All the evidence was accounted for. The friggin bags aren't the evidence. It's what's inside them."

"Yeah and what really bites is that now none of the evidence we've collected can ever be used in court again. Hardman has really put the screws to us this time."

"You mean to tell me that murdering bastard is getting a free pass on everything?"

"It appears so." Anderson shamefully responded.

"Isn't that just damned perfect?"

With venomous eyes, I stood and watched as Hardman finally gave up trying to control the situation, electing instead to climb down from his throne and retreat to his chambers where he would most likely get out of the building, post haste.

When he was gone, my attention turned to Hess. As I glared, someone behind me shouted. "If anyone should be held in contempt, it's you Hardman." Even though the judge was gone, the shout was loud enough that Hardman had to have heard it.

As for Hess, if he'd been a little closer, I would have likely got to him and killed him on the spot. Fortunately for us both, he wasn't. Seeing Coker standing next to Hess made me think back to his molestation of Kelly on the stand. He was fortunate too.

My staunch glare left the two of them and went back to the jurors who had been dismissed but who still sat there in total disbelief. Like us, they had had to endure the entire farce. Seeing their faces, I could tell they were in as much shock as we were.

By now, everything I saw was tinged in red. It was all I could do not to go after Coker or Hess from where I was. The one thing holding me back was seeing Kelly in front of me. She was a shattered soul who needed to feel strength around her. I knew I needed to be part of it. Lord knows I didn't want to be.

Just like that, the murder conviction that should have been as satisfactory an ending as could be expected was forever lost. There would be no death penalty for this poor excuse of a human being. Hell, there wasn't even going to be a verdict.

Leaning forward to speak to Anderson again, I said. "What a frigging mess! The case was airtight. I hope you kept the evidence from the rape case separate."

He shook his head no and turned back away. Upon hearing that, my anger ratcheted back up another notch. My steely stare shot back to the people who were still too far away, Hess and Coker, his high dollar attorney.

Hess was a leach of a man in his late thirty's. Standing barely five foot tall, his one hundred eighty pound body was overweight and unkempt. On a good day, his greasy black hair and devilish eyes made me want to puke on him. His ill fitting pale blue suit only added to his hideous appearance. As alluded to during Coker's cross of Kelly, he was black. By the looks of him, he was less than half black. To me, he looked mostly Hispanic. From what I'd dug up about the dirt-bag, he was just a no account lowlife who sold drugs to kids for a living. How the hell he could afford a big time lawyer like Coker was quite another matter.

As for Kelly, who'd been blind since we were in our teens, not seeing Hess's arrogant attitude during the trial was probably the first time the lack of sight had ever been of any benefit to her. Not seeing his cocky looks back at her now was the second.

Red glows from the pits of hell burned from my eyes as I watched Hess stroll toward the courtroom exit a free man. Still wearing his arrogant smirk, he sought out our group one last time to gloat before exiting the room. His smug pious look melted quickly when he saw the fire in my eyes. He could tell that as far as I was concerned this wasn't over by a long shot. He could tell that the courts wouldn't have the final word if I had anything to say about it.

For years, I had fought to control feelings that had become part of me during Viet Nam, but suddenly they were back. And they were back with a vengeance. They were the feelings you felt when killing a human being was as easy as stepping on a bug. Hess could see it in my eyes now. We both knew it. The day would come when we would meet again if Anderson didn't remedy the situation first. With all the evidence lost, that seemed highly unlikely.

Several seconds passed before I could get control of my anger once Hess left the courtroom. Kelly's pulling on my arm helped snap me back to where I was needed.

"You okay, Jared?"

My silence had caught her attention. "Yeah Kiddo. I'll be fine. How about you?"

"Stunned."

"Yeah. Me too."

Quickly, I became involved with those around us, trying for the moment to stifle the vengeful thoughts that tried consuming me.

Moments later, District Attorney Anderson made his expected apology and proclamation that they'd get Hess somehow. It was a pledge that left Kelly, me and everyone else feeling quite betrayed and with even less belief in our wonderful judicial system.

The State had had Hess dead to rights. Now they'd lost it all in one fell swoop of the judge's gavel. Even the rape case that never got off the ground was lost.

After Anderson left, Kelly's parents, John and Helen, Derek's parents, Glen and Dorothy, and Kelly tried to console one another while trying to decide what to do next. Unfortunately, there wasn't much in the way of solace for anyone and the only thing left to do was go home.

Once we all came to the same conclusion, we got our coats on and walked through the empty halls of justice to an especially cold January day outside. The afternoon sun was as non-existent as the verdict that we would never get. Chill shot through our bodies, already numbed by what had transpired inside.

My parents climbed into their car accompanied by Derek's parents. I had brought Kelly and her parents in their car, so I was taking them home again. As we pulled away from the courthouse, I glared at the imposing gray building in the rearview mirror. I'd always thought justice should be pure and white. I suddenly realized why the statue of justice stood blindfolded. She wasn't necessarily blind. She just refused to see, as such, gray seemed a fitting color.

The short ride to the James household was a somber one; our goodbyes, cool ones. After walking Kelly and her parents to the door, I walked to my truck and drove away allowing the rage that still boiled inside me to rekindle. This issue would not be resolved until Hess was dead or in jail. I vowed that if left up to me, it would not be the latter.

Chapter Six

Several days after the trial, Kelly and I drove to the prosecutor's office to meet with Anderson, hopeful of new developments. Unfortunately, the trial's screwy conclusion and legal mumbo jumbo was pretty much all there was and all there was going to be.

We did get to ask the questions that needed to be asked, "How could the evidence become switched and what really makes any difference as long as it's all there?"

"As far as the switch, we just don't know. We went ahead and re-tested the evidence from both the evidence bags in question. The glass shard was from a vase that Hess had picked up and broken during the attack. It had his finger prints and DNA on it. Because it wasn't all that necessary to the case, we had decided not to introduce it to the court." Anderson answered.

"Why wasn't the evidence in clear bags so this kind of crap can't happen?" I asked.

"DNA and other types of evidence will mold inside a plastic bag and become worthless. That's why it's always kept in brown paper bags and cardboard boxes in cool dry places."

"So I suppose it's also normal not to look inside the bags before taking evidence to court?" I asked.

"It's the first time we've ever had a problem." Anderson admitted. "The technicians are extremely careful not to let such things happen. I can't even say with any certainty that it was them and not someone else who had access to the property room who screwed up."

"Is there any good news?" Kelly asked sarcastically, her face sporting a look that showed her disdain.

I knew her pain and her despair. Biting my lip, I tried holding my contempt.

"I wish I could be more optimistic, but I'd be lying if I were. Courts work under rules of law. At one time, they referred to them as rules of justice. I'd be hard pressed to call them that these days, especially with judges like Hardman behind the bench. Even those of us who have studied law for years don't understand how some judges get away with bending the rules the way they do. More times than not, it seems those same judges are just using their courtrooms to do whatever they damned well please.

"And you wonder why people don't trust the court system?" Kelly piped in.

"I never said I didn't understand it. That's why I joined the prosecutor's office shortly after passing the BAR. I had no intention of allowing dirt-bags like Hess to usurp my intelligence to screw the system and good people like you folks. I'm just sorry that sometimes the bad guys still win. There are just too many unscrupulous lawyers like Coker out there whose only concern is how much money they can make and how they can screw the system even further." Anderson said with a dejected shake of his head."

"Isn't that just peachy?" I said, letting go of some of the steam that was building inside.

"You can say that again." Anderson noted, obviously sensing my need to vent. "Hess is a moron. Sooner or later we will get him or his own kind will do the job for us. The Hispanic community already has it in for the guy. Besides the drugs he was pushing, Hess had started pushing child porn in their community. When people found out about that, they went looking for him with a vengeance. If they'd have found him, we wouldn't be having this conversation now. Their pushing him out of their part of town is why he ventured into your back yard."

"That brings up another question. How could a good for nothing like Hess afford a lawyer like Coker?" I asked.

"That is an issue we are trying to figure out as well. Unfortunately, lawyers don't have to divulge who pays them for taking a case." Anderson said sporting a questioning look.

"Maybe he received a stash of drugs that hasn't been paid for yet." I suggested.

"That is indeed a possibility. One that we are pursuing in an attempt to see if he leads us to incriminating evidence that we can nab him with to put him away for at least a while."

That was about the extent of news, good or bad. We left Anderson's office with no more hope than when we'd arrived and without an answer as to what the hell made the difference with the evidence, seeing as it was all still tagged even if it was in the wrong bags.

I drove Kelly home to her parents' little story and a half brick house since she still didn't feel safe living in her own home. Now that Hess was back on the streets, who knew how long it would be till she was ready to return home. Her husband had been killed, the trial had fallen apart and there was nothing good to look forward to. And what little we learned from Anderson did nothing to alleviate any of her concerns.

There wasn't anything I could say to help, especially since I felt pretty much the same.

A few days later, I spotted my neighbor Joe McFarland outside and went over for a chat. Everyone knew Joe Mac. Since he was a cop, I walked over to get his take on the whole ordeal. He was appalled, but already fully aware of everything that had occurred. He remarked that judges like Hardman made it all the more difficult for police to do their jobs. Mac couldn't allude as to how the evidence could have gotten switched, but told of rumors flying around the precinct that big money had fronted Hess.

"I'll leave you to derive your own conclusions from that." He said.

The inference was that money had possibly passed through the necessary hands to make the evidence change containers.

Mac said it wasn't all that uncustomary for Hardman, who hated forensics in his courtroom, to demand that evidence be shown to the court that wasn't already out in the open like a gun would be.

Mac agreed to let me know if he heard anything new concerning Hess, but after the trial Hess had moved out of the city since those who had associated with him before his arrest were having nothing to do with him after he got let out. They had probably been freaked out by all the cops nosing around trying to keep tabs on Hess. And since the Hispanic community had already been out gunning for him previous to the shooting, he choice of place to go seemed to be limited.

Chapter Seven

    Lying in bed with my head propped up on a couple of pillows, I was left thinking about the months since the trial's ridiculous ending and our meeting with Prosecuting Attorney Anderson. The first anniversary of Derek's death quietly passed and the winter snows had melted away leaving hints of green popping up everywhere. Though spring was well underway, it hardly seemed like it to me. The trial or rather the outcome ripped at my soul everyday tinting all the colors around me in gray. People say time will mend our broken hearts. I would suggest that, mending takes more than just time.
    Last I'd heard Judge Hardman was in the process of stepping down amid allegations of judicial misconduct concerning this and other cases. To my knowledge, no one had inferred that he had accepted any sort of payoff for any trial's outcome, but he had supposedly improperly used his pulpit to manipulate trials in his courtroom. Whatever that really meant!
    The governor, on the hot-seat with his constituents having run on a ticket of being hard on crime and nearly a month ago, had asked for Hardman's resignation for his inappropriate handling of cases in general.
    Hardman might get away with being a liberal loon in New York or California, but in the more conservative Midwest, he'd have to find a new profession. Dog catcher was one that came to mind since he seemed eager to help those incarcerated out.
    According to the supposed legal specialists on TV, when the error with the evidence was discovered, Hardman should have removed the jury as per Anderson's request. His action, or rather his inaction, made it possible for Coker to make his motion. Even then, most concluded that Hardman could have just dismissed the motion or simply not taken any action on it at all.
    The State board was conducting its own investigation as to why and how Hardman made the ruling he'd made. According to those in the know, if the evidence itself had not been correctly tagged, his ruling would have been proper. But under the circumstances, with all the inside

tags being correct, dismissing all the evidence went against all criminal and ethical codes.

As for the prosecution, its hands were tied and had done squat with the case, at least to my knowledge. Not that any of us were all that surprised. We had all pretty much given up hope that any sort of justice would ever prevail at the hands of the courts.

Derek's parents and friends were doing their best to cope with the situation. And as always, Kelly had proved to be the strongest of us all. She'd continued to be everyone's rock. Over a month ago now, she'd moved back into her house armed with the gun I'd given and taught her to use since Derek's death. She was determined to live her life in spite of the crazy world around her. And of course, Derek was forever on her mind.

As for me, I'd begun planning for and anticipating the day when Hess and I would meet one last time. Without the benefit of his scumbag lawyer or the courts to protect him, justice would be swift. Well, maybe not too swift. I still read the eye for an eye part of the Bible. And what he did to my best friend would come back to haunt him big time if I had any say in it.

Though not officially family, I'd been adopted by Derek's family years before as the brother Derek had never had and vice versa. As a matter of fact, I had for years taken to calling him Derry like his parents always did. I still remember the first time I inadvertently called him that. He had simply turned his head slowly and looked at me in that ornery look that he could muster upon demand. Once his eyes stared into mine for a second he simply said, "Jerry, only family calls me that." And that was that. We were Derry and Jerry or simply Bro from that time forward.

As for Kelly and me, it went without saying that we were two peas in a pod, having grown up just doors apart. In more ways than either of us would care to admit, we had been and probably always would be each others rock.

Derry and I had made a pact years before in what seemed like another life to watch each other's back. As far as I was concerned, I hadn't been there when it counted for him on that occasion. I didn't plan on letting my friend down altogether.

We had both grown up in the greater Toledo area, but never met officially till we hooked up in boot camp on our way to Nam in '72. I say officially, because as it turned out, we had beat up on each other regularly playing sports in high school. Because we didn't attend the same school, we had been combatants. Who knew that in just a few short months, instead of being adversaries we'd become best friends?

Nam became the wildest senior trip ever for those of us who trudged off to war, or should I say police action? The insidious Russian roulette lottery draft system had left Derry and me very little choice. Our numbers had been so low that we figured the only way to get a decent break in the military was to enlist before marching orders made it to our front doors. As it turned out, the jobs we got weren't any better than the ones handed out to the draftees. They all sucked.

More than one guy from our unit didn't make it home alive. Some of the guys who did didn't make it all in one piece, whether physically or mentally. Nam ended up being a hell hole that sucked the life out of everything it touched. Anyone who arrived weak willed or as mamma's boys either grew up quickly or soon succumbed to the horrors that met them there. Those of us who made it out alive saw things we never should have seen and did things to survive that we would never speak of again.

Derry and I were lucky. The war had brought us together. We'd saved each other's asses more times than either of us would admit. Toledo and our friendship enabled us to make the transition back into society. It all seemed so long ago. In a way, I guess it was. It was Bro's lifetime ago.

The irony that he had fought for his country so scum like Hess could have rights and freedoms didn't escape me one bit. The way I saw it, judges and lawyers should have been put on the front lines over there. Maybe if they had been, they'd be less liberal with the rights of the guilty and actually try to protect the innocent like the laws were intended.

Over the years, Derry and I had remained close. Living only minutes apart, we worked out regularly at the local Y together after work. I towered over Derek by nearly a half inch and occasionally found a way to remind him of it. At five foot ten each, we each weighed in at just under two hundred pounds and could easily bench pressed our weight and about half again more.

It was easy to see that even in our fifty's, we were in better shape than most of the thirty year old kids who worked out around us. Unfortunately, that was probably what had gotten him killed. If he'd been a little more concerned about who was knocking that night, maybe he wouldn't have opened the door to a complete stranger and he'd still be alive.

But that was Bro to a fault. He'd been a friend to everyone he'd ever met. He'd sung in the church choir and along with Kelly gave lots of time to the youth ministry. They felt the call since they couldn't have kids of their own. Often times, he gave more than he should have to help someone who he thought was in more need than he. For that and so much more, everyone who knew Derek missed him.

As for myself, I was finding solace in planning my final confrontation with Clinton Hess.

Chapter Eight

Before turning the lights off, I checked the alarm clock setting. Though it was only Tuesday evening and there were still three days of work waiting for me, I anxiously looked forward to the weekend. The plan was to get away to do some fishing and relax. The latter probably seemed like a contradiction in terms since relaxing led to thinking which inevitably led to thoughts of eradicating Hess, the cause for all my stress in the first place.

But for now, I felt like I could relax a little. The details of my plan were nearly complete. The missing link was simply a call from Mac that Hess had returned.

As usual, my mind raced about and it took a while to fall asleep.

Late into the night, a faint voice broke the monotonous silence within the room.

"Jared. Jared. Wake up."

My eyes opened slowly. The voice sounded vaguely familiar, but for the life of me I couldn't quite place it. Weary eyed I looked around in the darkness. No one was there. Peering at the clock, I tried to make out the time. Straining my eyes, I could barely make out that it was 3:0'something or other. Figuring that I'd just been dreaming, I rolled over to go back to sleep.

"Jared. Wake up. I need to speak to you." The voice called out a little louder, seeming to echo through the night air.

I shot another look at the clock. It still read 3:0'something. I wasn't dreaming now. Nor was I asleep.

Reaching for and flipping on the light switch, I called out. "Who's there?"

I waited for several seconds, but there was no response.

The thought crossed my mind that possibly one of my buddies, who knew where the spare key was, had let themselves in. Still somewhat dazed, I got up and walked into the main part of the house. The lights were off throughout and no one answered my repeated calls.

"Must still be dreaming," I mumbled as I stumbled back to the bedroom, flipped the switch off and slid back under the covers.

"Jared, don't turn on the lights."

"Who the hell are you?" I asked. Looking around seeing nothing, I finished with, "Where the hell are you?"

In the same breath, my hand snapped the light switch back on. Again, no one was around and no one answered. I stuck my head out of the bedroom and turned on the hallway lights one more time. Still, there was no one around.

"This is starting to piss me off." I muttered aloud as I turned the lights off once again and sat on the edge of the bed. Before I could lie down, a voice protruded through the otherwise quiet darkness.

"Jerry, leave the lights off. It's me, Derry."

"Derry's dead and this is a nightmare,...or had better be." I rubbed my eyes with the palms of both hands hoping that would revive me. It didn't. "OK Bro, if it's you, show yourself."

"Look in your mirror, Jared. You can see my reflection there."

Without hesitation, my eyes sought out the oak-clad mirror that was attached to a similarly wooded bureau on the far side of the room. "This I gotta see." I knew I had to be hallucinating, but what else could I do at that point?

Sure enough, there was a hazy looking illumination of someone who could have been Derry barely discernible there.

"How's my old Buddy?" I asked.

"Look Jer. I know you think you're dreaming all this, but there's something I need you to do."

"I'm working on taking care of Hess for you Bro if that's what this is all about."

"I know you are, but you need to let God take care of him. There's already a plan in place for Hess and people like him. It's important that you don't take matters into your own hands. Besides, I don't want you to get in any trouble. I'm fine with where I am, but there is another matter I do need your help with."

"Whatever you say; go ahead and lay it on me." I responded, hoping to just get past this so I could go back to sleep, if I wasn't already that way.

"I'm still not a goat head, but listen up."

The fact that he used that same old corny "goat head" line startled me. That was something Derry had done for years.

"This better be a dream and be over when I wake up or else." I whispered to myself. But just in case, I listened a little closer.

"I'm going to give you the numbers to the Ohio Lottery tomorrow. Play them and split the winnings with Kelly. I want you to quit your job, buy a full sized van and take a trip to the Northeast. Do you understand what I've said so far?"

"Sure Bro." I assured him that I did, even though I was fairly certain that I didn't have a clue.

"Okay, the numbers are 1-7-10-26-42 and 45. Take the cash, not the monthly payout. Do you understand?"

"I think so. 1-7-10-27-42-45, is that right?"

"No, not quite, you never could remember anything. Take the pen and paper out of your night stand. Get it without turning on the lights. I've been told it will take some time before I'll be able to contact you in the light."

Shaking my head at his not remembering anything remark, I reached over and did as I was told. "Okay, Butthead, try it again."

"Oh Jerry, you were always so full of crap. I'll miss that the most, I suppose. Anyways, the numbers are 1-7-10-26-42-45," the voice repeated slowly while I wrote.

"Is there anything else?" I asked looking back towards the mirror where he'd been standing previously. "Derry?"

There was no Derry, only silence.

"Derek?" I asked again.

It seemed he or my imagination was gone. Reaching for the light switch, I flipped it on revealing the pad with the numbers on it there in my hand.

Expelling a deep breath, I studied the pad and wondered what to make of what had just happened. One thing for sure, I wasn't telling anyone about any of it.

Laying the pen and pad on top of the nightstand, I shook my head. That was way too much excitement for that or any time of the night. Reaching for the light switch again, I turned it off before rolling back under the covers to try to go back to sleep. Tomorrow, I'd have to attempt to sort it all out.

Thoughts of Derry and our good times followed me back to sleep as did his plea to leave Hess to God. The chances of that happening were still pretty close to slim if not none.

Chapter Nine

The alarm tripped on as it should have at 5:35 rocking me out of a deep sleep. My left hand instinctively found the more accessible snooze button before Mr. Bo Jangles could dance his way across the jail cell. It then searched for and found the harder to locate off switch.

Not bothering to open my eyes, I stretched my weary limbs to prepare my well used body for another day of light punishment. After my creaking joints cracked back into place, I sighed deeply sucking up the last few seconds of rest that I would likely get for the day unless I could sneak in a power nap after work.

As I lay there for those extra moments, Derry's visit during the night ran through my mind. I winced and chuckled all at the same time.

"Thanks for the visit last night, Bro. It was good to hear from you. At least it wasn't as bad as my usual one." I said aloud recalling the recurring nightmare that I'd endured on and off regularly for the past several decades.

Another few seconds and a big yawn later, I sat up on the side of my queen sized bed and flicked on the light switch. Figuring the dream had been just that, I looked in amazement when the glow from the lamp revealed the note pad sitting there on the corner of my little night stand. Curiously, I picked it up. To my dismay, the numbers 1-7-10-26-42-45 were written on it.

"Oh brother!" I rolled my eyes and shook my head in disgust.

Tearing off the top sheet, I wadded it up and tossed it in the trash can a few feet away before placing the pad back in the drawer. "I never played the lottery before. No sense starting now."

After making the bed and grabbing some clothes, I went to take a quick shower. Ten minutes later, dressed and ready for work, I passed the bureau mirror where I'd supposedly seen Derry's reflection a few hours earlier. For a moment, I stopped to peer into it. As I stood there, memories of him flooded my thoughts.

"I miss you old friend, but I could do without the late night visits. Besides, I hope you know I'm still working on it." I said with a snicker. Then with a shake of my head, I headed for the door. Before I got there, something stopped me in my tracks.

"What the heck?"

There on the bed was a wadded up piece of paper. I shuddered to believe what I was thinking. Taking one step closer, I leaned over to pick it up. Unraveling the crumpled up wad revealed the lottery numbers from the night before.

"I know I threw this in the trash." I told myself. "Man, you're spooking yourself out, Jer. Oh, what the heck! I'll play the dumb Lottery to prove the dream was just that."

Folding the paper up neatly, I stuffed it in my wallet for safekeeping. Then, with a shake of my head I turned off the lights and went to the kitchen to nuke some of the cold coffee from yesterday's pot before heading off to work.

By profession, I'd been a CNC production lathe technician for over twenty years, which simply meant I programmed, set-up and ran metal parts on a huge machine all day. It paid well and I kind of liked the programming side of the job. I could have stepped up to a salaried job as a full time programmer years before, but didn't need or want the hassles that went along with the job. As it was, when I finished at the end of the day, I was done for the day. No one called me about their problems and I didn't have to go back in to fix someone else's screw ups. It might not be everyone's cup of tea, but it worked for me.

Hump day was over in just eight hours of semi-boring normalcy. I heard the same old people complain about the same old things that they never really wanted to change, because then they wouldn't have anything to bitch about. Of course, I stirred the pot whenever possible just to keep it interesting for myself anyhow. As a whole, the day went pretty well. Because I'd kept busy, I forgot all about the dream and the numbers in my wallet.

After work, I drove to the local grocery store to pick up some things that I needed for home and the upcoming week-end. Passing by the Lottery counter on my way to check out jostled my memory about the dream. With only slight hesitation, I decided to keep my supposed promise. Grabbing a card, I pulled my wallet out to get the numbers off the somewhat crumpled paper inside. As I penciled in the numbers, 1-7-10- 26-42-46, I realized these numbers weren't just any numbers. They had personal significance. 1-7 was my birthday. 10-26 was Derry's. 4246 was Derek's address.

Looking at the ticket in my hand, I shook my head and rolled my eyes. This was just way too weird.

"Wouldn't this be a hoot?" I mockingly asked myself as I paid for the pleasure of donating a buck.

"Thank you, Sir. Good luck." The attendant said.

I grinned and nodded my thanks at hearing the standard cliché designed to make people feel good about giving their money away, still feeling like I'd been taken.

Oh well. I'd spent more for less, I guess. With a grin on my face and a thought of Bro in my heart, I dropped the stub into my wallet. Rolling my eyes upward, I walked away and whispered, "Okay. I did my part. It's up to you now."

After paying for the rest of my booty, I walked out to my truck and headed home. As I drove, I started thinking about Derry. The problem was, thinking of him generally led to thoughts of Clinton Hess. It seemed a natural progression that soon left me somewhat pissed off.

Here we were in the greatest nation on earth, with the highest crime rate in the world and the most liberal means of punishing the trash who continue making their living that way anywhere. It shouldn't take a genius to figure out what needed to be done and how to do it. If asked to do so, I would be all too willing to quit my current job and dole out punishments that actually fit the crimes.

Chapter Ten

"Another subject," I scolded myself, not needing the stress. Quickly, my thoughts turned to my only safe haven, Kelly. It had been over a week since we'd spoken.

Kelly was the one person I could turn to and always had been. We all have our crosses to bare and ways of dealing with issues. My ways were like most guys, I suppose. Bottle it up till it blows. When all else failed, though, I could always count on Kelly to calm me down.

I grabbed my cell and speed dialed her number. On the second ring, her sweet voice reverberated across the air waves from the other end.

"Hello Jared. What's up?"

"Hi Kel."

"I was just thinking about calling you. We haven't talked in nearly two weeks. What's up with that?"

I had to laugh. She always knew how to brighten my day. "I know. It's been too long, Kiddo. How are you?"

"It's great to hear your voice. I'm doing okay. Mom's been over about every day and work keeps me busy. How are you doing and what have you been up to?"

"About the same and not much. I'm going fishing this weekend. That's about it for new news. I was just thinking that it's been too long since we've gotten together. Are you busy Friday night? Thought you might like to go out for dinner?"

"I'd love to, Jer. What time are you picking me up?"

"How does six o'clock sound? We'll have plenty of time to chat while we're waiting for a table at that time of night no matter where we go."

"Sounds terrific, I'll see you then."

The conversation was over almost too quickly, but I felt better just the same. Kelly was such a sweetheart and it certainly wasn't difficult to see what Derry had seen in her. Sure, there'd been some obstacles to deal with in living with a blind person, but they had had a great life together, short as it was.

As for my personal life, my significant other, Brenda and I had gotten divorced nearly four years earlier after eight years of marriage, some of it good. Fortunately, we hadn't had any children. That in itself was a blessing. I hated to see families torn apart by divorce. It was hard enough on the adults.

From the outside looking in, we were both to blame or neither to blame, depending on how you chose to look at our relationship. From my male perspective, I felt that like a lot of women, Brenda married me for the man she thought I could become instead of the man I was. There just came a point when I couldn't change anymore. If you asked her, I'm sure she'd probably say that I hadn't tried changing at all.

In reality, the true reason was more than likely like two people's perspective of any incident, somewhere in between. That said, deep down inside, I knew I was more to blame than Bren. There were just some things from my past that kept coming back to haunt our relationship, no matter how hard I wanted or tried to forget them.

And in many ways I still loved Bren, but she had moved on. The last I'd heard, she was trying to make a new man out of some other poor stiff. We talked on rare occasions when we happened into one another someplace, but that was about it.

After a few more minutes in la la land, my mind returned to the present leaving Bren and the past where they belonged.

Wednesdays were my bowling night at South Lanes and this was the final night of the season. If our team won three or more points, we'd be league champions, again. Even though winning paid an extra hundred bucks per man, competitors really craved the prestige of winning more than the cash. Not that I would give any of it back.

After a ten minute power nap and another shower, I grabbed my equipment and headed to the center to catch a bite to eat before bowling. At the snack counter, Sam, obviously short for Samantha, met me with her usual zest.

"Tonight the big night, Jared?" She asked.

"You could say that, Kiddo. What's your special tonight or should I ask what aren't you burning?"

She laughed, knowing I was only teasing. Actually, the food there was always pretty decent.

"Throw me on one of your nearly famous chicken breast sandwiches with lettuce, tomato and mayo, please."

"You've got it." She said with a snicker.

Sam was a cutie. She was also a high school student who worked evenings at the center. Everyone liked picking on her, because she gave it back in spades.

While she worked on my food order, I walked over to the pro shop to check on the latest news in bowling. Trace Chandler ran the shop at the center and always had some new tidbit of information to share. He liked to jaw as I put it, which meant he liked to talk for anyone not up on country jargon.

Pretty much anyone who knew anything about tournament bowling in Toledo knew who I was. I'd won all the city events at one time at least once over the years. Outside the city, I had captured a state title, a runner up finish at National's and had dabbled on the pro tour when I was a bit younger. I wasn't as good as I was at thirty, but I still received a fair share of respect on the lanes. Thinking about it, someone will probably make a Country song about something like that someday.

Anyway, as Trace and I chatted, Sam blew in carrying my food along with a Coke that I'd neglected to order.

"I know how you get." She teased. "Once you start talking, your food would be iced cold before you came to get it. Then you'd blame me."

Of course, she was right. I gave her enough to cover the bill and delivery services. Then, like Tigger in Winnie the Pooh, she bounced away back to her duty station and her next victim; her cute little blonde ponytail bobbing behind her.

While Trace finished filling me in on the latest in equipment and gossip, I ate. We finished up at about the same time, me eating and him talking. Then, I headed out to the lanes to get ready for bowling and to chat with the guys as they came strolling in.

When the lights came on to start the match, I got the team fired up by rolling the first seven strikes and finished the game with a very nice 258. The rest of the night went pretty well for both the team and me. I banged off a 760 series and the team won all three games and totals.

After that of course, the night ended up in the bar where we celebrated our most recent victory over beer, sandwiches and tales of other victories. As our celebration wound down, the news from Channel 13 came on the widescreen TV that hung behind the bar. That was when someone yelled out, "Hey. Check this out."

We got just enough quieter to hear a little of what they were talking about. It seemed someone from the Toledo area had won the lottery worth over ten million dollars. I swallowed hard as I watched in disbelief as the numbers 1-7-10-26-42-45 scrolled across the bottom of the screen several times.

I didn't know whether to pass out, scream and yell, or die. Could it be that Derry had really visited me? The idea was too preposterous to believe and I sure as heck wasn't going to tell anyone about it. About the only person I could really tell would be Kelly. Even then, I had no idea how I'd begin.

The one thing I did know was that I needed to get out of there before I said something I shouldn't. Jokingly I said to the guys, "Well it looks like I need to go claim my winnings. Catch ya'll later."

Just like I would have, they all laughed as I pushed back from the table and headed for the door lugging my bowling bag behind me. Later when they found out the truth, they would crap for sure. The next time we got together was going to cost me big time. It would be beer for the house. A smile lit my face as I realized I could probably afford it.

Chapter Eleven

Long minutes passed as I sat alone in my truck trying to separate the known from the unknown. I couldn't for the life of me figure out where to begin. My mind kept going back to the vision that I wanted to forget. Derry had given me instructions on what to do with the money. At least that was a place to start. The next day I'd have to hire an attorney or an accountant to make sure I didn't screw this up. Come to think of it, I'd probably have to hire one of each.

Along with confusion, excitement started boiling up inside me. I found myself needing to tell someone. Before I knew it, I'd hit the speed dial on my cell phone.

After two rings a sleepy voice answered at the other end. "Hello."

I shot a quick glance at the clock on the truck radio. It read 10:45. Oops!

"Sorry Kelly. I forgot what time it was getting to be. Well, since you're already awake, put on a pot of coffee. I've got some news that can't wait till tomorrow."

A protest tried to erupt across the airways, but I didn't pay it any heed.

"I'll be there in about ten minutes. Make a full pot. You'll want some, too." I said.

Kelly knew me well enough to know there wasn't any reason to argue. I was coming over. She had just enough time to wake up and compose herself before I got there. Me on the other hand, I wasn't sure if it was enough time to figure out what I was going to say.

As I drove, more questions bombarded me. Should I tell her about my dream? Had it been a dream? Had it been a vision? Was it just a fluke? Even if it was, I'd made a promise. Real or imaginary, I fully intended on keeping it. Besides, I would have shared the money with Kelly even without the vision. She had always been my best friend and so much more.

The lights were on when I pulled into the driveway of her brick eighteen hundred foot ranch, not for her sake, mind you, but for mine. The door opened as I came strolling up the sidewalk and Kelly poked her head out. "This had better be good, Jared Maxwell. Waking me up at this time of night to make you coffee is going to cost you big time."

She was teasing and we both knew it. Her bark was worse than her bite, at least usually. She let go of the screen door just before I could get to it and it slammed closed before I could grab it. I heard her laugh as she walked away. I did too.

Walking into the kitchen to where she was standing with her arms folded to show her disdain for having to get up, I gave her a kiss on the forehead and laughed at her attempted display of anger. "Alright, how much is this going to cost me?" I asked.

Kelly already had a cup poured for me sitting on her oaken pedestal table. Before sitting down in front of it, I grabbed a cup out of the cupboard for her.

"Don't pour me any. I'll have trouble sleeping if I drink coffee at this time of night." She said in protest.

"Trust me Kel. When you hear what I've got to say, you won't sleep anyhow."

"Trust me. Now those are famous last words coming from you." She teased.

"Yeah! Yeah! I know." I said. I finished getting her coffee as she walked to her heavy kitchen table and took a seat.

"I've got some work that needs to be done around here. I'll figure out something." She said, letting me know the price of this coffee and conversation.

"Consider it done."

"Yeah, I know how quick that'll happen. I'll have to have your mother start bugging you."

"Ouch. Now that really hurts." I teased as I set her coffee down on top of the cloth flowered placemat that lie there before taking my seat across from her.

"Oh, right! So what's got you all fired up on a Wednesday night. You bowl 900 tonight or something?"

"Well, we did win the league tonight, but that's hardly new news. Actually, I thought you might like to know I'm going to take a vacation."

"You woke me up to tell me you're taking a vacation? Have you been drinking? Is that all I made you coffee for?"

"Now wait Kelly, that's not quite all."

"It better not be." She laughed, knowing that something else had to be driving this semi-unusual visit.

I sat there looking at her for a moment trying to figure out what to say. Finally, I decided to just start talking and see what came out of my mouth, full well knowing that at times that could be dangerous.

"Have you ever had a dream that was so real that you weren't sure if it was really a dream?"

A puzzled look came to Kelly's face and then a smirk. "You came here to talk about a dream you had? I've heard everything now." She said as she started laughing.

"Not yet you haven't." I assured her.

"What do you mean by that?" She asked still tee hee-ing.

"My dream was about Derry and he talked to me."

Kelly's exuberant laughter ceased with the mention of his name.

"Oh Jared, you and he were best friends. It's only natural you'd dream about him."

"You don't quite understand, Kelly. He woke me up out of a deep sleep to give me instructions."

"Instructions? What kind of instructions?" She asked, dipping both eyebrows to the middle.

I couldn't take it any longer and excitedly told the story of the night before to a quiet but interested listener; including Derry's ghostly image in the mirror to the numbers I had thrown away, but then played.

After I finished, Kelly remained silent for a moment before responding. "So, are you trying to tell me you won the lottery?"

"No Kelly. We won."

Tears began flowing down Kelly's cheeks as she tried smiling, even a she wanted to cry. I reached out and placed my hand on top of her hands that lie folded on top of the table next to her coffee cup.

"I need a hug, Jared." Her voice cracked.

Getting down on one knee next to her we hugged, each hoping that the strength of the other would somehow sustain them.

After a couple of minutes, she said, "I'm ready for that coffee now."

"I thought so." I said as I returned to the chair across from her.

Slowly, she took a sip from her cup while I sat quietly allowing her to have a little space. Floods of emotion raced across her face as I watched.

Finally, she spoke. "That's sweet of you Jared, but I can't accept the money."

"Why not? You don't believe me, do you?"

"It sounds so wonderful, Jared. Really it does. I don't know that I've ever heard of anything so sweet. I mean, concocting such an outlandish story and everything."

"Kelly," I stopped her. "I didn't... Wait a second, I'll be right back."

In the living room on the fireplace mantle next to Derry's picture was the Bible I'd given them as a wedding present so many years ago. I walked straight to it, grabbed it, carried it back to the kitchen and placed it in her hands.

"You know what this is, don't you?"

Feeling the edges of the book, she confirmed to herself what she already knew. A nod of her head acknowledged that she did.

"Now listen, Kel." I placed my hand on top of hers. "I swear with God as my witness that everything I told you, no matter how unbelievable, is what happened. I don't pretend to understand any of it. Frankly, it doesn't really matter anyhow. Even if I hadn't had the dream or vision or whatever you want to call it, I'd share the money with you. You have been always been my bestest friend all my life."

Again, Kelly sat in silence trying to think of what to say or believe. Out of the corner of my eye, I spotted her purse over on the counter. "Wait a second. I've got an idea." I said.

Getting up again, I grabbed her purse and sat it down in front of her. With her keen sense of hearing, she knew what it was.

"What's this for?" She asked.

"Give me a dollar." I said.

Unsure what I was getting at, she reached into her purse and did as I asked.

"Is this a dollar?" She asked.

"Yes," I said as I took the bill from her. Reaching into my pocket I grabbed my change. Picking out two quarters, I placed them in her hand.

"What's this for." She asked.

"That's your change."

"Change! Change for what?"

"You just bought half a lottery ticket and guess what, you're a winner."

Chapter Twelve

"You crazy wonderful fool, you..."

"Be careful now. Don't be bad mouthing your rich partner." I teased.

Tears rolled down her cheeks as she sat shaking her head at me. "Jared, you know Derek loved you like a brother. He told me more than once that his only regret in life was that he didn't know you when he was growing up. More than that though, you were the friend he counted on during the worst part of his life.

"As for me, I don't know what I would have done without you to lean on most all of my life and especially this past year. There's no way I can ever repay you. What's more, I know that if he was going to come back for some reason, he'd come back to see you." She stopped to take a deep sigh. "Would you just hold me Jared?"

There was no need to respond. I stood and took her hand. Together we walked into the living room. I took a seat at the corner of the big dark leather sofa. She sat down next to me. With my arm around her and her head resting against my shoulder, our thoughts of Derek echoed around us in the darkness. In a way, we were the three of us together again, if only in our hearts.

After a while, Kelly asked. "What are you going to do now, Jared?"

My hesitation in answering gave me away, I suppose.

"Is there something that you haven't told me?"

"You know, it's no wonder Derry loved you. I can't tell you how many times he told me how you could read his very thoughts. I know the feeling, because you've always been kind of that way with me too."

"I'm tele-sensitive not telepathic. So what is it you've left out?"

"In my vision," I stopped to clear the lump that suddenly grew inside my throat. "He gave me instructions. It sounded like he would contact me again. I know it sounds absurd, but that's how I took it."

By now, Kelly's head was off my shoulder and looking through me with her eyes that saw nothing or maybe..., just maybe, saw everything.

"What do you mean?" She asked.

"He said I should buy a van and take an extended trip. He even reiterated to buy a van and not a car. I have no idea why. If there's a reason, he'll have to tell me or let me know in some way. You probably think I'm totally nuts and need a shrink. To tell the truth, you're probably right."

Even in her blindness, Kelly's eyes looked at me as she searched for an answer, her eyes piercing through me all the while. "It doesn't hurt to dream. Derry would be glad you dreamed of him."

Kelly's facial expression suddenly changed as she reached out and took my hand in hers. "Jared?"

"Yeah?" I asked, wondering what was coming.

"Since I'm your partner and bestest friend, take me with you. A trip like that won't be any fun by yourself. Please?"

I had no idea what to say. There hadn't been anything said about taking Kelly, but on the other hand there hadn't been anything said about going alone either. Maybe this was part of a greater plan. Or maybe it was just a dumb dream and it didn't matter anyhow. Maybe. Maybe. Maybe.

"Please!" She repeated. "I know just where I want to go, too." She said sliding back against my left side, pulling my arm around her. "Niagara Falls. Wouldn't you like to go to Niagara Falls? The power of nature is so strong there, don't you think? Take me to Niagara Falls, Jared."

How could I say no? There are so many levels of love that most people never get to experience. I loved Kelly not all that different than Derry had. And I knew the feelings were mutual.

"Sure, why not? We'll start our trip by going to Niagara Falls."

It wasn't important to tell her that my vacation was supposed to start in the Northeast, anyhow. She never raised her head or shifted at all. She simply felt she had me wrapped around her little finger, which of course, she did.

"Thank you, Jared. We'll have a great time."

A few minutes of quiet followed before Kelly spoke again. "What are you thinking about?"

"Just my sanity. If it wasn't for the lottery numbers coming up, I'd have just written this whole thing off as a weird dream. Now, I just don't know."

"You're okay Jared. I'll let you know if you start cracking up. That's what partners are for."

"I feel better already, knowing you'll be watching over me."

She knew I was mocking her and elbowed me in the ribs for it.

"Well, I should probably leave so you can go back to bed. I'll swing by tomorrow so we can talk some more."

"If you think I'm going to be able to sleep now, maybe you really are crazy, Jared Maxwell. Let's go get something to eat to celebrate. I'll buy. After all, I'm a millionaire. I can afford it." She laughingly snickered.

"Sure, why not? Do you want to change first or go like you are? I've heard you rich bitch women are kind of eccentric, but I'm not sure I want to be seen with you in your sleeveless t-shirt and cut off gym shorts."

She elbowed me in the side again and laughed. "I'll eccentric you. Give me five minutes."

"Take ten. They're small and I don't have to work in the morning. I'm on vacation, permanently."

The idea of not working again amused me. In all actuality, though, I knew I couldn't vacation for the rest of my life. I'd have to do something with substance or I would go loony.

A voice shouted out from down the hallway as I sat there thinking about it. "By the way, how much did we win?" She asked.

"Around ten million!" I yelled back to her.

Her door opened and a stunned Kelly poked her head out. Her mouth was trying to say something, but no words were coming out.

I laughed at the sight. Deciding to give her a break I said, "Actually it'll be more like six since we're taking the cash."

"Oh, that's a lot better." Her voice returned. "I can say six million a lot easier than I can ten. Pinch me please."

"You want me to come in there or wait till you come out here?" I called out, realizing she didn't have a shirt on, if anything at all.

"Just wait where you are, thank you." She said as she disappeared back into her bedroom sporting a huge smile.

With a few minutes to kill, I picked up my cell phone and called into work. I wasn't going to be in, but I could at least give them a heads-up. After getting through to the third shift supervisor, I told him that I needed a vacation day. I just didn't bother telling him that it might be a permanent one. Whether I'd go in over the next few days was another matter. Everyone in the world didn't need to know why I was leaving. I'd have to give that some more consideration.

For now though, we were headed out to get something to eat and talk about our upcoming trip to Niagara Falls.

Chapter Thirteen

Neither of us particularly wanted to go into a neighborhood bar at that time of night so we headed down Reynolds to where most of the popular chain places were located. It took us less than ten minutes to get there and at Kelly's suggestion, since she was supposedly paying the tab, we decided on the Hut. After parking in front of the building that always reminded me of an enlarged Keebler Elf cracker factory for some reason, we walked inside and were ushered to one of their many empty booths. Once seated, we ordered a thin crust all meat pizza with extra cheese on her half and talked over our sodas while we waited for our late-night snack to arrive.

A few minutes after the waitress brought us our pizza, three young teens strolled in. Naturally they had to park it in the booth right behind Kelly.

Personally, I like kids. I coached them at the bowling center from time to time. But these kids acted like punks. They should have been home hours earlier since this was a school night. Obviously, there was a lack of supervision or caring; in their case, probably both.

I could tell right away that I was not going to enjoy their intrusion. Within seconds after sitting their butts down, the profanity started spewing from their dirty adolescent mouths. F this and F that became the natural introduction or end of every sentence.

Now, I really wanted to know where their parents were, but figured they wouldn't be of any help, anyhow. They obviously hadn't been too good at instructing them on how to act in public up to this point.

At first, Kelly and I both tried not letting them bother us. We tried to enjoy our pizza and our conversation, but before long, I'd heard enough.

"Excuse me, Kelly. I'll be right back."

Kelly raised her hand in protest.

I placed my hand on her shoulder as I walked by to assure her that everything was under control. She knew what was coming since it wasn't the first time Derry or I had dealt with problems in her presence.

I walked the couple steps farther to the boys' booth and stood in front of them without speaking. Their conversation stopped abruptly as they looked up at me with their cocky little attitudes plastered across their cocky little faces.

"What's your f----ing problem?" The leader asked.

Disregarding his smart mouth, I said. "Tell you gentlemen what. I'll buy your pizza and your drinks if I don't hear another F word for the rest of the evening. Is that fair?"

I no more than got the words out of my mouth than he began uttering obscenities again. "F---you. Who the F---do you..."

The little punk didn't get to finish his sentence, because at that point I had hold of him by the throat and his eyes were trying to bug out of his head. He was so surprised that I thought he was going to start bawling. A spanking was what he really needed. If offered the opportunity by his parent or parents, I would have gladly tendered my services.

Across the table, one of his punk buddies tried to intervene. Anticipating that, I gave him a shove back into his seat with my free hand. Putting my index finger in his face, I sternly said, "Sit."

Looking back at the boy I had a hold of, I relaxed my grip a bit before asking. "How about it, Son, do we have a deal?"

The cockiness began welling up in his eyes again, so I squeezed a little harder. Fear quickly took its place as he muttered a weak, "yes."

I relaxed my grip a bit and asked. "What was that? I didn't hear you."

"Yes sir."

"That's better. Now order what you boys want and I'll take care of the bill."

I let go of the young man and looked at him for a second before returning to my seat, all the while listening to be sure they didn't try something while my back was turned. To be honest, I half expected them to storm out of the place like babies, but they didn't. They took their punishment like men. I half respected them for that.

We ate a little more of our pizza, but the mood wasn't nearly as festive as before. Our appetites, as well as our conversation, also suffered on account of the little punks. When our wide-eyed waitress came around to see if we needed anything else, I asked for a box, our bill and for the boys' bill as well.

She returned a few minutes later with all three.

"Thank you very much, Sir." Was all she said before scurrying back to her safe haven back behind the counter.

After helping Kelly on with her jacket, I stopped to talk to the boys for a moment. Laying a twenty on their table, I said. "A lot of boys would have gotten up and stormed out of here. You boys took your medicine like men. That shows backbone. Here's for the next time you have a pizza. Remember to show a little respect for those around you."

We had only taken a step when the leader spoke. "Excuse me, Sir."

I turned to look at him. "Yes?"

"Thank you, Sir."

"What's your name, Son?"

"Tim. Tim White."

"Well Tim White. Remember what I said and have a good life. Maybe we'll see each other again sometime. If we do, I might buy you another pizza."

"Thank you, Sir. That would be nice."

When we stopped at the register to pay the tab, the cashier thanked us and apologized for the incident. I knew Kelly was rolling her eyes behind her darkly tinted glasses. I just smiled.

We weren't three steps outside the door before Kelly belted my right arm a good one.

"Ouch! What was that for?" I asked, rubbing where she'd hit me.

"You could have been killed!"

"I helped three boys become men. They'll thank me for it one day. I think the one already did."

"Still, that was a dangerous thing you did in there. Besides,...I don't have my money yet." She exclaimed, her snarl turning into a smirk.

"Oh! Now the truth comes out. All right! I promise to be more careful till you get your cut of the money." I said with a laugh.

"You'd better be. By the way, when will that be?" She asked.

"Tomorrow, we'll get a safety deposit box and a lawyer. We'll have to see what he suggests. I don't want any surprises or the world knowing we won, if it can be helped. My guess is it'll take a week or two, but I really couldn't say for sure."

"You've got it all under control, don't you? Just like Derry would have. You two are...were a lot alike. That's probably why you hit it off so well."

"Thanks for the vote of confidence, Kel, but I'm not so sure I've got it all under control. Let's just say I've got a loose grip on the handle. Hopefully, it's the right handle."

She just smiled.

Minutes later, we were back at her place. I jumped out of the truck and walked around to help her out. As was our norm, Kelly handed me her keys. I unlocked the door, then checked out the house to be sure no intruders were inside, before she came in.

"All's good, Kel. I turned all the lights off already and here are your keys. I'll be by in the morning to get you. What time would you like to get started?"

"Jared?"

"Yeah? Did I forget something?"

"Well," She stammered, searching for the words she wanted to say. "Could you stay the night? I know the couch probably isn't all that comfortable, but I..." She paused.

I put my finger on her lips to stop her from having to finish. "The couch will be just fine, Kiddo."

"You sure you don't mind?" She asked.

"Nothing's too good for my partner." I leaned forward and kissed her on the cheek. "I'll be right in. I need to roll up the windows and lock the truck."

A smile lit her face and whatever tension there had been because of the pizza place incident was forgotten.

After locking the truck, I paused for a moment to look up at the stars. I wondered if I would ever again see life as I did tonight. What was going to happen next would be a huge change for both of us. There was also the little matter of Clinton Hess that hadn't been dealt with yet.

I closed my eyes and thought of Derry. "I hope you haven't got me in too deep here, Bucko."

No one answered, nor did I expect them too. But I listened, just in case.

By the time I made it back inside, a bottle of water was sitting on the stand next to the sofa where a pillow and quilt lay. Kelly had already disappeared into her bedroom.

I slipped off my slacks before stretching out on the couch. Moments later, her bedroom door opened and Kelly called out. "Good night Jared."

"Good night Kelly."

Chapter Fourteen

The next thing I knew, the smell of freshly brewed coffee rushed through my nostrils and cranked my eyelids open. A moment later, I heard the sound of Kelly tinkering around in the kitchen.

Rolling off the couch and onto the floor, I worked on realigning the vertebrae in my back that reminded me why people should sleep in beds. The couch was nice, soft and saggy and definitely not a place I'd want to sleep on an ongoing basis.

When I finally made it to the kitchen, Kelly greeted me with a smile. "Sleep well?"

"Pretty good."

"Hope I didn't wake you. It's after eight. You usually get up earlier."

There were a lot of things she knew about me, probably too many for my own good.

"I must have been tired. The smell of coffee finally brought me to life."

"Did you get your back straitened up in there?"

"You hear too much." I teased.

"I suppose. What's your pleasure this morning, eggs, French toast or pancakes? I still owe you a meal since you ended up buying ours last night."

"That's right, I did. What was I thinking?" I said acting surprised.

"Silly Boy! So what do you want this morning?"

"French toast."

"Blackened?"

That got us both laughing, remembering the black smoke that had filled the kitchen the last time she tried making French toast for me. I was outside fixing something when I should have been inside watching.

"I prefer the word crispy." I corrected her.

"That's not what you asked for."

"Yeah, I know. I asked for burnt. It was my fault."

"Do you want bacon or sausage?" She asked.

"I'll have whatever you're having." I said.

"And what if I'm not?"

"Then I won't either." I said.

"You're a funny guy. I know you like sausage with your French toast and bacon with your eggs. I already have sausage ready to go in the microwave."

"Then why did you bother asking? You just like to torment me, don't you?"

"You need it." She said, sporting a wry grin.

"Thanks. I'm sure I probably do. Did you call into work this morning?"

Kelly worked at a little factory not far from her house where she did some sort of electronic sub assembly work. It didn't pay a lot, but it helped fill the hours. She normally walked to work on nice days and someone picked her up when the weather was particularly nasty.

"I called in before the alarm was to go off. I'll have to admit, it felt pretty good going back to sleep."

"Don't get too used to it. I like to get up early when I'm traveling."

Kelly laughed. "Liar."

True. She knew me too well.

"After breakfast, we'll go to my place so I can clean up. After that, we'll go to the bank before seeing about finding a lawyer."

"Who are you going to get?"

"I have no idea. I'll probably need to make a couple of calls to even have a clue."

"You can call while I'm changing." She said.

"That'll work."

As I thought about it, Anderson at the DA's office still owed us big time. Maybe he could steer us in the right direction on this.

I kept an eye on the progress of my French toast so that we didn't have another episode with the alarms going off throughout the house. After eating, I helped rid and do the dishes, which gave us more time to talk. It was just idle chit chat, but that's what friends do. When Kel went to get ready, I called Anderson at his office. With only one transfer and a thirty second wait, I was talking to the man.

"Mr. Maxwell, what can I do for you?"

"I need some advice and thought you could point me in the right direction."

"I'll try."

"I know this lawyer client thing doesn't work in our case, but I'd appreciate it if you could keep what I'm about to tell you between us."

"Sure Jared, as long as it's not illegal."

I laughed. "No, it's nothing like that. I or rather we, Kelly and I, won the Ohio Lottery last night. We need a lawyer and probably an accountant. Got any suggestions?"

"Wow! Good for you guys. I'd heard someone from Toledo had won. Let me make a couple of calls and I'll get back to you. Make sure you put the ticket in a lockbox at your bank until you can get everything settled."

"We're on our way to do that first."

"Good. Give me your cell number and I'll get back to you."

"555-1621"

"Okay. How's Kelly doing? Maybe this is just what she needs."

"It'll help, but what we both need is for Hess to fry or eat a bullet."

"I know what you're saying. We're still working on it, but I'll be honest, nothing much is happening right now. We won't give up till we put him behind bars for something."

I knew he meant well, but our call ended with my faith in the system still flittering away. I knew in my heart that money or no money, Hess's days on this earth were numbered.

Chapter Fifteen

I waited patiently in the living room as Kelly finished getting ready, looking around at all the memories staring back at me. I'd been a part of most of them. An outsider would never realize the pictures that weren't there. No pictures of us in uniform survived, either at my house or his. It was one of the ways we had dealt with that part of our lives even though it was what had brought us together in the first place. It had taken us a year after our return from Nam to realize that the pictures always reminded us of that place and kept pulling us down. Remembering kept the triggers on our tempers always half cocked and ready to blow. After getting rid of all the military memorabilia, we were slowly able to put that part of our lives behind us. In many ways, he succeeded better than I had.

Because of her blindness, Kelly kept her hair fairly short so she didn't have to worry about bad hair days or if she'd done something wrong. More than once, she got called spike because of it. That said, getting ready meant a change of clothes and brushing her teeth.

I watched as she walked down the hallway to the living room. She still had that same athletic build that she had when we were in high school. Her hair sported a touch of gray, but it looked good on her. In school, I used to tease her about her bust size, saying that she could shower with the boys because no one would ever know the difference. That was one thing that had definitely changer over the years. She couldn't be mistaken for a boy any more. That was for sure.

I smiled at my short journey through the past and at my current thoughts of Kelly. We really were great pals.

"You ready?" She asked.

"Born ready." I answered.

She smiled. I locked the door behind us and walked her to my truck. As we rode and chatted, the radio station repeated the numbers and the news that someone from the area had won the lottery twice before we got to my place. We teased each other about it like kids with a secret, saying, "who could that be" and "I know who that is."

The winnings ended up being larger than expected. Our share was going to be nearly seven mil in cash. Not that another million made any real difference, but the information was a pleasant surprise.

Brad Anderson called just as I climbed out of the shower.

"Jared, here's the scoop. Kimmel and Darden took care of a lottery winner a few of years back. They should have a good idea how to proceed with your needs. I took the liberty of calling them to schedule an appointment for a noon luncheon for you. I hope that's okay. They're located on the 3500 block of Sylvania."

"Thanks Brad. I appreciate it."

"I wish I could do more."

"Keep working is all I can ask, I guess."

"We will." He assured me.

"Yeah, but I won't hold my breath." I muttered, after I'd hung up.

When I came out of the bedroom, Kelly asked who'd called. She didn't flinch when I told her it was Anderson from the DA's office. I went ahead and told her what he'd said.

"That was nice of him."

I watched her expressions to see if there were any feelings she needed to talk out, but didn't notice anything.

She even laughed when I added. "We'll probably go to the Country Club for lunch."

When we arrived at the bank, I asked to speak to a Private Banker. It took a few minutes to see one without an appointment, but she was quite excited to have our business once she found out why we were there.

Ms. Linda Thomas set us up with a safety deposit box that required both our signatures to get into. We deposited our ticket in the box and listened as she spoke at length how she could help us with many of the transactions we would need to make in the future with just a call.

It's amazing the attention you receive for just having just a couple of million dollars to your name. The humor of it didn't escape Kelly either. I saw her snicker under her breath after she reached over and squeezed my leg. It was just to get my attention, but for some reason it felt somehow different than usual. And I liked it.

Chapter Sixteen

After leaving the bank, we headed down Central to cut over to Sylvania. Passing the car lots that line Central at I-275, a flashing sign caught my eye. Casually, I looked over to where it was coming from.

"I don't believe this!" I said out loud.

"You don't believe what?"

"I think I've found the van we're supposed to buy."

"You mean a van that you like?"

"Not exactly."

"Jared, you're kind of creeping me out." She said, gritting her teeth.

"You're not the only one." I said as I pulled into the car lot.

After parking the truck near the vehicle that had gotten my attention, I helped Kelly out so we could inspect the vehicle together.

"What's going on?"

"I'll tell you in a minute." I said as I took a closer look.

By then, a salesman was already on his way out to greet us. "Hello there folks. My name is Bill. May I help you?"

"You can get me the keys to this thing, if you wouldn't mind."

"Sure. I'll be right back." He said.

With Bill gone, I finished my preliminary inspection.

"What are you looking for?" Kelly asked.

"Something that isn't here."

"Now what do you mean?"

"When we were driving by, there was a flashing sign in the windshield that was saying, "Buy this one."

"So?"

"First there's no sign in the window."

"What's second?" She asked.

"Actually, it said, buy this one, Jared."

"Are you trying to insinuate this is more of your dream or vision? This is the middle of the day for Pete's sake!"

"Maybe our next stop needs to be with a shrink instead of a lawyer."

"I'm beginning to wonder." Kelly admitted shaking her head.

"Hold on, the salesman's coming."

"Here are the keys, Sir."

I pushed the button on the key fob a couple of times to unlock all the doors. After helping Kelly in, I got in myself. Looking around at the amenities that lined the thing, I couldn't think of anything it didn't have, except maybe a kitchen sink. But for all I knew that could be in the back somewhere.

"Should we take it for a spin?" I asked.

"Sure, why not." Kelly responded as she threw her hands in the air as if to say I give.

"You heard the lady. Get me some plates for this thing?"

Bill quickly responded. "Yes Sir. Drive it up to the front door and I'll hook you up."

"What color is it?" Kelly asked, as I started it up.

"The interior is burgundy with four Captains chairs and a full sized seat in the back that probably folds into a bed. The..."

"No! Don't tell me. The outside is white with multiple stripes of burgundy with black pinstripes separating the different colors and four large windows to view the outside from."

"How could you possibly know that?"

"It's what Derry always talked about getting."

"Now who's freaking who?"

"Why bother driving it, Jared? I like it already. Somehow, it just feels right. You know what I mean?"

I shook my head, because unfortunately, I did.

When Bill returned with the plate, a huge smile was plastered across his face. It seemed almost cruel seeing it disappear when I said. "We decided not to take it for a test drive."

I didn't let him hang long before adding. "The window sticker says 34.9. How much will it cost me today?"

His eyes quickly resumed their earlier glow. "Will you be trading in your truck, Sir?"

Frankly, I hadn't thought about that. Looking over at Kelly, I pondered the question for a moment. Suddenly, I had an idea about disposing of the truck. Looking back at Bill, I answered. "No. We just want the van."

"Let me check the books to see what kinds of rebates and offers go with the van today. I'll be right back."

With that he was off, leaving the two of us alone again.

"You're really going to buy this, aren't you?"

"Me? I thought this was a partnership. Weren't we going to buy this thing together?" I teased.

"Very funny, but you're right. We should buy it together."

"You know I was only teasing."

"Yes, but I kind of like the idea. It's what Derry always wanted us to have. It smells so nice and new. Tell me more about it."

I finished telling her where things were and helped her find the controls for the radio and CD player, the separate climate control buttons and the switch for the heated seat on her side. Then I helped her into the back so she could feel her way around her new van.

I saw the salesman coming and said. "If you can't keep that big smile off your face, look the other way so he won't jack the price up on us. Okay?"

"Ornery cuss!" She snapped.

The price ended up being $31.9, including taxes and matching tint for the front windows. The salesman had to chuckle at the ear to ear smile Kelly was wearing when I finally said she could turn around.

Because we needed to be somewhere, I wrote the dealership a check to hold the van till I could get back to take care of the paper work.

Kelly was giddy with excitement over the purchase. We laughed and talked all the way to the lawyer's office, but no one ever mentioned the flashing sign in the windshield that wasn't really there that made me stop in the first place.

I did, however, tease Kelly about her new job.

"What's that?" She asked.

"If you're going to be part owner, I expect you to help navigate. They do have road maps in brail, don't they?"

As expected, I caught the full brunt of the back of her left hand.

"You're awful." She laughed.

I obviously knew her well enough to say such a thing. I was the one waiting for her that fateful morning thirty some years ago when she lost her sight.

Our norm back then was me walking her to school. On that particular day, I yelled up to her to get her butt in gear because we were going to be late. The next thing I knew, she tripped over her own shoes and came tumbling down the stairs. I had been too far away to help break her fall. At the time, she didn't appear overly hurt, but her parents and I took her to the hospital just the same.

During her stay in the hospital, her head swelled from bleeding in her brain around her occipital lobe and she lost her sight. The doctors assured us it would return once the swelling went down. For some unknown reason, it never did and they were all left confused as to why.

I always felt guilty about the incident; even though Kelly had done her best to assure me it wasn't my fault. I didn't get to walk her to school after that because she had to go to a school for the blind to learn the things she needed for her new found condition. She vowed to never let the blindness get her down and it didn't.

For me though, it was never quite the same. I always held myself to blame for yelling at her to hurry up. At times, even now, I'd occasionally tear up as the memory of seeing her tumbling down those stairs replayed itself in my mind's eye for some reason.

Chapter Seventeen

A very attractive brunette dressed in a navy blue skirt topped by a conservatively professional off white clamshell top was seated behind her desk when we entered the lawyers' offices. Upon hearing the door open, she looked up to see who it might be before removing her glasses. Upon seeing it wasn't a delivery person, she quickly stood in her short matching navy heals and walked around her desk to greet the two of us.

According to the black lettered gold name plate on her desk, I could see her name was Gwen.

"Welcome to the Kimmel & Darden Law Offices. How can we be of service to you today?"

"We have an appointment. My name is Jared Maxwell and this is my friend Kelly Sims."

"Yes. Mr. Kimmel is expecting you. Please have a seat." She said motioning with her arm. "I'll let him know you've arrived."

She quickly turned and walked down the hallway to a closed door and knocked softly. A moment later, she disappeared inside.

I led Kelly to a pair of plush leather chairs across from Gwen's desk where we both took a seat. Our wait was rather brief. Within a minute, a sharply dressed gentleman in a several thousand dollar suit, who I guessed to be in his late forty's, came strolling down the hall led by Gwen to meet us.

"Good morning, Ms. Sims, Mr. Maxwell." He said, as he reached us.

I took Kelly's hand and helped her out of the chair.

"My name is David Kimmel. Brad Anderson said I was to take good care of you or he would be coming to see me personally."

We laughed as we shook hands. His easy going manner was very relaxing.

"Please follow me back to my office. It'll give us a few minutes to get acquainted while the car is being brought around."

We followed him to a massive beautiful office, adorned with wildlife and nature paintings. Outside his window was a fountain spraying water into the air from the middle of a small cement pond. A beautiful mahogany desk sat in the middle of the room, half facing away from the window. Around the room were the finest of leather chairs and a plush sofa to kick back in when he wasn't busy. I could tell he'd already made his millions.

At his urging, we took seats near his desk so we could talk while he took notes after he called his driver.

"My congratulations to you on your new found wealth. As Mr. Anderson may have mentioned, we dealt with a similar scenario a few years back. Hopefully, our background will enable us to offer the best advice to protect yourselves and your money. We have an associate accounting firm that we have worked with over the years that can handle your accounting needs. If you already have a CPA, we certainly won't have any problems working with them either."

We sat patiently listening to his spiel; only occasionally offering a response. Neither of us had ever needed an accounting firm. We had had our taxes prepared by tax people, but that was about the extent of it.

My thoughts rambled as we listened to Mr. Kimmel, hoping he wasn't planning on building another office from what he was going to make off us.

When it was our turn to speak as to what we were looking for, I spoke for the two of us. "What we want is fairly simple. Kelly will correct me if I'm wrong."

"Oh believe me, I will." She teased.

Mr. Kimmel and I both had to laugh before I continued.

"We want as much anonymity as possible. We don't want the rafters to let out from all the kooks who want money from us. Next, we want the money to be split evenly between the two of us, however that needs to happen. We each want wills that will take care of our shares in the manner we so choose when we are gone. And lastly, we don't intend to be extravagant with our spending or our investments. We will care for our families and give money to people and organizations we know of as we see fit, but we didn't win enough to be stupid. We've both worked hard to be where we are in life and neither of us want this money to be the crux of bad times ahead."

Mr. Kimmel smiled as I spoke. I wasn't sure if he was thinking I didn't have a clue as to how much money we had or what, but he listened intently until I was finished.

"Would you like to add anything, Kelly?" I asked.

She shook her head no. "Sounds good to me."

About that time, Gwen buzzed, letting Mr. Kimmel know that our transportation had arrived.

"All right then. The car is waiting for us. I hope you are hungry. I've made reservations at Clancy's."

With that, we followed him to the front door where a black stretch limo waited.

I whispered in Kelly's ear, "Don't get too used to this kind of treatment. You can't afford to have your own personal limo and driver."

She just smiled.

As we rode, David, as he asked to be called, commended us on our ideas. "Simplicity is the most assured way of enjoying your new found wealth. You would be shocked at the people who spend all their money in the first year and end up worse off than if they'd never won a dime. An elaborate scheme of investing and expensive purchases is a sure fire way of making a person regret ever having money."

Thinking about his office, made me wonder if he heeded his own advice.

As if reading my mind, he continued. "You're probably wondering about my own surroundings."

Noticing my immediate grin, he laughed.

"To tell you the truth, our well to do clientele demand extravagance. If I had the office of my choosing, they would likely go elsewhere, believing we weren't of their caliber, so to speak. We call it our dog and pony show. My paintings remind me of where my roots are. Frankly, I love fishing and camping."

"You don't say. I'm going fishing this weekend. If you ever need to get away, let me know." I said, throwing out an open invitation.

"You don't know how inviting that sounds, Jared. I know I'm booked for the next couple of weekends, but I'd be glad to take a rain check until I can schedule it in."

I assured him that the invitation was open ended.

Chapter Eighteen

Minutes later, we rolled into Clancy's on Phillips Avenue.

I, myself, had never eaten there. The food was supposed to be excellent, but pricey was said to be an understatement. There were plenty of nice places in Toledo where you could eat exquisitely for under a c note. Call me cheap if you want, but I'd never seen the need to spend a ton of money to enjoy good food. That said, I realized we were probably paying for this meal, one way or another, but not entirely. His other rich customers were going to be footing some of the bill. We hadn't committed to anything, yet.

"Tell me about this place, Jerry." Kelly whispered.

As David listened in, I drew a verbal picture of what caught my eye for her.

"We're driving up under a large car port adorned with all sorts of flowering plants. The primary colors are purples, greens and yellows. There is a doorman dressed in a red jacket coming out to greet us. The building looks like a two story building with a lot of black glass and gold anodized steel columns adorning the front. It's quite an extravagant looking place."

"Wait till we get inside." David interjected. "I think they were trying to compete with Trump, except they used anodized versions where Trump used real gold."

"Just out of curiosity, how much is this lunch costing us? We haven't hired you yet." I said with a grin.

Kelly gasped that I would ask such a thing and nudged me softly with her elbow.

David just smiled. "You're paying for the time at the office, but lunch is on us. Just so you know, if I catch a fish, you might be off the hook for that too."

We all laughed at his choice of words.

"If I have to tie it to your line, I'll get you at least one." I teased.

It really was too bad that Kelly couldn't see the ridiculously rich embellishments that garnished the place. I tried my best to describe our surroundings, but I'm sure I did a terribly inadequate job of doing so.

But she was pleased with my attempt and David added his own observations from time to time to help me out, which was nice. We really seemed to hit it off, even if we were from opposite sides of the tracks.

Once seated, David asked if we both liked Italian dishes. After we assured him that we did, he asked if it would be alright if he ordered for us. Whether it was to take the heat off us trying to order from a menu we'd never seen before or so I didn't have to read the entire thing to Kelly, didn't really matter. We accepted his offer.

As he ordered and kept on ordering, we both began to wonder if we'd made a mistake. We'd never be able to eat the six course meal that was on its way, starting with jumbo shrimp-cocktail.

Once the first entrée arrived, every entree was soon followed by another. I had no desire to gain ten pounds at one sitting, so I ate a bit of this and a bit of that. The shrimp cocktail, I will have to admit, didn't stand a chance. Not only was it good, but it was gone.

Somewhere during lunch, David asked what he must have thought was a logical question. "If you don't mind me asking, how is it you two aren't married? You seem so good together. I hope I'm not stepping on any toes asking the question."

Neither of us choked or gasped for air, so I'm sure he was relieved that he hadn't asked something terribly offensive.

"That's a long story. Would you like to take this one Kelly?"

"Actually, I think I'd like to hear your rendition." She said, grinning at putting me on the spot.

It really wasn't a spot at all. At least, I didn't consider it so. I gave David the short version of a life that encompassed over fifty years.

"He's really too modest." Kelly added when I finished. "Jared has been my rock nearly all my life and was the brother that my late husband Derek never had. He made me give him fifty cents when I wouldn't accept half the winnings. When I did, he said, you've just bought half of a lottery ticket and guess what? You've won."

"Wow. Now that's about as neat a story as I've ever heard." David said, echoing Kelly's earlier sentiments.

"Now don't be going there. I might blush."

"That'll be the day." Kelly giggled.

"So what are you going to do with your winnings, if I may ask?" I smiled. "Your turn, Kel."

Excitedly, Kelly took her turn in the limelight. "We're going to Niagara Falls. Jared and I just bought a new van on our way to your office."

"That sounds like a great idea. If I might suggest,..." David took time to give us advice on how best to deal with the purchase of the van and our other needs until we could get our hands on the money. He also informed us that it would take about a week to get the paper work drawn up that we required and get the money.

We had no place else we needed to be so the rest of the day was his to get whatever information he needed. The quicker we could get the legal work out of the way, the better it was for us.

As we worked away on lunch and afterward on the paperwork, I found myself asking the question that David had. Why? As I pondered the question, I didn't really have a good answer myself. Why indeed?

Chapter Nineteen

After a long afternoon at the lawyer's office with paralegal gathering information, I drove Kelly to her parents' house. Much like I had been the night before, Kelly was bursting at the seams to tell someone her news. As for me, I needed to let my parents in on it, too. So, on our way to the James household, I called to inform my parents that I was coming over as soon as I got away from Helen and John.

When we pulled into the James driveway, I asked Kelly if she wanted me to swing by later to take her home.

She smiled. "You've already done far too much for me today. I'll have Dad drive me home. You know, you really didn't need to do any of this."

"Now what did I do?" I asked, playing dumb.

Kelly tossed a smirk my way. "You really are the best." She leaned over and gave me a hug. Before retreating, she kissed me with a peck on the cheek like always. For the first time ever I think, I realized I liked it. At the same time, though, I felt a bit ashamed. Kelly was my life long friend and my best friend's wife.

Trying hard to distance myself from those thoughts, I jumped out of the truck to help her out. By the time I got to her side, she was already on the ground. In the background, I heard the wooden screen door open and slam closed. It was Kelly's mother coming out to greet us.

"Hello Mrs. James. How are you today?" I yelled back over my shoulder, then braced for the ear pinching and hug I was about to receive. It was a game we'd played for as long as I'd known her.

"How many times am I going to have to tell you to call me Helen? You're going to lose that ear one of these days. Mark my words."

We all laughed and I got my hug, just as I expected. Right after she let go of my ear, that is.

"How's that old coot husband of yours?" I asked.

"Oh! He's over at the lodge playing cards. He should be home soon. Are you staying for supper? We've got plenty."

I chuckled to myself about the word supper. In Ohio, most of us refer to supper as our nighttime meal if we're eating in and dinner when we're eating out. City folk probably think we're from the hills calling it supper. That's okay.

"Thanks Helen, but I'm heading to Mom and Dad's. Tell John I was asking about him. I'll be over to whoop on him in checkers."

"He'd like that, Jared. Tell your parents we said hello."

"I certainly will. You folks have a nice evening. I'll call you tomorrow Kelly."

They both said goodbye and headed up the drive to the front door while I got back in the truck. As I watched Kelly climb the stairs of the porch with her mother, I had to question what was happening to me. Between the dream, the vision, the van, my feelings and everything else, I wondered if I really was starting to lose it.

I was still watching when Kelly turned at the top of the steps and waived goodbye. She knew I hadn't left yet, because she could hear my truck idling in the driveway. How she knew I was still watching? That I didn't know. I guess she just knew.

Mom and Dad had owned a small laundry and dry cleaning business up until a few years back. They had sold it to an oriental couple who were doing alright with it as far as I knew. I'd never entertained the idea of joining them or taking over the business, because there wasn't enough income to support me as well as them over the years. That said, there wasn't a lot that they were ever in want of. Like me, they were simple folk who had simple needs and desires. More than likely, Dad would have a fit when I offered to give them some of the lottery money to make their retirement years easier and more enjoyable. He'd simply have to get over it.

As I pulled into the driveway, Dad came walking out of the house wearing a blue checkered flannel shirt to greet me. "Hear you guys won last night." He said, as I got out of the truck.

At first I was taken back, till I realized he was talking about bowling and not the lottery. How soon we forget.

"Oh, yeah, we kicked butts last night. What have you been up to, Dad?"

"We went over to see Uncle Ben and Aunt Noma this morning. How about you?"

"Well, that's a good question. I spent most of the day with Kelly. I've got some news to share."

"Come on inside. Your mother is whipping up something to eat. There's nothing wrong with you or Kelly is there?"

"No Pops. Everything is fine." I said with a grin as we walked inside, his hand on my shoulder.

Mom greeted me with a big hug when I entered her kitchen before barking orders to get washed up. "I've got food a cooking and coffee's 'bout done brewing."

There was no since arguing. Besides, I'd already spotted an apple pie simmering on the stove. I'd have to find an empty spot to stuff more food into if I wanted any of that. And I did want some of that.

After washing, I took my seat at the table in front of a plate that got there before I did. Even with as much as I'd eaten earlier, it still looked darned good. As I picked up my fork to dig in, I said, "By the way, Helen and John send their best."

"When did you see them?" Mom asked.

"I just dropped Kelly off there before I came here."

"That's nice." She replied.

"Ma, Jared has something he wants to tell us."

Mom looked at me with worried eyes. "What is it, Jared? Is something wrong?"

"Nothing's wrong, Mom. In fact, things couldn't be better."

I waited for a second for Mom to sit down to hear the news. After all, I didn't want her to fall and hurt herself from the shock.

Not knowing how to start, I decided to just tell them the way I did Kelly. Well sort of. "Kelly and I won ten million dollars in the lottery last night."

After saying it, I sat and waited for their reactions. It took a few seconds to sink in. Mom just sat there not knowing what to think. Dad, as expected, was the first to pipe up.

"What in the world are you going to do with that much money?" He asked.

I should have, I suppose, but I hadn't seen that one coming. I laughed out loud.

"Who knows? Pretty much anything I want, I guess. The good news is you and Mom will never have to worry about anything concerning money ever again. Maybe you can finally take that vacation out west like you've talked about."

As I watched, they just sat there quietly looking at me. I think I saw the slightest hint of a tear welling up in Dad's eyes before he reached over to take Mom's hand. "Your mother and I don't need a thing, but it's nice to know we have a son who cares."

That was about what I'd expected so there was no since in arguing. I would just slip Mom money now and then. Sooner or later, she'd talk Dad into taking the trip. The main thing was I wanted them to know I was there for them, even though I knew they already did.

"So how is it that you and Kelly won together?" Dad's quizzical mind asked.

That caught me off guard, too. Needing to come up with a believable story quickly, I stuffed a bite of food in my mouth to buy a few valuable seconds to work up an answer. By the time I finished chewing, something came to me. "We play the same numbers every week together."

"Well, I think it's wonderful that you two keep so close." Mom said.

I sold one, but the expression on Dad's face said he wasn't so sure. I think he doubted whether I ever played the lotto. It really didn't matter and I sure as heck wasn't going to tell them the truth.

Quickly changing the subject or at least the direction, I told Mom and Dad about our upcoming trip to Niagara Falls. Since they had been there a time or two, we got to talking about one of their trips. Before long, the matter of money was the last thing on anyone's mind.

We chatted at the table for nearly an hour, long past that wonderful piece of apple pie with vanilla ice cream. Then Dad and I were shushed out of the kitchen so Mom could clean up. I had nowhere I needed to be, so I kicked back with Dad in the living room while Mom straightened up the kitchen. I would have offered to help, but knew Mom wouldn't have heard of it.

This was something I hadn't done nearly enough of over the past few years. I decided to rectify that situation in the future. Supper at least once a week needed to be the norm, after we got back from our vacation.

When Mom finished up, she made her way into the living room with Dad and me. The three of us finished the evening off in good old family style.

It was nearly ten by the time I headed home, well past my parents' normal bedtime. As I drove, I had time to reflect on the day's events. I'd won ten million dollars, given half of it away, bought a new van, had lunch at probably the most expensive place in Toledo if not the state, ate supper with my parents and planned a vacation with Kelly. I'd call that a pretty full day. I figured on sleeping well tonight, once I got past the unusual feelings I was having towards Kelly.

Chapter Twenty

As I passed through the kitchen door into the house, it donned on me that tomorrow was Friday and payday.

"How soon we forget." I said with a smirk.

Taking a second to consider everything, I decided I might just as well take care of retiring, picking up my check and tools all at the same time. Telling my co-workers goodbye still required some sort of cover story. The first idea that popped into my mind had a good ring to it. Since everyone knew I still had a lot of contacts in the bowling industry, I could say that I'd been hired to rep for one of them. Only the guys at the pro shop would ever see through that little white lie and even then, not immediately. If a better idea didn't present itself, I decided to go with that.

Sitting in my easy chair to relax for a few minutes before turning in, I turned on the news. Within minutes, I was out. Around four o'clock, my kidney's asked for a breather. I turned the TV off before stumbling off to the bathroom. When I looked in the mirror as I washed my hands, I was momentarily startled by my reflection.

"What the heck?" I said, shooting a hard look at the front of me. But what I saw was nothing, at least nothing out of the ordinary. I then shot another look into the mirror. The sawdust covered reflection that I'd seen just a second before was no longer there. As I peered into the mirror though, a faint recollection of a dream began taking shape in my mind. It was one of Derry and me building something. What did he call it, an Ark I think? In my dream, I had crap all over me. So why did I see it when I looked into the mirror just now?

Perplexed, I sat down on the stool, aghast of what seemed to be happening, again. The truth is I'm not even a good carpenter. I'm a machinist. I work with metal, not wood and there are few similarities in the two. Derry, however, had been good with wood, though.

As I sat there, more haunting recollections of the dream started filtering into my consciousness. After a few seconds, I sort of remembered it all or at least most of it. Derry had somehow taken me to a shop where all the tools we needed to do a project were at our disposal.

He had worked with me through each step of the building of this...this box-like thing.

"This is absurd. You just don't go somewhere in the middle of the night and work on projects, especially in your sleep." I scolded myself.

Getting up off the stool, I washed my face, dropped my pants on the floor and went to bed. Switching the alarm to on, I dropped my head onto the pillow and struggled back to sleep.

In the morning, I realized my night hadn't exactly ended with the earlier sawdust incident. I awakened to find myself drenched in perspiration when the alarm sounded. Tossing the covers off, I looked down at my wet sticky clothes.

"At least there's no sawdust." I said, shaking my head in disgust. "A few more nights like this and I won't have to wonder if I'm nuts."

After grabbing fresh clothes, I climbed into the shower, eager to wake up from whatever it was I'd done this time. With the warm shower flowing over my tired body, visions began filing past my mind's eye and I sort of remembered staining or painting whatever it was that Derek and I had made. I quickly checked my arms to see if there was anything on them. I was relieved to not find anything.

As I finished getting ready for work, the thought crossed my mind that maybe I should keep working if just for my sanity's sake. A brief chuckle ensued as I answered myself.

"Nah."

When I got to the kitchen, I poured a cup of cold coffee from the three day old pot into my plastic insulated cup and nuked it in the microwave. When the dinger rang, I grabbed the hot cup of jo, placed its lid on top and headed for the door. As I started to close the door behind me, something stopped me cold.

Eerily, my eyes locked onto something that couldn't possibly be there. But there it was. Sitting on the table by the far wall was the Ark from my dream.

For several seconds, I couldn't move. A whirl wind of thoughts tore through my soul. When I finally collected myself, I walked back in and turned on the kitchen lights to get a better look at this...this thing. Sitting down in front of it, I fearfully admired the marvelous piece of workmanship, that I could almost remember doing. There were inscriptions all around its outside. Some of it I understood. Most were symbols that made no sense at all.

On top was inscribed, "Vengeance is mine sayeth the Lord." On the front, along with other symbols, was the Bible scripture, "Confess your sins unto the Lord, for He alone is Holy." On one side were pictures of little children, the significance of which totally eluded me.

The finely crafted piece of wood was stained in light oak and finished with a protective coating of what seemed to be polyurethane. Even if I could have made such an item, which I couldn't, it would have been tacky for at least a day. This, on the other hand, was completely dry to the touch.

The more I looked and marveled at the piece the more I recalled vague recollections of the dream or whatever I should call it. I remembered Derry trying to tell me things about the box, but they were just too far out there to grasp. One thing I did recall, he said I would know what was needed when I needed to know it because he would be part of me at times in the near future, or some such non-sense.

Closing my eyes, I shook my head and wondered if any sane man could be expected to believe any of this. Impossible wouldn't even begin to explain any of these happenings.

"I have to get out of here." I muttered aloud as I placed the thing back on the table and headed for the door. There had to be a logical explanation to all of this. Somehow though, I seriously doubted it.

Chapter Twenty One

At 6:50, I clocked in at the factory and got into my morning routine of chatting with the usual people. As I made my way to my four axis Okuma machining center, my foreman came strolling down the aisle. Seeing me, he strolled over and stopped to talk, which was good, because I needed to talk to him.

"Jared, I'll bring you out a vacation slip for yesterday."

"Thanks Joe. Actually, I need to talk to you about something. I got a great job offer from someone in the bowling industry. They want me to start right away. I know this is really short notice, but if possible, I'd like to make today my last day. I could probably postpone starting for a week or two if it's going to put you in a real bind."

"Well congratulations, Jared. It'll probably put a crimp in things for awhile, but we're about as slow now as we ever get. I certainly hate to see you leave, though. You've been a good worker over the years. We'll miss you around here. Are you planning to stay the whole day?"

"Yeah, that's my goal. I'll try to give you a decent day of it."

"I appreciate that. I'll let personnel know so they can get whatever forms around that they need signed."

"Thanks Joe. You've been a good foreman to work for."

We shook hands and he left me to get to my work. He probably realized that the afternoon would be pretty much a bust, between signing forms and seeing my work buddies one last time.

The morning moved along pretty good as work occupied my thoughts instead of the box that sat at home on the table. The busier I was, the better I felt.

During lunch, I called Linda Thomas at the bank to get the title cleared on my truck by using money out of my savings. I decided to take care of that situation today, as well. I'll have to admit, it felt pretty good having people run errands for me. Too bad you needed to have a lot of money before they would.

News traveled quickly around the shop that I was leaving. One by one, most of the guys I'd worked with over the years came around to blow me crap for leaving them there to carry the load. It gave us time to laugh and flip about the past.

Near the end of the shift, I hunted down Paul Brown. As usual, he was busy working away at his machine. He was a devout family man who loved his wife and kids. He and his family had fallen on hard times a few years earlier when his wife and daughter were involved in a bad accident. The resulting medical bills nearly wiped them out financially. They were both still going through some sort of therapy.

When Kelly and I got back from our trip, I'd have to see what I could do about helping out with his medical bills without him finding out about it, because there was no way he'd accept my help directly.

"Paul, got a minute?"

"Sure Jared. Word has it you're leaving our merry band of tradesmen. Taking a job in the bowling industry, I understand. Congratulations. I've enjoyed working with you."

"Same here, Paul. By the way, they're giving me a vehicle to drive. Would you be interested in having a newer truck?"

"Sure I would, but I really can't afford it."

"You can this one." I quickly asserted.

"How's that?" He asked.

"Even trade, yours for mine."

Paul immediately started laughing. "That's a good one."

"No Paul, I mean it."

Paul looked at me with unbelieving eyes. "You're kidding me. Your truck is worth over twenty grand. Mine is worth about twenty bucks."

I chuckled because he was probably about right on both counts. His truck wasn't just pretty nasty, it was nasty.

"Paul, I know you've had a tough go of it lately. Besides, you'd be helping me out. I need to get rid of the truck."

"Oh Jared, I...I really can't accept it. It's worth way too much."

"Paul, let me do this for you. Your family needs a break. All I need in return is help getting my tool box home after work. What do you say, we got a deal?" I asked, stretching my hand out to seal the deal with a handshake.

Paul's eye's started welling up from the emotions he was feeling. Unable to say anything, he just shook my hand and nodded.

"Meet me back at my tool box at 3, okay?"

He nodded, still not able to speak.

If nothing else good came from this money, I'd touched the heart of a good man. It felt pretty special for me too.

A few minutes before 3, Paul timidly walked down the aisle to my machine. I'm sure he half expected this to be a bad joke or something.

Together, we pushed my toolbox out to my truck and got it loaded. Not a lot of words were spoken. I'm sure he was still thinking this couldn't be real.

"Follow me to my place and help me unload this thing. Then we'll go to the bank." I said.

"Whatever you say, Jared."

Twenty minutes later, we pulled up to the front of my eighteen hundred foot ranch. Paul waited on the street while I backed my truck up the driveway toward the slowly opening automatic garage door before pulling into the driveway in front of me. Three minutes later, we were back on the road and heading to the bank.

When we walked into the bank, Ms. Thomas had the paperwork in order and quickly escorted us into her office, where we signed the necessary papers. In no time at all, everything was finished.

Paul was nearly stoic as we walked out of the bank together.

"Here's your keys. Let's swap plates and she's all yours. There's a screwdriver in the glove-box."

"You're really doing this, aren't you?" He asked.

"No. It's already done. Just don't forget to bring your title over sometime so I can get legal plates for this thing." I said with a smile.

After changing plates, Paul gave me a hug when I offered to shake his hand. He still couldn't believe what was happening. I saw him wiping tears from his cheeks as he drove out of the parking lot and down the street in what used to be my truck. It kind of got to me, too.

Looking at my new ride, I chuckled. It had little if any of the original twenty some year old paint left on the vehicle. What paint there was remaining was faded to such an orange that you could never have guessed the true red color it probably had been, once upon a time

"Maybe I should just drive it to the bone-yard, instead of home. What a heap." I said with a laugh and a shake of the head. I wasn't really sure they'd even want it.

Jumping in and starting it up, I was just pleased to hear it start. Before I shoved it into gear, though, I realized it still actually ran pretty darn good.

"Hopefully the drive train runs as good as the engine." I said as I let out the clutch and the truck began rolling out of the parking lot.

Chapter Twenty Two

Ten minutes later, I arrived home safely and nothing had fallen off the old clunker along the way. There had been a slight blue haze in the air, though, that trailed behind us from the tired engine that still purred like a kitten. Pulling into the driveway in front of the garage, I felt pretty fortunate and quickly parked the beater in the inside, not wanting the neighbors to see it. They might think someone was breaking in and call the police. More than likely, I'd end up giving it to the Salvation Army or taking it to the dump. That said, I had to wonder if I'd been a bit hasty in getting rid of my truck so soon. Kelly was expecting me to pick her up in a couple of hours for dinner.

I chuckled to myself as I toyed with the idea of picking her up in the beater and wondering if she'd know the difference. It was such a heap! It had holes in the seats and probably a few in the floor boards. As I peered at the truck while the garage door closed behind it, I decided to make other arrangements.

With all the commotion at the end of the day, I'd forgotten about the Ark. That changed abruptly when I opened the door from the garage to the kitchen. Like a bad surprise, it beckoned to me from its resting place on the table. Pulling up a chair, I sat down to examine it, again.

Tracing the finely crafted details with my fingers, vague recollections of how we had built it started playing in my mind. I sort of even remembered doing the carving, even though it was totally impossible. First, I don't have access to those kinds of tools. Second and more importantly, I couldn't even draw a good stick man, little lone do the kind of intricate work this piece entailed.

As I studied it, I realized it was supposed to go on the trip with us. Why? I couldn't say or remember if it was ever really said. The question of whether I'd made it seemed suddenly irrelevant, but did little to quell my fear of it.

Taking a deep breath, I sat the box down out of my way. I still needed a way to pick up Kelly. Whipping out the phone book, I called for a rental car. Since it was particularly warm for late April, I ordered up a convertible. I had to pay a premium to get it at this late notice, but I didn't mind. They said they'd pick me up in about an hour. After giving Kelly a call to confirm our date, I hit the shower.

The car I drove to Kelly's was a bright red Chrysler convertible with a black top, which was already tucked away beneath the rear lid. It was kind of a chick car, but the place I called didn't have a Vette coupe or convertible available for rent.

Kelly heard me pull in, but didn't come outside to greet me. When I knocked on the door, I called out so she'd know it was me.

"Jared, you didn't drive your truck. Is that our new van?" She asked.

I snickered. Obviously, she would have figured out the beater, too.

"No, not yet. I thought you might like to feel the wind in your hair."

"You said Derek told you not to buy a car."

"He didn't say I couldn't rent one till the van was ready."

She laughed at the idea of driving around with the top down, but I could tell she approved.

As she went to grab a light jacket, I told her about giving the truck to Paul. She just smiled, accepting my giving nature as being what it was. After all, I had just given her a sizable chunk.

As we walked to the car, she said. "You know what I'm really hungry for, Jared? Topak's. I haven't eaten there forever."

I had to snicker. It was our first night on the town as soon to be millionaires and she wanted to eat at a hotdog joint. Go figure.

"Sure, why not?" I said, as I opened the car door for her.

With top down and hair blowing in the wind, we cruised to the other side of town to a place made famous by a local celebrity who starred in Korean War episodes years earlier. At one time or another, all the cast members had eaten there. Quite a few other notables had visited the place as well over the years. Their autographed pictures adorned the walls of the place.

During the drive over, Kelly teased that maybe someday they'd put our autographed picture up on the wall now that we had all this money and everything.

Of course I said, "The only way they'll put our picture up is if we bought the place and put it up ourselves."

She slugged my right arm and we laughed together at the idea.

The place had changed some over the years, but for the most part it had just gotten larger so they could serve even more people. Rustic would be my first choice for describing the place as we drove up.

Kelly asked, "Has it changed any since we were here last Jarrod?"

"Not that I can tell." I assured her.

Once we were seated, we sniped back and forth with our typical friendly banter that we always enjoyed. The dogs and chili came before long and weren't bad either. She had kraut with hers. I didn't. It truly was a meal fit for the common people we were and always planned to be.

Afterward on our drive back to her house, I asked Kelly about Derek's woodworking. The change of subject put a slightly darker tone to our festive mood.

"Why do you ask?"

"I had another dream last night. This morning, there was a gift waiting for me on the table."

"What kind of gift?" Kelly asked. Her lowered brow let me know she wasn't really sure if she wanted to hear anymore, but I couldn't keep it to myself.

Even though there wasn't much I knew for sure, there was plenty that I sort of remembered. The Ark itself gave obvious credence that something had occurred so I told Kelly everything that I knew.

I finished my story with, "This whole thing is getting crazier by the day. I'm really beginning to wonder if I should even take the money."

"Don't be going there, Jared. Remember, half that money is mine." She said, sporting an ear to ear grin that at least got us both snickering.

After a moment to think about it, Kelly went on to say. "Maybe we should just see where this thing leads us before we make any snap judgments."

Listening to her words, I wasn't sure if she was being placating or if she actually believed some of my outlandish story.

I, myself, wasn't entirely sure there could possibly be an end to be led to, but as usual, I bowed to her usual wisdom and agreed to see what happened next.

Chapter Twenty Three

A week passed with no further supernatural visits intruding on my otherwise insane world. During that time, the lawyers and accountants had worked together to work out what they thought would be best for us. At the end of that time, Kelly and I had signed the necessary paperwork with the state lottery people. We were officially rich.

We had also taken time to sign the necessary forms so that during our upcoming travels, Ms. Thomas from the bank could keep both our accounts solvent.

First thing upon receiving our money, Kelly and I went to the bank and paid off our new van. Kelly was grinning ear to ear at the thought of being half owner of her very own van. Seeing her write the check for her half made me smile at the thrill she was getting out of the whole thing.

Kelly and a couple of her girlfriends had gone shopping during the week. Needless to say, she was sporting a brand new wardrobe for the upcoming trip. I reminded her more than once that we were only taking a van, not a semi. She found my teasing humorous, but actually did a pretty fair job of packing light, or at least lighter than I was expecting.

During the week, I'd replaced or added a few things to my own closet as well. There were also a few items that I'd bought, not necessarily for the trip. Among them was a new 9mm Glock.

It took a couple of days to get through the customary waiting period involved in obtaining a gun, but it was well worth it when I finally got to fire it. The Glock more than tripled the stopping power of the little .22 revolver that I'd given Kelly and more than complimented the J frame revolver that I'd replaced that piece with. It was probably more gun than I would ever need, but what the heck? Maybe I'd want to stop a Mack truck with a certain dirt-bag driving it someday.

A friend of mine, from where I used to work, had a place outside of town where I could go shoot. I spent several hours there getting comfortable with the new piece.

Because of the difference in gun laws across the country, I knew I couldn't take it on the trip, even with the Ohio permit that I had to carry that was legal in over twenty some states. Gun rights in the northeast were nearly non-existent for private citizens. I guess only cops and criminals were supposed to have them in most of those states. It seemed myopic to me to think that a utopian world could be created where none existed simply by taking away peoples' guns. But, what do I know. I'm only a pistol packing NRA member and a UAW union member, which in some circles is a contradiction in terms.

Over the year plus since the rape and murder, I'd taken Kelly to the same place out in the country and taught her to use the little .22 I'd given her. Being with Kelly and teaching her to use the gun was one of the few things that had kept me from going off the deep end and going after Hess wherever he was.

She had taken to shooting like a kid to water. She simply learned to do what she did best, listen and know her surroundings. At first, we practiced with an empty gun so she could get a feel for it and I didn't get shot in the process. With her hearing as acute as it was, we played games to help her hone in on a target. We next went to throwing rocks to see if she could target where they'd hit. As the training progressed, I threw things everywhere, some landed between us or behind me. She'd start to point her empty gun, then stop.

"You're there, Jared."

"Exactly! That is a deadly instrument in your hands. You must remember who is around you at all times and where." I warned. "You have to be absolutely certain what you're doing before you ever pull that trigger."

In no time at all, she'd become amazingly proficient at targeting a sound. Before long, she was using live ammo. At thirty feet, she could hit within a foot of a sound every time. At ten feet, she seldom missed by more than an inch. Kelly soon began carrying the piece in her purse along with the permit she'd earned to carry it.

Brad, from the DA's office, had helped us out with that. She'd proven her proficiency in the up close and personal range through the special schooling she'd enrolled in and passed easily.

As expected, Kelly's parents had been more thrilled with our good fortune than my folks had been. As promised, I'd eaten supper with them one night and played checkers with John. It was something I did occasionally, but I got the feeling this time it was so they could implore me to take good care of their daughter on the trip. That was fine. They cared for their little girl. They knew I did too. I even let John win a game or two. Actually, he kicked my butt.

Chapter Twenty Four

The night we actually received the money, I surprised Kelly with a special night out on the town. I'd already taken delivery of the van, so the convertible was long gone. All Kelly knew was that I was picking her up at seven and she needed to be dressed up.

When we were a block away, I called to let her know I was almost there. It wasn't something I usually did, but tonight wasn't usual. Kelly walked outside onto her porch when she heard the car drive in. Besides the beautiful green dress she wore, there was also a quizzical look plastered on her face.

As I walked up the sidewalk, she spoke her mind. "Jared, that's you isn't it?"

"It's me."

"What are you driving? That's not the van and you already took the convertible back."

"Actually, I'm not driving tonight. We're riding. I rented a limousine for the evening, complete with chauffer."

Kelly began laughing. "Didn't you just tell me only a week ago that we couldn't afford this type of lifestyle?"

"This isn't a lifestyle. It's a night out on the town with my rich bitch partner."

Of course I was too close when I said that and she let go with a left jab that landed squarely on my chest. A laugh from each of us followed.

"Let's get your doors locked so we can start enjoying this thing. I'm paying for it by the hour." I teased.

Kelly didn't argue. She just chuckled and tossed me her keys. Once I took care of checking all the locks, we walked arm and arm to the car.

"What color is it, Jared?"

"It's a white stretch that seats twelve. The interior is burgundy. And here is our driver, his name is Jackson."

Kelly held her hand out to greet him. I'd already informed Jackson about her blindness. He was right on cue to get in front of her when I introduced him.

"Nice to meet you, Ma'am." He said taking her hand.

Once seated, Kelly's smile lit up the inside of the car and she wanted to know where everything was and where I was taking her. I'd made reservations at The Wharf. Just to watch her squirm though, I told her we were going to the Café of Arches.

Again, I was too close. A serious slap landed on my left leg in protest. "We are not going to a place with plastic benches in a limo."

"Come on Kelly. We've always talked about doing that, remember?"

"I didn't get all dressed up to go have a Big Burger, but maybe we could use the drive-through later to get a dessert." She said with a giggle.

"Alright! Now that's what I'm talking about. We're going to The Wharf."

"That's better. Just don't push your luck." She warned.

Accepting that as a challenge, I reached over and grabbed her knee where she was the most sensitive. She was soon laughing hysterically and fighting to get to my ticklish spots. Once she couldn't take it anymore, she walloped me a good one to get me to quit. Knowing the warning sign, I did. A woman who can't take it anymore is like a pinned cat and Kelly was one feline I didn't even want to spare with.

After things settled down, she asked. "When are we leaving on our trip, Jared?"

"Well let's see. Today is Friday, tomorrow is Saturday, next month is summer and your birthday is coming up shortly after that. Maybe we..."

Kelly had heard enough. She gave me a push and pounced on top of me, dress and all. I was laughing too hard to fight back.

"I said, when are we leaving?"

"I'm trying to answer."

"Answer faster or I'll tickle you and you know how good I am at that."

"Okay I give, anything but that." I pleaded.

"That's better." She didn't get off till I said we could leave as soon as Monday if she wanted.

As she climbed off, she said. "See, now that wasn't so bad, was it?"

"Not for you." I laughed.

Twenty minutes of more bantering later, we arrived at The Wharf. After taking time to straighten our clothes from our tussles, we went inside. Our table wasn't ready quite yet, so we walked around the place whose exterior looked like a fishing schooner that might have been used in an 1850's adventure like Moby Dick while I tried articulating our surroundings. She touched the roughhewn wooden walls, paintings and the plants to help envision the place as I did so.

When our table was ready, we were escorted to a large table for two up at the bow of the ship. The piped in violin music and the adorning art work gave the place a romantic allure that I wished Kelly could see to appreciate. The rustic architecture and the waiters dressed in Tuxedo's gave you the feeling you needed money to dine there. Looking at the prices, I quickly realized you did.

I wasn't sporting a tux, but I did wear a suit. I wasn't a complete oaf. I had nice clothes and unlike some guys actually like to dress for an occasion.

Kelly's dress of emerald green sparkled like the twinkle in her eyes. The glittering necklace that she wore was one of the last things Derry had ever given her. She was more radiant than any woman in the place. And that wasn't just me thinking. I saw the looks she evoked from most of the men and several of their wives. She'd even done something different with her hair, short as it was. I definitely approved and told her so.

An expensive bottle of Merlot started our dining pleasures accompanied by shrimp cocktail as our appetizer. For the main dish, Kelly decided on lamb while I chose the filet mignon done medium rare. Through our salads and beyond, we talked and laughed and thoroughly enjoyed ourselves. Naturally, our upcoming trip was a major topic in our conversation.

Afterward, Jackson drove us around the better parts of town before heading to Mickey Dee's and our long awaited ice cream treats. When we arrived at the golden arches, I got the bright idea to open the moon roof and order from there. It didn't take much coaxing to get Kelly to join in.

As I was ordering, I popped my head back inside the car and yelled. "Hey Jackson, do you want a sundae?"

He snickered before calling back. "Sure, why not? Make it hot fudge with nuts."

So that Jackson could enjoy his treat, we had him park the beast while Kelly and I sat our sundae dishes on top to eat. Still standing, we ate, watched and listened to the traffic as it drove past.

For a while as we rode back to Kelly's, we stood with our heads sticking out of the moon-roof and our hair blowing in the breeze. We laughed and called out to people walking down the sidewalk. You'd have thought we were teenagers the way we were acting. In a way, maybe we were. At least for a few minutes, we got to live a little of the time we'd been cheated out of years before. Nam had seen to that.

It was nearing 11 o'clock when I walked Kelly to her front door. I unlocked the door and checked out her house before allowing her to enter. She gave me a hug along with our customary peck on the cheek. After bidding her good night, I walked back to the limo and sat up front with Jackson as he drove me home.

"Did you have a good time tonight, Sir?" He asked.

"No Jackson, my friend, I had a great time."

Chapter Twenty Five

Late morning Monday, Kelly and I headed out of town, destination Niagara Falls. Within minutes of leaving Kelly's house, we were on the Ohio Turnpike heading east. Though Kelly was the co-pilot, the navigator's responsibilities still fell on my shoulders. It seemed they didn't do road-maps in braille, after all. I'd ragged her that she needed to sit in the back since she wasn't contributing anything useful to our trip. That, of course, only got me clobbered and hugged.

I'd already mapped out our route and had a cheat sheet close at hand to follow sitting on the center console. At the I-80 and I-90 split near Cleveland, we took I-90 northeasterly towards the falls. Because we hadn't gotten an early start, we knew we would probably end up stopping along the way for the night. And since we weren't on any particular schedule, we had already decided to check out any sights that sounded interesting along the way.

As always, it was my responsibility to share the scenery and the road signs. I was only too happy to accommodate. We were going to have fun, even if that little wooden box was packed in amongst our belongings. What it foretold, I had no clue. But how apprehensive could I feel? It was just a little box.

Nearly four hours into our trip, Erie, Pennsylvania was coming into view in our windshield. I started talking about the past when I'd bowled professionally. I had made the cut at Erie in one of the PBA stops there and nearly made the show. During our conversation, I remembered a great place to eat where nearly all the bowlers went. At Kelly's urging, we decided to see if it was still around and if we could find it.

The place wasn't far off I-79, as I recalled. I thought I might even remember the exit when I saw it. Fortunately, there was a sign displaying the restaurant's name visible from the expressway that made it simple to find.

Beef's back in the day was kind of a red neck joint that served some of the best ribs I'd ever eaten. I call it red neck because there were always more motorcycles and trucks parked around the place than cars. As far as I knew, none of the bowlers ever had any trouble there.

Everyone drank and ate in peace. It wasn't really a bar as such, so things didn't get out of hand, too often, as I was told. Maybe as bowlers we fit right in. We weren't of the uppity crowd, as it were.

I warned Kelly before we arrived that she might have to be wary of peanut shells on the floor. She laughed a discerning laugh that suggested she wasn't sure what she was getting herself into.

As we pulled in, I noticed some major changes in the place. Vinyl siding adorned the outside instead of the rough sawn wood that used to be there. Black top replaced the old stone rutted parking lot. Though there were still a few bikes parked out front, most of the vehicles were cars, vans and SUVs.

As we walked in, more differences stood out as the peanut shells were now gone. So, too, were the wooden benches and picnic tables that used to clutter the dining area. Wooden booths, square and round tables for four to six were arranged neatly around the large hall for a little more customer enjoyment and privacy. Yes, the place had changed significantly and all for the better. Fortunately, the food had not. It was as good as I remembered, maybe even better. We enjoyed a fun time and a great late lunch before heading back out on the road.

An hour later, we crossed the state line into New York. There were still three hours of driving left to get to the falls and it was nearing 5 o'clock. Kelly and I began discussing if we should stop for the evening. Out of the blue, the right turn signal started blinking as we neared an exit.

My eyes danced back and forth between the signal and the switch to see if I had inadvertently bumped it. When I tried turning it off, I realized it wasn't even on and yet the signal kept blinking.

"I think we're supposed to get off here." I said to Kelly.

"What do you mean by that?"

I told her about the signal.

"You sure there isn't a short or something?"

"Your guess is as good as mine. I don't know anything for sure at this point. Let's just see what happens when we turn off."

The expression on Kelly's face mirrored the feelings I was having.

At the stop sign at the end of the ramp, the signal kept blinking right. I held out a glimmer of hope that it was, as Kelly suggested, just a short. I tried turning the switch off again, but the signal persisted. Following its direction, I turned right. Once I made the turn, the signal stopped.

Kelly heard it stop blinking and asked, "Did you turn it off, Jared?"

"No."

"This is getting a little weird." She said rolling her eyes.

"You think? I guess we'll just drive a bit to see what happens next." I said.

After several miles, the left turn signal came on as we neared an intersection. Near the corner was a sign telling of a lodge five miles ahead near Chautauqua. Grabbing the map, I looked to see what else was around there.

"Besides the lodge, there's a lake ahead, but that's about it." I told Kelly.

"Do you suppose that's where we're going?" She asked.

"Beats me! I suppose we'll have to wait and see, I guess."

Our wait wasn't long in coming. As we neared another crossroad and another sign directing vacationers to the Chautauqua Lodge, the signal did likewise.

"We must be headed to the lodge. According to the sign, this is a dead end." I told Kelly.

She remained quiet, not sure what to think. I certainly understood her feelings.

Two miles down the road, we pulled in and parked out in front of the lodge office. There was the small matter of the no vacancy sign flashing in the window that had me a bit puzzled.

"I don't know, Kel." I said, informing her about the sign. "Do you want to stay in the van while I check it out?"

"Not hardly! I can't wait to see what happens next. Besides, I need to stretch my legs."

Together, we climbed out of the van and after I stretched my legs I walked around to get Kelly. We walked up the wooden steps that led into the office. At the front desk, I rang a bell summoning the clerk.

When she arrived, I said. "Hello. We stopped to see if you have a room for us?"

"What is your name, Sir?" She responded.

"My name is Maxwell, but we don't..."

"Oh yes Mr. Maxwell, your cabin is waiting for you. Will you be leaving this on your credit card or paying in some other way?" She asked.

As I reached for my credit card, Kelly's finger nails dug into my right arm. I was a bit perplexed myself.

"Can you tell me when the reservation was made?" Kelly asked.

"Actually yes, I remember taking the call myself nearly two weeks ago, I think. Wasn't it you who placed the call Mr. Maxwell?"

"No. It was a friend of mine."

"Your friend must have stayed here before. He seemed quite nice and insisted on reserving cabin number seven for you."

Chapter Twenty Six

As we walked back to the van, Kelly's finger nails sunk deeper into my arm as she fought the urge to scream. Once we got in, she quit fighting and let me have it.

"How could we have reservations since before we won the lottery? Were you planning on taking a trip that you didn't tell me about? What is going on? What, who...?" She rattled off one question after another, each being just another one without an answer.

I took Kelly's hand in an attempt to comfort her. "I don't have any answers, but maybe now you can understand what I've been going through these past ten days."

"Oh Jared. I really never doubted you. Well, maybe a little. But I was sure it was just the stress of losing Brenda, Derek's death, and the whole trial ordeal. Now, I don't really know what to think."

"At least we're on the same page now. We might just as well go in and check out our accommodations. Heaven knows what they might be. If there's only one bed, I want you to know it's mine. I paid for the room."

Of course, the seat belt restraints made it impossible to miss the thump I got from the back of her left hand.

After driving the van over in front of our twenty five foot square-ish wooden cabin, we got out and walked inside together. I sighed a breath of relief at seeing two full sized beds in the room. As a matter of fact, that was the first question out of Kelly's mouth upon entering.

She then proceeded to tell me which bags she wanted brought in from the van. While I went to retrieve them, Kelly mapped out the place in her mind by feeling her way around. Nothing else was said about what would have happened if we'd have had just one bed to share. I knew I would have just taken one for the team and slept on the floor and that would have been that.

Before going to dinner, we took a quick stroll around the complex, as it were. The evening temperature was cool here near the mountains so we wore sweatshirts topped by light jackets. As we walked, I filled Kelly in on the wonderful scenery. Because of the elevation, the spring colors were only just starting to come in. The grass was green, but the trees that weren't some sort of fir were only just beginning to bud. I figured the fall colors were probably very beautiful and suggested we might want to come back to check them out in the fall. The aroma of the fresh pine was stimulating.

Just after 7 o'clock, we walked into the lodge restaurant to enjoy whatever they might be serving. By no means did we expect to find lobster on the menu and we weren't surprised. Our waitress read us the available entrees from the back of her guest check tablet. They consisted of pork or beef manhattans or some sort of chicken and rice combination. We ordered coffee and she scurried away to give us time to consider our choices.

"I wonder why we were supposed to stop here." Kelly remarked, almost nonchalantly.

"I wouldn't worry about it, Kel. I'm sure we'll know when the time comes. It may not even involve this place or today at all."

Though meant to appease her concerns, I totally shared her sentiments.

We both decided to pass on the entrees and opted for dessert instead. Because of our earlier late lunch, neither of us was all that hungry. Once we finished our pieces of homemade pie and decaf coffee, we walked slowly back towards our cabin. In the quiet of the night as we neared it, I heard something muffled.

"Did you hear that, Kelly?"

"Hear what? I didn't hear anything."

"Listen! There it is again. Did you hear it that time?"

"No Jared. I can't hear anything."

"Listen carefully." For several seconds we strained together to hear what it was that I was hearing quite clearly.

"There it is again. Certainly you heard it that time."

"No Jared, I don't hear anything."

"It's coming from over here by this car." I pulled her along to where the sound seemed to be coming from. As we got closer the sound became stronger. I became excited, but Kelly became scared. She still couldn't hear anything and began to cry, thinking that maybe I had finally lost it completely.

I hollered for someone to bring me something to break into the trunk. People started piling out of their cabins and gathered around us. Kelly became hysterical and grabbed onto my arm.

"It's all right Jared, it's all right." She shouted in hopes of snapping me out of whatever possessed me. But no one would help me. I started screaming for help, but no one could hear what I was hearing. Maybe I had lost it, but the sound was too strong in my ears to dismiss.

Finally, two Park Rangers came running over to us from wherever they'd been to see what was going on. When they arrived, they pushed me up against the car to subdue me.

"Calm down Sir." They shouted.

But I couldn't let it go. "You don't understand. You don't understand." I shouted again and again. "There it is again. There's someone inside that trunk."

"We'll check it out, Sir. Just settle down." The Ranger demanded.

By now tears were rolling down my face and I saw the same when I looked over at Kelly's. I quit yelling and worked hard at staying calm, but it was tough because I could still hear the muffled voice in my head. After several seconds, I took a breath and said. "That's all I want. Please check it out."

"Who owns this car?" The Officer barked, but no one came forward.

"If I let you go will you wait for us to do our jobs?" The officer who still had hold of me asked.

"Yes Sir. Just get that trunk open, please." I begged, half crying.

"We're working on it."

After releasing me, he watched for a moment to make sure I didn't start anything again. After a few seconds, he stepped back and waited while the other officer went to see if the license plate number showed up on any of the overnight guest's registration forms. A minute later, he walked past where we were all standing and headed to cabin six. When he arrived there, he knocked on the door and waited.

Moments later, a man answered. It appeared that he had been sleeping, though I couldn't imagine how with all the ruckus I'd been making. I heard the officer ask if he would mind stepping outside. The man did.

"What's this all about?" The man asked.

"This man over here," the ranger said, stopping to point at me, "says he heard something coming from inside the trunk of your car."

"What is he, a loon?" The man scoffed.

"That's what we're trying to determine, Sir. Would you mind opening your trunk for us?"

The man seemed to change his demeanor at that point. He started acting really nervous, shifting his weight from side to side. I could tell he was fighting to remain calm in front of the officer.

After some hesitation, he said. "The keys are in my room."

The officer followed him inside. Moments later, the two returned with the keys dangling from the officer's hand. When they were within a few feet of the other ranger, he tossed the keys over to him to open the trunk. Almost everyone huddled around to see what might be inside.

The man from cabin six stepped back from the crowd as the ranger inserted the key into the lock. When the trunk lid was finally opened, he took off running towards the hills behind the cabins.

A second later, the ranger who opened the trunk exclaimed. "My God, there's a little girl tied up in here." Feeling for a pulse, he continued. "She's alive. We need an ambulance."

Everyone's eyes shot back to where the man from cabin 6 had been, but he was long gone.

"Did anyone see where he went?" One of the officers shouted.

Someone said they saw him take off running and in which direction. A few of the younger men started to run after him, but both rangers yelled for them to stop. "We'll handle this. First we need to focus on taking care of this little girl and get her to a hospital."

As one officer ran inside to call for assistance, the other stayed with the little girl. Looking up at me he said, "Thank you. More than likely you saved this little girl's life."

"I'm sure I got a little carried away. Thanks for checking it out." I said wiping tears from my cheek with the back of my hand.

He grinned, but said nothing more as his attention went back to caring for the little blonde haired girl.

I walked over to Kelly and took her hand in mine. Before I knew it, she was in my arms and crying. We both were.

"I couldn't hear her, Jared. I'm so sorry I doubted you. I was so scared, but I couldn't hear her."

"I don't know that I did either, Kelly. She's unconscious or sleeping and had tape covering her mouth when the officer opened the trunk. I'm not sure I ever did hear her, at least not in the natural sense of the word."

Kelly was stunned. She pushed back as if to look at me as she tried to understand what she'd just heard me say. After a moment to comprehend it, she grabbed me and gave me another big hug.

Before long, sirens screamed in the distance. Soon they could be seen racing down the road towards us.

As the crowd started to break up and head to their cabins, I felt pats on the back and words of thanks for getting involved and holding my ground even when it got a little dicey.

I took a deep breath and thought if she was why we were here, she was in someone else's hands now. Someone's a whole lot better than mine.

With that thought, I shot a look upward and whispered. "Thank you Bro. And thank you too God."

Chapter Twenty Seven

Once the ambulance hurried away with the little girl, the rangers asked their questions which, of course, had no answers. After that, Kelly and I walked to our cabin.

Inside, Kelly was quick to ask, "Is there anything you haven't told me?"

"Like what?" I asked.

"I don't know, but this is getting crazier than I could have ever imagined."

I assured her that there was nothing more that I knew. Instead, I suggested, "Perhaps this little girl is why we were supposed to take this vacation."

Kelly was too fast to fall for that. She quickly reminded me about the box.

Of course, the box! Who knew what that foretold? The problem was neither of us really wanted to know more than we already did or guess what else this trip might have in store.

When we turned in for the evening, a restless night followed for both of us. In the morning, we ate an early breakfast at the lodge eager to move on and hopefully put the night before behind us. One thing we hadn't counted on was the press.

Several local papers had gotten hold of the police report about the child and before we got out of there, several reporters cornered us to do a story. Fortunately, we weren't close to any major metropolitan area, so they were only from small town papers.

Their questions started out fairly innocuous, as did our answers. Our story remained that I'd heard something and caused a ruckus till someone responded. That was it.

I suppose I could have shocked the pants off the world and told them the real story. That would have either made the national news or got me locked up in the loony bin for sure. Maybe both.

They came close to a real story when one of them asked why we were there in the first place. The canned answer, of course, was we were just on vacation, heading to the falls and happened to take a side trip for the evening.

During the so-called interview, we were able to glean some information about the little girl. Her name was Molly Loriman and she'd been kidnapped the day before from the Buffalo area. The fugitive was still on the lamb, but the FBI and Rangers had helicopters scouring the area around the lodge and would no doubt capture him before long.

It seemed from the car he'd left behind that he was local to the Syracuse area. What affiliation he had to the little girl or the Loriman's and why he'd come this way was still just speculation.

"The little girl is doing fine and the family had offered a reward for her safe return." One reporter noted. "How can they contact you?"

"Tell the family to keep the reward for a college fund for Molly. We don't need the money. We're just happy to have been able to help."

Perhaps, I'd used the wrong choice of words when I'd answered them. They suddenly got hung up on why we didn't need the money and started badgering us about our monetary situation.

"Look, it was just a figure of speech. We do all right and don't want to take a reward for saving a little girl's life. So drop it already." I told them.

The interview finished soon enough after that, with them heading to their cars to call in their stories or ask for other assignments.

Kelly and I quickly got packed and headed out ourselves before one of them got the bright idea to pursue the story even further. Driving back to the interstate the same way we'd come, no more funny things happened with the turn signals. Three hours later, we pulled into the Embassy Suites at the falls, hoping to find a suite looking out towards the falls.

As I helped Kelly out, she smiled and said rhetorically, "Maybe we have reservations here, too."

"At this point, I wouldn't bet against it." I said with a smirk.

But that wasn't the case. At the check in desk, I asked for the nicest room available with two bedrooms and at least one room facing the falls. Perhaps, I had been a bit impulsive again in my choice of words. I ended up paying five bills a night for the penthouse suite.

The bellman eagerly came out to the van and moved our luggage to the room while we walked around outside listening to the sound of nature billowing in the background. As usual, I told Kelly about the majestic scenery.

Kelly could still remember what colors looked like, even after all these years so I was sure to include the green of the beautiful lawn, the blue of the sky, the reds, yellows and purples of the planted foliage and the white stone adorning the sidewalks.

She had told me at times she could still visualize the scenes in her mind when we drew gave her enough information. More than once, she'd told me of dreams she'd had in color. Maybe they helped keep the colors vivid and alive for her. What she couldn't envision, she liked to touch or smell. In many ways, she was freer to experience nature than many of us who couldn't appreciate what we saw through our own eyes.

Before heading upstairs to our room, we took a seat in the restaurant overlooking the falls in the distance. The splendor of the falls was magnificent. The natural power emanating through the air gave self-evidence to the power of God over mankind. Man could produce momentary bursts of destructive energy, but this was life giving power that remained constant for centuries upon centuries.

We decided a light lunch of soup and salad was just what we needed before heading up to our room to take a short nap. I told Kelly that I'd familiarize her with our hotel later. She was fine with that.

It was important for her to have some control of her surroundings. It was a game she'd played to be able to get from her room to the front desk and back. It was a goal that she always won, providing she was staying for more than just one night. It usually took about three trips before she'd have the route mastered. We could only go one way and in elevators on only one side of the hall.

Once when we were all traveling together, Derry and Brenda included, I had fooled Kelly by taking a west side elevator down to the desk and an east side elevator back up. I had done that several times before she caught on.

As you can imagine, Kelly got confused and became totally disoriented until she finally realized what I had done. I thought it was funny. Kelly had her own thoughts about it. Let's just say she got even, big time. I had the runs for two days the next time we got together for a meal at their house. I sure wouldn't be doing that again, but we all did get a chuckle out of the story from time to time. Me included.

When we got to our suite, Kelly took a few minutes to familiarize herself with it. The inner room was a living room with a giant flat screen TV and wrap around sofa. The outer rooms on either side were both bedrooms, each having a king sized bed. A large split bathroom was located off each bedroom. With dual sinks in a common area, one person could use the shower or facilities while another spruced up.

Kelly laid out her bathroom supplies while I put my stuff away in my bathroom. Most of her stuff was shape identifiable. Those that weren't, she figured out by smell or taste. My stuff was easier to put out. I simply dumped my ditty bag contents onto the counter, then shuffled things around till they were in the order I would need them.

After I finished, I went out to the living room to see what was on TV. From where I was, I heard Kelly walk into her bathroom once she got all her stuff in order. She soon appeared from her room ready for a nap.

"Wake me when you're ready to venture out." She said.

"Sure thing, Kiddo."

I watched as she disappeared behind her bedroom door before getting up to do the same. Dropping my jeans on the floor next to the bed, I stretched out on the bed. Peaceful thoughts and memories lulled me to sleep.

Chapter Twenty Eight

It was nearly two hours before I emerged from my room fairly refreshed. Kelly was sitting on the sofa patiently waiting; her fingers reading her a story. After taking a few minutes to discuss what we would like to do next, we decided to take our first navigational trip to the front desk and back. During our second trip, we included a stop at the concierge's desk to see what tours were available to and around the falls. We were both eager to begin our vacation and took information with us to mull over during dinner.

Before heading to the dining room, we stopped at the front desk once again so Kelly could get her bearings and also to find out where the workout room was located. We were both concerned about pounding on the weight because of our new life style. Not working and still eating is a weighty combination.

From the front desk, we went to the dining room. Once seated, we each ordered a salad. Since we had just sought out the workout room location, we decided to share a main course which neither of us would likely finish. As we ate, though, we discussed the trip brochures we had grabbed. The concierge had made several suggestions; among them were a day trip to the Canadian side and an evening dinner cruise.

I'd always heard the Canadian side was even more breath taking than the American side. Whether it would be for Kelly was yet to be seen. Most times, she just enjoyed hearing how other people responded to the sights around her.

The dinner cruise intrigued us both, so after we finished eating what we wanted of our meal we revisited the concierge to sign up for the cruise for the next evening. After that, Kelly took her first stab at making it upstairs without assistance.

I watched admiringly as Kelly unfurled her new state of the art walking cane that she had purchased for the trip. It sprung out of her hand as if it had come from a magic show. Using it, she followed the walkways to the elevators.

Her attention to detail was awe inspiring. Meticulously, she retraced each distance and direction she'd put to memory. Starting from the south corner of the front desk, she made her way to the elevator. Recognizing the difference in the flooring kept her directions in order. Once upstairs, she counted the doors down the hallway to our room.

There was never a doubt in her mind or mine but that she would prevail. Stubbornness is a good quality in the hands of the right person. On another person, it might be construed as being a bullhead. You just had to love her for it.

Once we walked into our room, I noticed we had a message waiting on the hotel phone. I pressed the button to see what it was. I was a little surprised to find it was Molly's parents thanking us for having saved their little girl before terrible things had happened to her. They said that Molly wanted to meet us in person and that she was doing fine.

How they'd figured out where we were staying didn't matter much. Between the newspaper people and the police, there were plenty of ways of figuring it out. They left a number to call that I wrote on the hotel stationary next to the phone. I had reservations about making the call and I definitely didn't want the press involved, if it could be avoided.

"What do you think, Kelly? Should we call them?"

"I don't see why not. They just want to thank you."

She was probably right, but I decided to sleep on it. "A good night's sleep usually yields better results than impromptu decisions." It was a saying my Grandpa had taught me as a youngster. I always thought of him when I needed to use the wisdom of his adage. "Thanks Grandpa." I whispered.

Opening the patio doors, I walked Kelly out onto the cement veranda outside our room and leaned against the railing to listen to the thunderous roar of the falls in the distance. The closest thing I could equate the sound to is the roar of a locomotive passing by and passing by and passing by. It was almost too loud to carry on a decent conversation, so we ended up back inside after a few minutes.

At 10 o'clock, we called it a night. While Kelly went into her room to change, I did the same in mine. After hanging up my slacks and donning a T shirt, I dropped into bed.

A few minutes later, Kelly poked her head inside my open door. "Jared?"

"Yes?"

"Thank you."

"For what?" I asked.

"For bringing me."

"You're welcome Kiddo. Thank you for coming."

Chapter Twenty Nine

Around 5:00 in the morning, the relative quiet inside the room was replaced by a soft voice whispering for me to wake up.

"Jerry. Hey Jerry. Wake up Bro."

I didn't want to open my eyes, but I did. There didn't seem to be any reason to pretend it wasn't happening, again. Not after everything else that had happened thus far. Scanning the room, I saw a halo of light emanating from nowhere with no physical substance that I could tell.

"What is it this time Derry?" I whispered, so as to be sure I didn't disturb Kelly.

"Take the Ark to room 348."

"Do you want me to leave it in the hallway or what?"

"No. Place it on the bed."

"How am I supposed to do that? The room will be locked."

"Use your room key."

"How's that going to work?"

"Think back to the night we made the Ark."

"What about it?" I asked.

"I told you that you would know what you needed when you needed to know it."

"So?"

"The Ark is a power unto itself. Made by human and spiritual hands together, it will help you do what would otherwise be impossible. No one, besides you, can open it without God's permission. It cannot be destroyed by anything of this earth, but has the power within to do His bidding."

"So what does He need me for?"

"I need you Jerry. Think of yourself as my courier, helping me take the jury to the accused. God has allowed me a certain time here on earth to do His work."

"That didn't really answer my question!"

"Okay. Think of it this way. We are helping reshape the future the way it was intended. Because of our free will, God has to occasionally set things back on course again. You and I are helping."

"Yeah? What about the child at the state park?"

"My guess is it wasn't her time, but it could have been more about stopping the guy himself before he did something to some other child. I don't really know. Only God knows for sure. I'm just doing my part with your help."

"That takes me back to my original question. Why do you need me?"

"The thing is, only God and the higher Angels can be subjected to the amount of evil found in that room."

"Well, that certainly sounds reassuring. Why is it okay for me to go in there?"

"Things on earth are different than in heaven. Evil that strong is like a deadly virus to those like me. I would be forced to go back to heaven for a long time to recover."

"So you just need me to go where you can't?"

"That's about right. At times, I will live in your spirit and you will hear my voice. Other times, you will be directed by the Keeper of the Ark. But know this, no matter what happens, trust what you see or hear and know that I am forever close by. Not everything will happen as you might expect, but things will happen for a reason. As always, the reason may not be clear to you right now. God's time is not the same as our time."

"I've heard that somewhere before."

"Yes, I'm sure you have. Now take the Ark to room 348. Trust me on this."

Like Kelly, I didn't especially care to hear those words, even from Derry. Good Samaritan that I am, though, I got dressed as quietly as possible.

I didn't even make it to the door though before I got startled out of my mind.

"Where are you going, Jared?" Kelly snapped from her open doorway.

After my heart regained a proper rhythm, I answered. "I have an errand to run. I'll be back in a few minutes. Go back to sleep."

"What kind of errand?"

"We'll talk about it when I get back. I have to go."

Grabbing my room and car keys from the stand by the door, I headed out. The Ark was still in the van so the first thing I had to do was go to the parking garage to get it. Fortunately, the van wasn't far from this end of the building. No one passed me in the hallway along the way, which was understandable since it was the middle of the night.

At the elevator entrance on the first floor, I peered around the corner at the front desk. Only the attendant was in sight taking care of some paper work. Taking a deep breath, I turned and headed for the van which was parked on the second floor of the garage about a dozen spaces from this end of the complex.

Within minutes, I was retracing my steps back to the elevator. I had no idea what to expect with this delivery or what would happen if someone was in the room and awake.

Inside the elevator, I pushed the third floor button using the knuckle on my index finger. The less evidence I left connecting me to this floor, the better I felt. If cameras operated on the elevators, which they probably did, it wouldn't matter much, anyhow. As I rode along in silence, I found myself wondering if I should be treating this whole thing as some sort of covert operation.

Like everyplace else, no one was in the corridor when I stepped off the elevator and no noises were being generated from any of the rooms I passed. At 348, I pulled my key from my pocket and pushed it into the key reader. The green light came on signifying that the door was unlocked. I swallowed deeply, unsure of what was waiting for me on the other side.

Slowly, I opened the door, hoping that its hinges wouldn't squeak. I drew a deep breath once that was accomplished without sound and walked on in. My knees wouldn't have been shaking badly for someone with palsy. If someone would have said something, I'm sure I would have wet my pants for sure as I walked inside and slowly closed the door behind me.

Chapter Thirty

Just enough light streamed through the curtains from outside lighting for me to see where I was going as I walked to the bed. As I started to set the Ark down I suddenly realized someone was in the bed.

"Derek!" I yelled silently. "You could have warned me."

Softly, I finished placing it on the bed before back tracking to the door and getting out into the hallway as quickly as possible. Closing the door behind me as silently as I could, I immediately began giving Derry a tongue lashing as I scurried back to the elevator for sending me into the room with someone inside. He probably wasn't around to hear me, but it made me feel better.

Standing there waiting for the elevator door to open again after pushing the button, I took a moment to peer back down the hallway towards room 348. What I saw scared the begeebees out of me. There was a brilliant light emanating from underneath the door that lit up the entire hallway outside the room. Even the door itself seemed to glow as though a bright light was passing through its steel skin. I took a big gulp and turned my back to it all. I was pretty sure that I didn't want any part it.

I wasted no time getting on the elevator when the doors finally opened and quickly pressed the button for the eighth floor as I entered. Impatient for the doors to close again, I hammered the door close button a half dozen times before any movement happened at all. Distance from whatever was going down in 348 was my only desire.

Before the doors could close a howling sound filled the hallways of the third floor. I didn't want to know what it meant and could only guess as to where it emanated.

Once back on my floor, I tried getting into the room without making a sound. Unfortunately shaking as badly as I was, I couldn't do anything without making a noise. The fact that Kelly heard everything and was already awake when I left made my attempt a moot point.

"What's wrong, Jared?" She asked from her perch on the sofa, somehow sensing my trembling.

Even my voice shook as I tried to answer. "NNNothing. Go bback to ssleep."

Almost instantly the light came on, so I'd know that "nnnothing" was an answer that wouldn't result in sleep or time alone anytime in my near future.

"Do you want to try again? Your voice is shaking like a leaf. What is it?" She demanded.

Walking over and standing next to her, I tried to formulate an answer, but I couldn't imagine how to begin.

"Sit here Jared." she said, taking my hand with one and patting the sofa beside her with the other.

Maybe she thought if she could touch me, she could read my mind or something. Who knows? Regardless, I did as she asked. With her hand resting on my shoulder, I fought to come up with an answer.

"Take your time. It'll be fine." The calmness of her voice and the touch of her hand helped, but not much.

"I'm not sure, Kel."

"What do you mean?"

"I think someone is dying or about to die."

"What makes you say that?"

"Were you awake before I left or did I wake you when I got dressed?"

"I was sort of awake. I thought I heard you talking to yourself. Why?"

"Did you hear anyone else?"

"No. Why? Was there someone here?" She asked, seeming puzzled by my question.

"Sort of, Derry spoke to me."

"What about?" She asked, sounding almost like it was no big deal.

Slowly, I replayed the conversation for her along with the events of the past fifteen minutes.

"So what makes you think this person is about to die?"

I fought to come up with an analogy that befit the picture I had in my mind. Amazingly everything seemed to fall sadly short. Finally, a picture came to me that depicted what I wanted to say.

"Do you remember when we went to see Indiana Jones a long time ago?" I stammered.

"Sort of. Why?"

"Do you remember what I told you happened when the Germans opened the Ark of the Covenant?"

"You don't really think your little box is the resurrection of the Ark of the Covenant, do you?" She said with the slightest hint of a snicker.

"I don't know, Kelly. Derry told me it has a power unto itself, but other than that I just don't know."

She put her arms around me to help settle me down. I was still shaking uncontrollably. Being held by her slowed the shaking, but did little to diminish the anxiety that I felt.

We wouldn't know until the next day if I was completely out of touch with reality. I hated to think what the maids might find when they went to clean 348, if I was right. Maybe, they wouldn't find anything at all. Maybe, he'd just be gone. Maybe, he'd be fine and nothing will have happened. How would I know? Did I need to know?

Well. I needed to know. That was the one thing I was sure of. I did need to know.

Kelly took my hand and led me into her bedroom. She tossed open the covers and told me to lie down next to her. After dousing the light, her arm draped over me. Under her protection, I felt secure. A kiss on my shoulder helped calm my fears, if only a little.

Though slow in coming, sleep finally came in her protective arms.

Chapter Thirty One

At 7:15, we were jolted out of deep sleep by an alarm clock that was purposely set the night before to get us ready for our workout. Aided by the heavy drapes that blocked the early morning light, darkness still consumed the room.

Neither of us gave it any thought at 5:30. Being the closest, I reached over and turned it off. Kelly's arm was still draped over me and barely moved as I did so.

"We'll work out tomorrow, Jared. Go back to sleep."

I was in total agreement as far as the workout. Sleep, however, was altogether another matter. Too many questions bottlenecked in my now awakened brain. Along with the unanswerable questions about my early morning jaunt, something else disturbed me terribly. Kelly's holding me felt incredibly good. What bothered me the most was I didn't know whether to feel angry, ashamed or elated.

For twenty minutes, I fought to find an answer to any of it. All that came were more questions. At 7:40, I couldn't stand it any longer. I told Kelly I needed to get up. Rolling out of bed, I went back to my own room, grabbed some clothes and hopped in the shower. Steam from the hot water rolling down my back relaxed my muscles, but did little to lessen the mental anxiety I was feeling.

After getting dressed, I knocked on Kelly's still open door. "I'm heading downstairs."

"Are you alright? I was worried about you last night."

"Me too. I'm glad you were here. I really needed you." I said.

She smiled.

"I'm going to go get a paper. I'll be back in a half hour or so."

"I'll be ready for breakfast when you get back."

A USA Today was on the floor outside our room so I didn't have to go far for that. I didn't give a thought to going back inside to read it. I knew I needed distance more than anything right now. Downstairs, I found comfy chairs in the sunlit atrium that made for great reading. I sat in one with an ottoman and kicked back to see what kind of news I'd been missing. I didn't expect to see anything about Hess in it, but I could hope.

The front page was covered with mostly national news. One item that did catch my eye was a story about a confessed child molester who had been let out of jail in Syracuse, New York, on some sort of technicality. The guy had been on trial there, but someone had forgotten to dot an I or do something equally stupid. Now he was out.

Friggin perfect! I thought.

Since Derry's death, I'd been doing a lot of scanning on the internet about criminals, especially the predatory types, who had gotten off for idiotic reasons. On the website Injustice-in-America.com, I found actions regularly that culminated in hardened criminals escaping prison terms because some slick lawyer had figured out another new way to screw the system.

How lawyers could live with themselves after putting scumbags like them back on the street was beyond me. I often thought that it would be the ultimate payback if those same molesters started targeting the kids of the very lawyers and judges who had screwed up the system in the first place. How sweet and just would that retribution be?

On the sixth page, I found an article about our little Molly and her parents. They had finally caught the bum who had abducted her. By all accounts, it still appeared to police to be a random abduction.

"Maybe to them it was random, but someone certainly knew it was going to happen, Little Molly. You had an Angel looking out for you. Hopefully, you'll get the chance to live a long normal life and have little ones to whom you can tell your horror story to some day." I said quietly to the only interested person there, me.

As I turned the page, a bustle of activity around the front desk caught my attention as anguished faces began speaking on telephones and pointing for people to go here or there. I quickly got the feeling that room 348 might just be the topic of their discussions. No one was screaming or raising a riot, at least not down here, but if that were the case, upstairs could be quite a different matter.

After a few more minutes, I folded the paper under my arm and headed to the elevator area. Pressing three instead of eight, I decided to take a quick look-see for myself. When the door opened, an immediate sense of urgency loomed in the air. I heard crying and someone in authority giving people directions. I didn't bother stepping off. I'd heard quite enough.

In case there was a camera scanning the action on the elevator, I acted a bit surprised at the door opening on the wrong floor and corrected the situation by pressing eight.

Within another minute, I walked into our room to a patiently waiting Kelly who had found a cooking show to listen to on TV. She greeted me with a smile.

"Get your paper read?"

"Most of it. Ready for breakfast?"

"Just waiting for you. How are you doing this morning?"

"Somewhat better thank you."

Seeing what she'd been watching, I asked. "Find any new recipes to try on me?"

"As a matter of fact, they just had a segment on making the perfect burnt French toast." She said with a snicker.

"Yum, I can hardly wait." I said with a chuckle. "Maybe it'll be on the menu downstairs."

"I'm sure."

"Let me get the brochures off my dresser to go over while we eat."

"Okay."

Walking into my bedroom, I was stunned to see what was waiting there on top of the brochures.

Chapter Thirty Two

"Did someone deliver something while I was out?" I asked over my shoulder.

"No, why?"

"Well,… I don't know how to put this, but…the Ark is back. It's sitting on my dresser."

"You're kidding me, right?"

"Unfortunately, I'm not."

"What in the world do you think that means?" She asked.

"Oh Kelly, if I only had a clue. The way things are going, I'm afraid we might find out sooner than we'd like. Just so you know, while I was reading the paper downstairs, a commotion started taking place around the front desk. It was worse on the third floor when I stopped the elevator there on my way up here."

"This is getting to be quite the journey you've brought me on."

Her tone was matter of fact and seemed to be letting me know that she was in this for the long haul. I had to admire her for that.

Grabbing the brochures that I'd come to get, I shot the box one more look. More questions was all it brought. Two seconds later, I took Kelly by the arm. We then left the room in search of food.

As the elevator opened onto the first floor, a sense of urgency filled the air. Police scurried through the complex to get to an awaiting service elevator. I whispered the news to Kelly, who was already acutely aware that something was happening, just not sure what.

Figuring that news travels at the speed of sound in small places, I assumed we'd confirm soon enough what had happened. More than likely, someone would have leaked enough information to staff to calm anxious patrons. I highly doubted the word murder would be used in order to prevent mass exodus.

Of course, when newspaper people got hold of the story that would be quite another issue. They lived on hype. The more inflated they could spin an article, the better their ratings. I'd always figured in many cases their motto must be something like, "the hell with truth, full exaggeration ahead."

Putting aside our questions for the moment, we casually walked to the restaurant amidst the controlled chaos. The waiting receptionist took us straight to a table in the moderately full dining room. As we were being seated, I asked about the ruckus. As expected, she had a coined response.

"It seems someone has died on the third floor. That's all we know right now."

She didn't seem overly concerned by the news. I wondered why, but perhaps it wasn't all that unusual since the place attracted so many senior citizens.

As for the two of us, we didn't hold out much hope that old age was the culprit this time. With everything that had happened in the past several days and Derry's words to me, I was beginning to wonder if we were on some sort of Divine mission. As absurd as it sounded, it was as plausible an explanation as any. By some of Kelly's comments, I believed she was beginning to come to the same conclusion.

We ate a quiet, nearly somber breakfast, not at all like our normally jovial selves, before heading for the tour bus that took people to and from the falls hourly. By the time breakfast was over, we had resolved that we were tourists, here to witness the splendor of this magnificent place. To that end we were determined to do so unless otherwise directed. Unspoken was each person's desire that we wouldn't be any time soon.

We found that though the crushing sound of the falls could be heard for miles, the true splendor didn't truly hit you till you arrived on site. The thunderous crushing of the millions of tons of water forced you to shout to be heard.

Kelly kept a firm grip on my arm once we got off the bus. Although the power was exhilarating, I could tell that for her it was also somewhat frightening. She used her ears to hear and see. The falls made that quite difficult, causing her to feel terribly vulnerable.

Feeling her concern, I said. "Don't worry, Kelly. I won't let you get anywhere near the edge."

"I don't know. You might want to reclaim all that money you gave me."

"Now who's being funny? Besides, it's too late, isn't it? You didn't include me in your will, did you?"

She gave me a quick slug to the arm with her free hand that was accompanied by a friendly hug.

As always, I did my best to describe our surroundings. I'm afraid I was terribly inept at doing this particular place any real justice. Even so, we both enjoyed the trip about the falls, which made us eager to see what awaited us on the evening dinner cruise. It also helped us put aside, temporarily at least, the night's prior incident.

Besides, with Kelly by my side, I didn't worry about the box or what might be happening back at the hotel. And as far as I was concerned, I knew nothing, nothing for sure anyhow.

Chapter Thirty Three

When we returned to the hotel, we quickly got filled in on the latest concerning the morning upheaval on the third floor by the maid who was still working in our wing. She seemed quite excited to have someone to tell her account to.

"A child molester, who was released by the courts just yesterday up in Syracuse, was found dead in his room. His screams around 7:30 a.m. woke up neighbors who called security. When they arrived, they first had to get past the inner security lock on the door.

"Here's where things get really weird." She said. "Rumor has it that when they finally got inside, it was like the guy had been scared to death. His eyes were wide open. His hands and arms were out in front of his face like he was warding off evil spirits or something. It's all really quite interesting, you know, the stories that are coming out of there." She said.

"The police are trying to keep a tight lid on things so as not to frighten the other clientele. I know I really shouldn't be telling you folks about any of this, but it's the strangest thing I've ever heard."

Myself, I thought it quite curious that the security lever wasn't in place when I'd made my delivery. Depending on what cameras the facility had in place and where, I had to wonder if I was going to be interviewed about my late night trip. Chances were probably pretty good that I would. I decided I probably needed to come up with a plausible explanation, just in case. Until that time, though, I wasn't going to get all worked up about it. According to the maid, the screams had occurred hours after I'd left the floor.

We thanked her for being honest with us and walked on to our room. Of course, when we got inside we had our own rather brisk discussion about the maids account. Kelly wanted to know more than there was to know. Or at least more than I knew.

In the end, without anything new that I could add to what we already knew and what the maid had told us, we were left with the decision to either go home or continue on about our vacation as though nothing had happened. With possibly less than total conviction, we decided on the latter. Whatever had been done hadn't been done by either of us.

Though easier said than done, we endeavored to kicked back to relax a little before getting ready for the dinner cruise. She sat in her bedroom and read while I watched a movie on the boob tube in my own room.

Though I'd showered once already, around five, I decided to take another one before getting dressed for dinner. As I dried off near my bed, I heard the water come on in Kelly's bathroom. Just as I dropped my towel to the floor, Kelly stuck her head inside the door that I'd neglected to shut to ask a question.

The sudden realization that I was standing there in the nude shocked me as I temporarily forgot she couldn't see. Reaching for the towel in a panic, I banged my right shin against the bed frame. Gritting my teeth, I tried not to let on what had happened.

Kelly in her never ending awareness of everything figured it out immediately and started laughing hysterically. "Why Jared, now that's a picture for our vacation scrap book!"

Standing there in the doorway, she pretended to take my picture with a make believe camera, just laughing away.

"Very funny. Have your laughs."

"Oh I will. By the way, what are you wearing tonight, besides the nothing you have on now?" She laughed.

"Hah! Hah! Slacks and a blazer."

"Thanks. Now, put some clothes on, will you?"

I smiled as she closed the door behind her. She'd gotten me a good one. Needless to say, I was dressed completely and watching the news out in the living room by the time she got out of her shower.

From behind her door, she called out in jest. "Are you decent yet?"

"No, not yet!" I yelled back.

"Too bad." She answered, as the door opened anyway.

"Maybe, I'll pull your towel off so we'll be even." I teased.

"Only if you can sleep with one eye open, if you know what I mean."

I did know and bowed out of the dare. I'd taught her too well growing up on how to get even. The problem was, she had figured out how to improve on my own ideas. I didn't really want her owing me anything.

We laughed at the cat and mouse game we'd been playing. Each of us knew where we stood with each other or at least where we'd stood up to now. I watched as she disappeared back into her bedroom to get ready. The thoughts that followed her ingot my heart racing more than it should have and I knew it.

When she reappeared, she took my breath away. The black and white floral patterned dress she wore looked stunning on her. Though the cuts weren't overly deep, enough skin was exposed to make you think about what wasn't. I'm not sure which of her friends had helped pick it out, but I approved of their taste.

"Do you like it?" She asked.

Noticing that I had to clear my throat in order to speak, she answered herself. "I'll take that as a yes."

Chapter Thirty Four

A few minutes before six, we headed downstairs to wait along with about thirty other people for the bus that would take us to the boat and dinner. Kelly had the eyes of everyone upon her as we walked to the waiting area. In her all-knowing way she probably realized it, but didn't let on. She kept hold of my arm as I led her to a pair of empty chairs to relax in while we waited. The one thing she probably didn't realize was that she also had hold of my heart too. For that and a few other reasons, it was as uncomfortable a feeling as it was wonderful.

While we waited, we began chatting with a couple who were about our age that happened to sit next to us. Their names were Jim and Cindy McDonald, from outside of Joliet Illinois. They were on their second honeymoon.

Our own story was that we were lifelong friends going on a much needed vacation. It wasn't all that far from the truth. We had only left out a few minor details.

While we chatted, Jim started watching me curiously. I could tell something was puzzling him. Finally, he said. "I think I know you from somewhere."

"Unless you're a bowler, I can't imagine where. I used to bowl some pro stops when I was a bit younger."

"Well, I do bowl, but only in league. No, I've seen your face somewhere before, recently I think."

"Maybe, I've got a twin." I jokingly commented.

"No, I don't think so. It'll come to me." He said.

They seemed like nice people and Jim was a funny guy, so we continued talking to them and found seats near one another on the bus. Since we were getting along so well, we asked them to join us for dinner on the boat, as well.

As we enjoyed our salads before dinner was served, we all got to talking about our trips thus far. Kelly inadvertently made mention of our stay at the lodge, just inside the New York border.

In a flash, Jim's eyes lit up like a bulb had gone off in his brain. "That's where I know you from."

"What do you mean?" I asked, startled.

"Your picture was in the local paper today for saving that little girl's life. You're a real hero."

"Oh please. I didn't even know they'd taken my picture, let alone put it in any newspaper." At least none that would have reached here, I thought.

"Oh man! That must have been really exciting. I mean, hearing the little girl calling from inside the trunk like that and everything. That had to be a special feeling, saving her from that Son of a you know what."

I couldn't argue with that. It did feel pretty good. Trying to avoid talking about the incident any further, though, I shrugged my shoulders, hoping to dismiss it at that.

"I saw from the article that you aren't going to accept the reward." He continued anyway.

Kelly and I smiled at one another and at our new friends.

"A reward isn't necessary. Saving her life is plenty reward enough." I assured him.

"Good Samaritan or not," Jim continued. "I'd have to think long and hard about turning down fifty thousand dollars."

I nearly choked on the food in my mouth at the sound of that. After a short coughing spell and a drink of water to clear my throat, I said. "I didn't realize it was that much."

Stopping to cough again and taking another drink of water to sooth my now raw throat, I said, "Still, I doubt if it would have made any difference."

Without notice, Jim stood and tapped his water glass with his knife trying to get everyone's attention. Soon enough he achieved his goal. There was nothing I could do at that point to stop him. I pretty much knew where this was headed.

"Could I have everyone's attention, please?" He called out.

To my dismay, everyone got really quiet so he could say his peace.

"We have a real honest to goodness hero among us. This gentleman," he said, stopping to point at me, "is the man responsible for saving the little girl who was abducted from Syracuse two days ago. I think we need to give him a big round of applause for having the courage to get involved."

It was too late to object as everyone applauded and shouted their praises. I sheepishly stood up to take a bow; anything to get this over with as quickly as possible. Hoping that was now behind us, I sat down intending on resuming dinner and changing the conversation to something else.

Jim, however, having the attention of the assembled, continued. "He is such a hero, that he isn't going to accept any of the reward offered by the family of the little girl."

At least he didn't mention the fact that the reward was fifty grand. Applause shot up again. This time, I just waived my hand to those in attendance in thanks. Throughout the remainder of the evening, we had to deal with people coming up to praise us for having saved little Molly. Although I wasn't a totally private person, I wasn't really up for a show like this one. And I could tell that Kelly wasn't enjoying the attention much, either.

Cindy apologized several times for Jim's exuberance. "He's a salesman and can't help himself."

We just smiled and said it was alright.

Despite all the attaboys, we did enjoy the remainder of dinner and our cruise around the falls. After dinner was complete, Kelly and I got cozy next to the railing outside so we could watch and listen as the falls came ever closer. Like always, I did my best to paint a portrait of everything I saw and what Kelly heard. I described the beautiful boat and told her all about the people, their dress and their behavior as we traveled near the falls. She hung on my arm and on my every word, trying to visualize what it must be like, but the pounding in her chest from the intensity in the air was probably the best picture of all.

As for me, I knew the pounding in my chest wasn't all because of the falls. I enjoyed having her on my arm more than she could imagine or I could understand.

After the cruise, the McDonald's, I'm sure at Cindy's insistence, offered to buy us drinks for having embarrassed us on the boat. Though I wanted to decline, Kelly had other ideas. She was on vacation and decided it would be nice to socialize a bit longer. Who was I to object?

When the bus dropped us off at the hotel, we walked to the bar, where unfortunately, instead of a band, they had karaoke singing. I have no idea why vacationers love trying to be someone they aren't, especially when they aren't around anyone they know. But that seems to be the nature of the beast. A few of the singers actually did a fair job, but the majority should have paid us for having to listen.

At Kelly's urging, I got up and participated. I sang in the choir at church and had even played in a band back in high school, so I could actually sing albeit a little. Jim and Cindy were thrilled that I did so well.

I laughed at their response then chided them. "Now you know why I'm not taking the reward money. I'm holding out for a call from my agent." Which, of course, got us all laughing.

Around 11:30, Kelly started running out of steam, so we called it a night. Thanking the McDonald's for an enjoyable evening, we got up to leave. They decided they were tired as well and followed us to the elevator. Once inside, they pressed the fourth floor button. When we pushed the button for the eighth floor, Jim took notice.

"You must do alright for yourselves to stay in the penthouse suites. No wonder you didn't take the reward."

I hesitated, not knowing what to say. Fortunately, Kelly came to my rescue. "I received a large insurance settlement when I lost my sight in an accident a few years ago."

Jim didn't know how to respond to that and didn't. When we got to their floor, they smiled and said good night as they exited the elevator.

After the doors closed, I looked at Kelly. "Quick thinking," I said.

"You've taken enough heat for one day." She said with a wink. Putting her head on my shoulder, she put her arms around me and gave me a hug.

Little did she know my heart skipped at least one beat, leaving me pleasantly terrified.

Upon entering our room, she gave me a kiss on the cheek, said goodnight and walked straight to her room while I walked directly to mine. Less than five minutes later, I was out.

Chapter Thirty Five

The sandman left gritty granules in my eyes through which to view the morning streams of light that penetrated the narrow gaps in the drapery. Rubbing the remnants away, I searched out the numbers on the alarm clock not far from my face.

7:30 something. That was close enough. Today I had to work out.

Rolling out of bed, I limped into the bathroom with muscles that didn't seem all that eager to be moving quite yet. Maybe they knew what was awaiting them. As I walked out of the bathroom, I heard movement in Kelly's room.

"Good morning, Kiddo. Ready for a work out?" I yelled through her closed door.

"More or less. Some of me more, some of me less."

"I know the feeling."

We both decided on the mouthwash method of getting ready, knowing the full treatment would take place after our workouts. When we arrived at the thirty by thirty workout room on the second floor, I gave Kelly a tour of the machines there. Afterward, I jumped on the elliptical trainer before moving to the weight machine while Kelly burned calories on the rowing machine before moving over to my just vacated elliptical trainer.

We worked out for a half hour, sparring verbally just to keep it interesting. As we did, I watched as she pushed herself to a hot dripping sweat. Seeing her that way started to heat me up on the inside and resurrected the memory of how her hug had terrified me just last night. I tried to turn away but couldn't bring myself to do so. Realizing that I couldn't, I pushed myself a little harder. It didn't help much.

After our hearty workouts, we went for a cool down by taking a stroll around the complex. While we walked, I noticed and told Kelly about the police cars still parked near the front entrance. Evidently, they were still investigating room 348.

Good luck with that, I thought to myself.

After showering, we strolled back downstairs to enjoy a light breakfast. As we ate, we talked about our options for the day. Traveling to the Canadian side seemed to be the odds on favorite. Little did we know that our day would end up going in a whole other direction.

As we headed toward the elevator to grab our jackets after breakfast, we were stopped by reporters near the front desk. We could have walked through them, I suppose, but Molly's parents were among them hoping to extend their gratitude to us. Why the reporters had to be involved in the deal, I could only guess. Personally, I thought it was a bit distasteful.

Though it was a reporter who first spotted us as we neared them, the true culprit was obviously the photo taken without our knowledge. After the reporters stopped us, Donna and Chuck Loriman stepped forward to introduce themselves. They seemed like a nice couple dressed in casual money, not flaunting it.

If I had to guess, Chuck was close to my age, in his early to mid-fifty's. His slightly graying hair was receding somewhat, but his torso wasn't. Dressed in khaki slacks topped by a red polo shirt that was covered by a golfing wind breaker, he seemed quite relaxed with the media and quite fit.

As for Donna, she was a bit younger, probably in her late forty's. I'm sure she probably used hair color, but the ash blonde looked very natural and she seemed fit, as well. She was had on tan colored slacks with her short heals, a pastel blue button down shirt with a very light in color draped across her shoulders neatly tied around her neck.

After initial introductions, they asked us to join them at their home for the day. Molly wanted so much to thank us for saving her life. As much as we would have liked to side step the offer, we found it impossible to do so without offending the Loriman's or giving the press any more reason to ask more questions than we didn't want to answer.

I only hoped that once we were left alone with them we could bypass the question of the reward. If push came to shove, I guess we could just accept the money. I'd never said we had too much.

While Kelly chatted with them, I made a trip upstairs to get our jackets. When we walked outside with the Loriman's, a limo was waiting to take the four of us to their estate. The caravan that followed included several press vans of one kind or another. At least there weren't any national television crews working the story. I was thankful of that. These people were just local. My goal was to be so low key that they wouldn't even think of sending this story farther up the food chain.

Inside the limo, Chuck apologized about the press and the hype. "The fact is, I'm a state representative on the ballet for congress this fall and the press has been hounding us to meet the man who saved our daughter's life. There is also the matter of the reward." He said.

We side stepped the issue of the reward for now, opting to talk about Molly instead. They filled us in on Molly's scholastic achievements and interests as well as how she'd been doing since the abduction.

After a half hour or so ride to just outside of Tonawanda, north of Buffalo, the limo passed through the front gates of the Loriman estate. I snickered under my breath and squeezed Kelly's hand let her know we were nearly there. The mansion itself as we passed through the security gates was smaller than the estate that surrounded it would have suggested. Jed Clampit's place on TV was probably larger than the house we faced, but the ground around it was massive. That's not to say the place was small by any means. It was just somewhat smaller than some of the homes we'd just passed that were also gated along the way.

At first glance, the house looked as though it was a three story dwelling of probably twelve to fifteen thousand square feet on the first floor. After closer inspection of the window placements as we drew closer, I guessed it was more than likely a large two story with a high ceilinged first floor.

I whispered to Kelly about the red brick monstrosity as we drove up the long gated driveway.

"How many servants does it take to manage a place like this?" I asked.

Kelly elbowed me, thinking it was an improper question. Whether it was or wasn't, it was too late to retract it. At least I hadn't used a southern drawl when I asked or I probably would have really sounded like a kick.

Chuck smiled before answering. "We contract the outside maintenance, the chauffer second's as our butler and a rotating maid during the morning and early afternoon hours rounds out the troops. It's actually fairly modest in comparison to a few of our neighbors who have round the clock employees."

"Occasionally, we have an evening function that requires staff, but we try to limit those." Donna added. "When we need them, we contract them through a catering service."

"Interesting." I commented, having no desire to own this much home for any reason, even if I was filthy rich, which I wasn't.

Before getting out of the car, Chuck assured us that after the press got their story, they'd leave and we would spend a relaxing afternoon with them, alone.

I will have to say, he was quite assertive with the press and controlled them as well as could be expected. Before going inside, he set ground rules for how long Molly would be scrutinized and what types of questions could be asked. Anything too personal would end the interview process immediately. Previous to seeing Molly, Kelly and I took our turn with the press.

Much like our earlier interview, I told how I'd heard a muffled noise from inside the trunk of the car, which turned out to be Molly. I said I responded like anyone else would have under the circumstances.

The questions got tougher when they zeroed in on the fact that Kelly and I weren't married. Kelly's story from the night before gave us direction to build on. Hopefully, this story didn't make it back home or we would be screwed. People who knew us obviously knew about her vision. If national TV cameras ever homed in on us, we'd have to come up with a better version. I didn't even want to think about that.

"What about the reward money? Are you accepting it? We've heard you aren't."

"We really haven't discussed that yet." I said, attempting to dismiss it.

"So you are accepting the reward?" Another reporter interjected.

"No. What I said was, we haven't discussed it yet." Not confirming nor denying it seemed to work at least for the time being.

After our two minute interview, the press was anxious to get a picture of Molly and me together. Chuck took a minute to look in on Molly first. He soon returned down the long semi-circular staircase to inform us that she was up for a five minute interview and that was all. We were then all escorted upstairs to meet the little princess.

When we entered her bedroom that was about a third the size of my whole house, it seemed, a beautiful little blonde haired brown eyed girl was sitting up in her four poster pink bed leaning against a half dozen fluffy pillow. She was dressed in her pretty pink American Girl pajamas holding a Winnie the Pooh bear against her chest and smiling.

"You must be Jared, the man who saved me from that awful man." She said, sort of asking, sort of proclaiming.

"There were a lot of people who worked together to save you, Honey. I just got the ball rolling."

She placed the bear next to her and held her arms out so she could give me a hug. I walked over and sat on the edge of the bed next to her. As we hugged, cameras flickered in the background.

While we embraced, she squeezed me tightly and whispered in my ear. "Thank you Jared Maxwell. An angel named Derek came to me when I was in that dark and dirty trunk all tied up. He told me not to worry because you were coming to save me."

Chapter Thirty Six

Tears instantly welled up in my eyes at hearing Derek's name. Before I stood up, I looked at little Molly and whispered. "We all have guardian angels, Sweetheart. He was mine too over the years. More than once."

As I stood up and backed away, I had to wipe the tears from my cheeks with the back of my right hand. The cameras flickered again behind me. Then she spoke up so everyone could hear her in her little lady like manner. "The way I hear it, Mr. Maxwell, you are far too modest. The officer I talked to at the hospital said it was only because of your assertiveness that anything was done at all."

Kelly snickered, not so much under her breath that Molly couldn't miss hearing her.

"You're a lot of help." I scolded Kelly, who just laughed a little more and a little louder.

"I think your friend is attesting to your true actions, Jared. Your name is Kelly, isn't it?" Molly exclaimed, holding out her arms asking Kelly to also come give her a hug.

I took Kelly's hand and whispered that Molly wanted to give her a hug as well and then led her to the little girl's side. As they hugged, I saw Molly whisper something in Kelly's ear just as she had mine. I also saw Kelly flinch ever so slightly at whatever it was she had been told. I'd have to ask her about that later.

After their embrace ended, Molly exclaimed. "Daddy said he didn't think you were going to accept the reward for saving me. Why not?"

"Well Honey, we really haven't talked about that yet. But I really don't want to take money for doing what any person would have done in my shoes."

"But why not? You saved me." She asked.

"Not really Sweetie, I only helped. Besides, seeing you sitting there so full of life is plenty payment enough and makes me feel better about a few things in my life that didn't turn out so well."

"Like what?" She asked.

"It's kind of a long story, Honey, but quite a few years ago, I was a soldier who fought for people in a far off land so that they could be free. In the end, that didn't fare too well. I still believe people should be free. And that goes double for kids. You should be free to enjoy the things God has in store for you. That may not always happen in today's crazy world, but my real reward is in knowing that today you're safe."

"Thank you so much Jared. You will always be in my thoughts and prayers as I grow up and I will never forget what you did for me. I hope you'll come back to visit me some time."

"It would be my pleasure, Precious."

She reached out to give me another hug. I held her for a moment and kissed her on the forehead. "You get your rest. I'll talk to you again before we leave, okay?"

"Promise?"

"I promise." I assured her.

With that, her father asked everyone to step outside, figuring Molly had been through enough. I wiped several more tears from my cheek as I walked through the door, which of course at least one photographer had to catch.

Once Donna tucked Molly in, leaving a nanny to watch over her, she and Chuck joined the rest of us in the hallway. From there they led us back downstairs to the foyer. He then told the reporters to wrap up their interviews with any last questions so he could entertain his special guests.

After several more questions concerning the money and what Molly had whispered to me, which I of course said was none of their business, the reporters flocked out the front door. For time being, they were out of our hair.

After escorting the news crews to their vehicles, Chuck returned and said. "You really did my family a great service by coming today. I hope we didn't inconvenience you too much."

Kelly and I smiled and did our best to assure them they hadn't.

"If you don't mind us asking, off the record if you'd like, why is it that you really don't want the reward money?" Donna asked.

"Off the record?" I asked.

"Of course."

"Derek, Kelly's former husband and my best friend, and I served in Nam together. He was killed just over a year ago by scum like the trash who kidnapped your little girl. I wasn't there to help him, but today one little girl is safe because I happened to be at the right place at the right time. It helps make things a little better."

"Why didn't you want the press to know that? That would have made a fantastic story." Chuck said.

"The dirt-bag who did it got off scot free because of some legal bull crap. You don't even want to know..."

Kelly cut me off to spare the Loriman's my tirade. "We also won ten million dollars in the Ohio lottery two weeks ago."

"Oh! Now I understand. Nobody knows about the money." Chuck said, nodding his head.

"There's that too." I smiled, squeezing Kelly's hand to thank her for stopping me.

"Well, if you ever need anything, even if it's only information, I hope you'll call. I have contacts in some pretty high places." Chuck said.

"I'll remember that. Thank you. I may just take you up on that someday." I replied.

"Could we ask just one more question, if you wouldn't mind?" Chuck continued.

"Sure, why not."

"Molly told us that someone came to her while she was kidnapped. She said this, let's say person, told her that you specifically were coming to save her. Do you know what she's talking about?"

"Kids are closer to God than us adults. Maybe her guardian angel knew more than any of us. Heaven knows why I heard her. Kelly couldn't, even with her acute hearing. And when they opened the trunk, Molly was gagged and sleeping. You'll have to derive your own conclusions from that, I guess."

"Is that what she whispered to you?" He asked.

"You should probably ask Molly that question."

The Loriman's were confused but not put off by my answer, and respectful of my privacy and Molly's.

Over the next few hours, we got to know our hosts and them to know us. They started by splitting forces. I walked around the huge estate with Chuck, enjoying the beautiful sunshine while Kelly stayed at the house with Donna which gave them plenty of time for girl talk.

During my time with Chuck, I found that he'd only been in political office for a few years. Prior to that, he'd been a successful businessman, owning a fair sized construction company employing nearly one hundred fifty people. His family had had money which helped, he noted, but he had been determined to make a name for himself.

As we walked, I shared some of my life story with Chuck, keeping the highlights away from Nam, focusing instead on my earlier bowling career and my high tech machinist's job.

"Did you pick the numbers or did the computer pick them?" He asked.

Not wanting to talk about it or make up another story, I said. "Let's just say they were special numbers." Hopefully, Kelly would do similar if asked. I realized we should probably put our heads together and work on a solid story that dealt with all the details of the money and our trip in general for future use.

What the girls talked about, I had no idea. More than likely, Kelly's blindness and our relationship would have been highlights in any conversation between two or more women. Children or the lack of might have been a close third. When we got together later, Kelly didn't volunteer any information and I didn't ask.

The four of us enjoyed a late afternoon lunch together that Donna helped her day help prepare. Afterwards, Chuck and I went into his study to enjoy an expensive cigar and a snifter of brandy while the ladies enjoyed a cup of coffee.

As we finished our drink and smokes, Chuck said with a tear welling up his eyes, "Let me reassert my earlier offer. If there is anything in this world that I can ever do for you, all you have to do is ask. I don't know what my wife or I would have done if we'd have lost our little Molly. She means everything to us."

"I can't even begin to imagine the horrors that you and Donna must have gone through, Chuck, but you have her back now. That's what's important. If I can ever use your help, though, I'll be sure to call."

We shook hands and he thanked me again before we went back to join up with the girls. A half hour or so later, Kelly and I decided it was time to get back to our own business.

Before leaving, I was sure to say goodbye to Molly. During our goodbyes, she made me promise to call from time to time. It was a promise that I intended to keep.

Chuck rode with us back to our hotel, though his chauffer, Norm, would have been adequate company. He was a colorful old guy who gave us an area history lesson as we rode along. We learned things we never would have discovered on any tour. We teased Chuck that we wanted to borrow Norm as our travel guide for the day.

He laughed and said, "Sure why not. Norm can pick you up in the morning and drive you around."

Even though we were sorely tempted to do so, we assured him that we were only joking and declined the generous offer.

At the hotel, Chuck handed me his business card with all his numbers on the back. "Would you mind calling Molly from time to time?"

I smiled. "Absolutely, it would be my pleasure."

I borrowed a pen from him and wrote down both my home and cell numbers as well as those of Kelly's.

We shook hands and he said, "Thank you" one last time. But as he turned to walk away, he suddenly turned around and gave me a big hug before walking away. As he did, his hand wiped away the tears that were streaking down his face.

Tears were running down ours faces too as he hurried away. Even Kelly who couldn't see what I saw was crying.

As he got in his car, I heard Molly's words playing one more time in my mind. "Thank you Jared Maxwell. Derek told me not to worry because you were coming to save me."

Chapter Thirty Seven

Twilight had befallen the area by the time we returned to the hotel. Artificial light lit up much of the outdoor surroundings almost as if it were daylight. There is just something magnificent about seeing light refracting through watery mist at night. The radiant natural colors were just plain awesome and something I couldn't even begin to articulate to Kelly. Heaven knows I tried.

Between the rides to and from the Loriman's and everything else, it had been an exhausting day, both emotionally and physically. Tired as we were though, it was a bit early to turn in. As we passed the bar, we heard a live band playing inside.

"Wanna sit and listen for awhile, Kelly?"

Her smile lit up the night as a most assured yes echoed without a word.

I escorted her across the same wooden floor that the McDonald's and us had walked across earlier after our dinner cruise together. We sat in an open booth at the far end of the room where we ordered up a pitcher of frozen margaritas and a basket of chips and salsa to munch on.

The band played a little bit of everything; oldies, blues, country and a little soft rock thrown in for good measure. Fortunately they played it all at a decibel low enough that allowed for reasonable conversation.

At Kelly's urging, we joined those already on the dance floor. After we had danced to a few songs, the band started playing a slow song. Kelly didn't bother asking me if I wanted to dance to it or not. She just snuggled up close and put her arms around me. I didn't offer up any protest. I found myself liking the feel of her there in my arms.

More and more, I noticed the desire of wanting to feel her close to me. Along with those feelings came feelings of guilt. The signals I was getting from Kelly didn't help matters, especially since I knew Derry's spirit was always nearby.

After the slow dance ended, we walked back to our seats to listen and chat. Several more hours of listening and dancing followed before we finally headed back to our room, laughing and cutting up as we walked. As enjoyable as the evening had been, we were both tired and ready for a good night's sleep. Like today, we hadn't made plans for tomorrow.

Unfortunately, sleep wasn't going to be the first thing on our agenda. Walking past the mirror in the living room as Kelly headed for her room, I jerked to a stop. It seemed we had a message. Much like the hazy appearances by Derry some weeks back was a halo-ish looking note appearing on the mirror which simply read, "It's time."

Beneath the eerie message was the Ark, not at all where it had been earlier. I guess if it could rematerialize itself back into my room from five floors below, it could certainly move to wherever it wanted within.

I reached out and touched the mirror to see if the writing had any real substance, but as expected, it did not. As I peered at the message, it slowly vanished back to wherever it had come. I wondered if it had ever been there or if it was simply a figment of my imagination. Real or imaginary, I had gotten the message.

As I stood there perplexed, Kelly stuck her head out of her bedroom door. "Good night Jared. I had a great time today. Thank you."

"Don't mention it Kiddo. I had a great time too. Just so you know, we have a message, or at least had one." I said.

"What was it?"

"It's time."

"Time for what?"

"Your guess is as good as mine, but I wouldn't plan on doing anything around here tomorrow."

"What do you mean by that?" She asked with a frown.

Walking over to where she stood, I took her hand and walked her to her bed. Sitting down beside her, I told her what I'd seen.

"I'm not sure I like this merry go round we seem to have gotten on." Kelly murmured.

"I'm with you there. I kind of think I liked my old job better."

Kelly sheepishly nodded in agreement.

Even though we were both dead tired, we suddenly weren't ready for bed. We tried talking about the message, but had no idea what to talk about. When we did finally retire, it took forever for me to get to sleep. I expect it was the same for Kelly.

In the morning, I awoke to Kelly's shaking and calling to me.

"Jared! Jared! Wake up! It's okay. You're having a nightmare."

"Wha...what?" I shouted with my eyes suddenly wide open and looking around, searching for whoever I'd been searching for in my dream, finding Kelly's concerned face hovering over me.

"You were yelling. It woke me up. Who is Sergeant, Jared?"

"Uh...er...ah...someone from the past, I guess. I'm sorry I woke you."

Light breaking through the draperies let me know it was already morning. Taking a quick look at the clock, I was shocked to see it was already past 8:30.

"Do you want to tell me about it?" Kelly asked, not ready to let go of the subject quite yet.

"No thanks. I'm good. It was just a bad dream. I'll be fine. Thanks for waking me, though. I'm sorry if I scared you."

"It did a little, but only for your sake. Are you sure you don't want to talk about it?"

"No, I'm okay. How did you sleep before my tirade?" I asked.

"I've slept better, but I did get some sleep."

"I know the feeling. As long as we're awake, we might as well go have breakfast. Maybe there'll be another clue waiting for us when we get back."

"I can hardly wait." She said getting up and rolling her eyes.

Chapter Thirty Eight

We both took our time getting ready for what would be by our standards a rather late breakfast. The long hot shower that I treated myself to helped clear some of the cobwebs out of my head. It also helped release some the anxiety that was left over from my reoccurring nightmare.

Already half past nine when we arrived downstairs, we had to wait to be seated because of the large crowd already assembled. While we waited, we walked around the atrium and talked about what was going on, which wasn't much. For the most part, people were just passing through, waiting to eat like we were, checking out or waiting for a tour bus to take them somewhere.

Once our table was ready, our little hand held buzzer went off and we walked back to the restaurant. We were seated at a table far from any window, but with a terrific view of the huge buffet that we weren't going to indulge in. When our waitress arrived, we ordered coffee and menus.

Before opening the menu, I flopped the paper that I'd picked up outside our door down on the table. It rolled itself open. Before my eyes could move to the menu, the bold headline and lone story caught my attention.

A smirk came to my face as I stopped, put the menu down and took a closer look at the whole front page, such as it was.

"I think we're going to Frederick, Maryland." I said.

"Why do you say that?'

"The front page of the paper only has one story on it."

"So?"

"The story only covers a forth of the page. The rest is blank."

"Maybe it's a misprint?"

"Do you really think it's a coincidence that we just happened to get a misprint today?"

"What's the story about?"

"Terrance Godfrey. He's a no good convicted child molester who just recently got out of prison. For some reason he moved to

Frederick and the people there are hot about it, and rightly so. I sure as heck wouldn't want someone like him living around my kids and family."

As we spoke, someone in a cheap navy blue suit came strutting deliberately up to our table. When he reached us, he stopped to speak to us.

"Excuse me, are you Mr. Maxwell?" He asked.

"Yes."

"Hello. I'm Detective Weber. Would you mind if I asked you a couple of questions?"

"Sure, why not? This is my friend Kelly Sims."

I watched with some interest as Kelly held out her hand in the general direction of the officer. It took him a moment to recognize her condition for what it was and to shake hands with her. "Pleased to meet you, Ma'am."

"What can we do for you Officer?" Kelly asked.

"Well, as you may have heard, there was someone found dead on the third floor early yesterday morning."

"We heard something about it at breakfast yesterday, but that's about it." I answered. "I don't know how I can possibly help. I haven't even heard who he was."

"I just need a little clarification if you don't mind. The elevator camera has you getting off on the third floor at around 5 a.m. Can you explain what you were doing up then and why you got off on the third floor?"

I chuckled to myself. Good thing I'd thought about it.

"Actually, Kelly had left something in the van, so I went to get it for her. On my way back, I inadvertently pressed three instead of eight. I'm a little dyslexic. Matter of fact, I did the same thing yesterday morning after I came downstairs to read the paper, while Kelly got around for breakfast."

"I see." He responded. "Well, I'm glad we could clear that up. Sorry to interrupt your breakfast. Thanks for your time. Oh, by the way Ms. Sims, what was it you needed from the van at 5 in the morning?"

Kelly smiled. "I couldn't sleep and wanted my book to read. In all the commotion of getting our luggage, I'd left it in the van. As you can tell, I can't read just any book. Jared was nice enough to run down to get it for me."

Reaching into her yellow Vera-Bradley bag, she held a book out for the officer to see.

"Would you like to read it?" She teased.

"No, that's quite all right. Thank you for your time. You folks have a nice vacation. Bye now."

With that he walked away.

I watched as he left the dining room, still in my line of sight over Kelly's right shoulder the whole way. He didn't stop to take a second look back to see if I was still watching him.

"You're pretty quick and what was the deal with that handshake? I've never seen you miss your direction that far."

"Who said I did?" She asked sporting a wry grin.

"Remind me to never play poker with you. I'm afraid you'd bluff me out of the other half of my money." I teased.

Kelly simply smiled. "I did almost leave my book in the van the other day when we got here. It came to me when he started asking questions. Anyway, do you really think we need to go to Frederick, Maryland because of this Godfrey fellow?"

"Between the message last night and the paper this morning, it seems fairly clear to me. I suppose we can wait until tomorrow if you'd like to see if anything else manifests itself."

"I suppose we really should go. Who knows? There might be another little girl to save along the way." A hint of sarcasm laced her retort.

"I'm not touching that with a ten foot pole." I responded.

We enjoyed our breakfast in spite of our reservations. Afterward, we walked outside to enjoy a few minutes of sunshine and the distant roar of the falls before heading up to our room to pack.

As we walked through the lobby to the elevator, her arm was hooked in mine. Resting her head on my shoulder, she said. "I really like it here, Jared. Do you suppose we could come back sometime?"

"It's a date. Besides, we will probably want to come back to see Molly some time."

"Sounds wonderful. Thank you, Jared." She said, giving my arm a passionate squeeze.

After a short ride up in our floor, we walked to our room where we were greeted with another interesting sight, or at least I was. As Kelly started to walk past me when I opened the door, I had to stop her.

"Wait a second." I said grabbing her arm.

"What is it, Jared?"

"I don't want you to trip."

"Over what? Are the cleaning ladies here or something?"

"Not exactly, Kiddo."

"What do you mean, not exactly?" She asked, her face going into a bewildered contortion.

I took a moment to look past Kelly at the view behind her, before answering.

Shaking my head, I said. "Our bags are packed and waiting for us on a cart just inside the door. I guess it's time for us to go, now."

"You're kidding me, right?" She gasped.

"Not hardly."

After a quick check of our rooms to make sure nothing was left unpacked, which there wasn't, we wheeled the cart to the elevator and down to check out. Once the bill was paid, I pushed the cart outside leaving Kelly to guard it while I went to get the van.

Fifteen minutes after leaving our room, we were ready to hit the road. Before pulling out of the parking lot, I got the atlas out to see where we were headed. I grimaced when I opened the page to the New York state map. Our route was already highlighted in yellow.

The highlighted route was probably at least a hundred miles farther out of the way than the route I would have chosen, but at that point I wasn't asking any questions and didn't bother telling Kelly about it. This was one 400 mile trip that, for now, I wasn't looking forward to. But I was certainly glad to have Kelly along for the ride.

Trying to make light of the situation as I pulled out of the parking lot I said, "I guess we'll just drive till we get tired or the turn signal tells us to stop, whichever comes first."

Kelly's smile was a snarly one with teeth showing. "How many hours will it take us?" She asked.

"Never been through the mountains up here in New York before, but I'm guessing it'll take around eight hours of driving time plus stops. Maybe we can stop in Scranton, Pennsylvania for the night and finish the trip in the morning."

"Jared?"

"What's up?"

"Thanks for bringing me along and being so honest with me."

"Sure, Kiddo. Besides, you were my alibi this morning. Without you, I'd probably be down at the police station trying to answer questions that have no answers."

A grin took shape on her face as she fashioned a remark in her mind. "We do make a pretty good team. Don't we?"

I had to smile. "Yes, that we do. By the way, what did Molly whisper in your ear yesterday?"

"I don't recall you confiding in me." She snapped.

"I guess we never did talk about it did we?"

"Not that I recall."

"She told me that an angel came to her and told her that I was coming to save her. Not that someone was going to save her, but that I personally was going to save her."

"Let me guess, this angels name was Derek."

"Bingo. So what did she tell you?"

"She said that Derek told her something to tell me and that I wasn't supposed to tell you."

"WHAT?"

"That's all I can say, at least for now."

"Some friend you are." I chided her.

"Hey! I have to follow orders too."

"Whatever." I said and let it drop. I knew her well enough to know she would tell me when and if she was ready and not a moment earlier.

Chapter Thirty Nine

The sun was bright in the late morning Spring sky as I pushed on the shades and settled in for the long drive. Kelly took care of our listening pleasures for the next several hours by loading the multi-disc CD changer before plucking a book out of her bag as I called it to read.

"You really like your butt bag, don't you?"

Her bright yellow Vera-Bradley bag was the one that only showed the animals from their behinds. So obviously, I had dubbed it her butt bag. We had had a lot of fun with it over the years as she took it with her most of the time.

"Yes I do." She smiled.

So that I could get the weather conditions ahead of us and the news, we listened to the radio stations she could find from time to time. Through the mountains, though, it was all CDs. Fortunately we enjoyed the same kind of music, so there wasn't any dissention within the ranks about what we listened to. Between my menial collection and hers, we'd brought enough CDs to keep the 5 disc in dash CD changer busy.

On the outskirts of Syracuse, a couple hours into the trip, we caught the wrap around that took us to I-81. Once we were headed south, we got off the Interstate for a bite to eat and a break in general. Pulling into a Lucky's Steakhouse parking lot, we clambered out onto solid ground, stretched our wings and rubbed our tired behinds.

It seemed quite warm for a northern New York spring day. Not that I really knew for sure what the weather should have been, but 80 degrees was warmer than I would have expected for this time of year this far north. Only intermittent clouds blotted the sky's otherwise clear blue hue. In the distance, the green mountain tops reached up towards the heavens.

Kelly had slipped to the ground and waited for me just outside the door till I could help guide her through her new surroundings. Once I had the kinks worked out of my own body, I strolled around to take her hand.

"Can you see the mountains from here, Jared?"

"They're in the distance. It's a lovely view." Since she asked, I took a minute to give her my typical oral slide show of the distant tree topped Appalachians and of the valley that was closer.

I knew that just around the corner out of sight was a lot more that couldn't be seen, but she always appreciated listening to the imagery. I could tell she missed her sight, but she never complained. More than once I thought it was too bad that all this money we had couldn't restore her sight. I suppose we could have another go at it with the doctors, but the last time we'd checked nothing had changed and it just ended up being another hurtful experience for Kelly.

After I was done painting pictures, we walked inside. Of course, the first stop was at the restroom facilities. She waited at the door while I retrieved a hostess to escort her inside.

Because we'd eaten at a Lucky's Restaurant before, I didn't have to read the entire menu to her. Besides, she just wanted a salad while I chose their scrumptious sirloin steak sandwich that I'd had before. We both nibbled on the peanuts from the metal bucket on the table and drank our ice teas till our entrees arrived and chatted.

Our conversation started out a little subdued because of the nature of this second leg of our trip, but after a few minutes, Kelly got inspired for some reason.

"What do you think Brenda will do when she finds out you're rich?" She asked, sporting an ornery grin.

"Where in the world did that come from?" I asked.

"I don't know. Just popped into my head, I guess."

"Beats me! She's pretty busy molding her newest victim the last time I heard."

Kelly laughed at my choice of words. "She was kind of pushy, wasn't she?" She said with a smirk.

"A big dog is pushy. She's more like a ram." I joked back.

"Oh now, Jared, she wasn't that bad. I mean she never made you wear a skirt or anything."

"That's what you think."

That got us both howling with laughter. Then we started trying to outdo each other's last comment with something even more outlandish.

It felt good to laugh, especially together. Then Kelly got started with the remember when's of times when Brenda went off halfcocked on some stupid tantrum about nothing. That got us roaring even louder as we again tried to outdo each other's memory.

Funny how at the time, those incidents hadn't been all that funny. I really had loved Brenda and tried like crazy to change myself to suit her. In the end, I finally realized that sometimes there just wasn't anyway of pleasing people who aren't please-able. I guess she just never liked herself enough to accept other people for who they were. At least that's what our counselor told me after he tried in vain to help us.

Of course, she wasn't entirely to blame. I did have issues, but I really did try. At least I believed so.

After what started out as a gloomy lunch turned out to be the laugh we both needed. Both of us left the restaurant with an uplifted feeling about the trip in front of us. At the van, as I opened the door, Kelly stopped to give me a hug and a kiss on the cheek before getting in.

"What was that for?" I asked.

"Just because, Jared, just because."

I couldn't say I didn't enjoy it. As she climbed in, I gave her a pat on her behind.

"What was that for?" She shrieked acting shocked.

"Just because." I replied with a smile of satisfaction. "Just because."

"Very funny!" She sniped back. Though she pretended to protest, I could tell she enjoyed it too.

For several more hours, we drove on down the highway, barreling along at seventy five miles an hour. From time to time, I turned down the music to tell her about something interesting that I saw. The rest of the time, she read by the light of her fingers and we listened to whichever disc was playing.

Just north of Scranton, my right turn signal came on.

"Are we stopping for the night?" She asked.

"It's possible. We're getting off here, anyways."

"Not again."

"Yes. Again."

Kelly marked the page in her book before placing it back in her bag. She then became an interested participant in the present goings on around us. At the end of the exit ramp, the signal kept pointing right, so I followed its lead. As we neared a Bed and Breakfast Inn less than a block down the road, the turn signal came on again. I proceeded as directed and parked the van.

"Suppose we have a reservation here?" I joked before getting out.

"I wouldn't doubt it at this point. Take me with you, Jared. This I have to hear."

Hand in hand we walked into the office. The dude inside looked at us pretty funny when Kelly snickered as I asked if we had reservations.

"You don't know whether or not you have reservations?" He remarked.

Kelly and I both laughed. It did sound kind of funny now that he mentioned it. I'm sure our laughter left him wondering what the joke was.

As we chuckled, he checked the computer. There was none.

Next, I asked the logical question. "Do you have any rooms available with two full or two queen sized beds?"

"Nope. Got one room and it has one king sized bed. That's it. Someone just called in a few minutes ago to cancel or we wouldn't even have that."

"Imagine that." Kelly snickered.

"We'll take it." I interjected before the clerk could ask what she meant by that.

"Where's the best place to eat around here?" Kelly asked as I pulled out a credit card to pay.

"Depends on whether you want chicken or hamburger." He replied.

"What?" Kelly cackled.

It was almost cruel since I hadn't told her anything about the eateries at this particular exit.

"That's about all that's close. There is a truck stop down the road about three miles east of here on the state road. It's the only real sit down restaurant near this off ramp."

"I guess that'll have to do." Kelly said, shaking her head in disbelief while I collected the room key and directions.

Once we walked outside, she poked me in the ribs. "You could have warned me."

"Right! And miss the look on your face when he asked if you wanted chicken or hamburger? It was priceless!" I laughed as she tried in vain to clobber me.

I can occasionally get out of the way if I really try.

Chapter Forty

"So which is it, hamburger or chicken?" I teased, as we climbed into the van.

"Hopefully neither! What kind of place is this, anyhow? It's not a hotel is it?"

"It's a three or four room Mom and Pop Bed and Breakfast."

"You could have warned me about that too." She said, sporting a fake snarl.

"Yeah right and I've got dibs on the bed since I paid for the room."

This time, because of the seat belt constraints, I couldn't escape her wide swinging left hand. Besides, I was too busy laughing to try.

"Just take me to dinner and I'll think about it." She said feeling somewhat vindicated since she'd landed a good one.

Dusk had already begun to fall and there wasn't much to see as we proceeded down the shadowy covered state road to the truck stop just outside the next small town. Because of the earlier turn signal taking us off the interstate, we expected something to pop up at us at any moment. Nothing did. Without incident, we drove to and ate a typical truck stop meal, which like usual, was very good.

I got a chuckle out of Kelly's order because she ended up having double chicken; a chicken sandwich with a cup of chicken noodle soup.

As for me, I opted for the meatloaf. Wherever we ended up in Frederick needed to have a workout room. Neither of us left anything for the dog which we didn't have anyhow.

As we left the diner, we intently waited for something that again never materialized. Even back at our room, we more than expected something to happen. But again, nothing did, leaving us to finally give in to the exhaustion that consumed us.

With one king sized bed in the room, I started tossing a homemade sleeping bag on the floor.

"What are you doing?" Kelly demanded.

"What do you think I'm doing? I'm making up your bed on the floor."

"Yeah right! Get into bed Silly. Just make sure you stay on your side of the bed or else."

I didn't ask or else what, because I knew better. I did have to wonder, however, what would happen if I accidentally strayed by mistake.

The morning sun was high in the sky when I finally awoke. A delicate arm was draped over me. Peering at the clock, I saw a eight in front of whatever other numbers were registering. My stretching to see the clock got Kelly's attention.

"I thought I might have to wake you for lunch." She said.

"You should have awakened me."

"I tried, but you were sleeping too soundly. I even molested you twice and you never even flinched."

"That's what you think. I watched it all and enjoyed every minute of it."

Whack! She couldn't miss at that range. "Liar." She shouted with laughter.

"If you say so, but I swear I'll never tell anyone about that little tattoo on your butt."

A pillow hit me, quickly followed by Kelly jumping on top of me. Then the tickling began and I was in deep trouble. I pleaded for her to stop to no avail. When I couldn't take it anymore, I had to get physical to stop her. Pinning her to the bed was the only way I could get her to quit. She hated that as much as she liked it.

Yeah, I knew all about her little tattoo. After all, I was the one who egged her on to get it, way back when in a lifetime long long ago.

"Enough screwing around already." I said, as I held her down.

She laughed as she struggled, but finally she consented to call it quits, if only for the time being.

Getting off her and off the bed, I asked if she wanted to shower now or wait till we got to Frederick.

"Well, of course I need to shower now. I have to get your bodily fluids off me."

"Oh brother! I'll go get a paper to read while you try to clean up."

Slipping on my pants and shoes, I grabbed my billfold and room key before leaving her to do her thing. At the office, I picked up a USA Today from the counter, poured a cup of free coffee, grabbed a free Danish and found a place to read in the breath taking scenery that lay just outside the large office window.

On page two was another story about the guy who was presumably our next victim, Terrance Godfrey. It wasn't all that different than the one from the day before, except it included that he was staying at the Maryland Vacation Inn just off the interstate. He was still making life miserable for everyone by being there and there wasn't anything in the article that suggested why he'd chosen Frederick in the first place. Since there was no mention of a job or anything like that, why he was there was as much a mystery to me as why we were going there. If I had to guess after reading the article, the Maryland Vacation Inn was probably going to be our next stop in our adventure as well.

As I sat there scanning the rest of the paper, someone turned up the TV that had been on but had sat nearly muted. The local lady news anchor seemed all excited about some breaking news. Her enthusiasm quickly gained my attention. As I listened, I too became intrigued.

Her story was about a little girl who had been missing in the area for several days. As I listened to the story replayed, I learned that little four year-old Tabatha Turner had evidently wandered away from the family's campsite two days earlier.

As I listened, I had to wonder if maybe she was why we were brought to this place and if our services just hadn't been needed this time around. The park where she'd wandered away from was less than ten miles from here. Where she'd been found was really close to the truck stop where we'd had dinner last night.

As I watched, I thought I recognized the people who had found her walking near the highway in tall grass. I wasn't 100% certain, but they looked like the family who'd paid their bill just in front of us as we were leaving the diner.

Thinking back to their conversation as we waited our turn to pay, they were trying to decide which way to go home. The wife wanted to go through the hills. The husband wanted to go some other quicker way.

As I speculated, they showed a close up of the couple telling their story. Then I knew I was right.

The lady, Nancy Overmeyer, by the subtext, said, "If I hadn't overruled my husband, that little girl might still be out there wandering around. I don't even know how I ever saw her at all. The grass moved about twenty or thirty feet from the edge of the road as we went around a bend in the road and our lights flashed for just a moment on her long blonde hair. I knew in my heart it was the little girl. My husband, John, said I was seeing things, but I made him stop, anyhow. We were both shocked when I called out Tabatha's name and she called back. I cried as I ran to gather the poor little thing up in my arms. I know in my heart that God sent us there to save her."

The lady's eyes were filled with tears and so were those of her husband as she finished telling her story. I'll have to say, mine got a little misty too.

Under my breath I agreed with Mrs. Overmeyer supposition. Yes dear, I do believe you were directed to save the little girl last night. But just so you know, if your husband had won out on which way to go, we would've had your back.

When I told Kelly about the news story and my hypothesis, she was amused and possibly even intrigued. I was pretty sure her conclusion, however, was less assured than mine even with what had happened thus far on our trip.

We tossed the incident around for a while as we drove, but then decided to let it drop in favor of listening to the music she played, the friendly banter we'd always enjoyed and the descriptive dialogue of our ever changing surroundings when something breath taking caught my eye.

Chapter Forty One

It was after 4 o'clock when we pulled off I-70 onto the city streets of Frederick. With only one stop for a potty break, gas and a quick bite to eat along the way, we'd made pretty fair time. Having seen the Maryland Vacation Inn signs along the Interstate, I simply followed them, assuming that if that wasn't where we were supposed to stay our trusty turn signals would re-direct us accordingly. They didn't.

At the front desk of the four story brick building, I asked for their best room. They didn't have any suites or adjoining rooms available, and didn't say if they had any period. The best they had at that time was a room with two queen sized beds.

Before taking the room, I asked Kelly, "Do you want your own room?"

"No silly. I'll share one with you."

They then asked how many nights we were staying. I looked at Kelly who was in turn waiting to see what I was going to say.

"Who knows? We may be here a day or we might be here a week. Depends on what we find to do. Do you have weekly rates?" I asked.

"Sorry Sir, no. We do have different rates for the weekend, though."

"Well, whatever. We're here till we leave."

After picking up the keys, we walked back to the van and drove around the building to our entry door which was near the too cool to open pool. Finding a cart inside shortened the moving process considerably.

Once we got everything moved to the room, Kelly asked. "What should we do now?"

"Live like tourists, I guess. While you get yourself situated, I'll go back to the office to get some brochures and a map."

"Okay."

As she went about her business of unpacking and mapping out the room, I went to move the van from the no parking zone it was parked in. When I opened the door, I was greeted by a surprise sitting on Kelly's seat. It was the Ark. Sticking out of it was a slip of paper of some kind. I pulled the note out and opened it. It simply read, Lacombe Restuarante'.

There was no since asking where in the world it came from, it would obviously be a redundant question. I knew where and it wasn't from this world.

After re-parking the van, I took the note inside the office with me and asked the attendant about the place.

"Oh it is one of the finest restaurants within a hundred miles of here. There are pamphlets about it along with our other local travel folders over in the corner there." He said pointing a finger in its general direction.

Picking one up from out of the rack before heading back to the room, I glanced at it and realized this was going to be an expensive dining experience. I also decided to tell Kelly she was paying the bill since I found the note on her seat.

Even though our night was tentatively planned, I grabbed a few other brochures along with a general map of the area. It seemed that most anything of any interest wasn't really located in Frederick. It was, however, centrally located to a lot of things to do. One thing that did peak my interest around Frederick was a duck pin bowling center. I figured even Kelly might get a kick out of doing that. I knew I would.

Walking the hallways back to our room, I knocked before entering.

"It's me. Are you decent?"

"Come on in."

"Hope you're hungry. We're going to dine high on the hog and you're paying."

"Why's that?" She asked with a frown.

After explaining about the note I'd found, she responded. "I can't see how we can possibly get into any trouble at a restaurant. I'll be glad to pay."

"Yeah right!"

We laughed because we both knew who'd end up paying.

Needing to offset the lag of the long drive, I stretched out on the bed to take a nap. It was nearly six o'clock already, so I asked Kelly to wake me up at 6:30. Within seconds, I was out.

At 6:15, the alarm sounded, blowing me out of a deep sleep.

"Did you set your alarm, Jared?"

"No." I said, reaching out to check the switch on the clock, which wasn't turned on. "It must be time to get around. Evidently, we're on some sort of time schedule tonight. You can shower first, if you'd like."

An understandably perplexed look was pasted across Kelly's face, but like the trooper she was, she didn't say a word as she set about getting ready.

As I waited for my turn in the shower, I couldn't help but wonder what this night might bring. After all, we were going to a fine restaurant, not a biker bar.

When Kelly came out of the bathroom wrapped in a towel, I got up to take my shower. She was stopped at the counter where all her cosmetics were. As I walked past her, I playfully tugged on her towel. For my effort, I received a swift elbow and a meaningless scowl that turned into a grin.

"If you want to see, just ask." She teased.

"I'm asking."

"Just ask someone else is what I meant to say."

"Figures." I said as I closed the door behind me and locked it.

A rap on the door followed.

"What is it?" I asked.

"Make sure you knock before you come out." She said.

"I'll think about it." I replied.

She barked something catty and we both laughed. We both realized I knew better than tread those waters.

After a nice warm soothing shower, I felt refreshed and ready to take on the world, as long as it wasn't too big. When I knocked on the door to be let out, Kelly was already dressed in a new dress that I hadn't seen before. The deep red velvet glistening next to her naturally dark skin took my breath away.

"Whoa!" I said when my eyes saw her standing on the other side in the light.

"Does that mean you approve?" she asked, sporting a wry grin.

"I don't know who helped you do your shopping, but I'd keep them around."

She smiled appreciatively and sat by the table so she could read while I got ready.

Ten minutes later we walked out to the van arm in arm. Using the directions I'd gotten from the front desk earlier, we drove through downtown to the other side of the city.

I'm sure we hadn't taken the fastest route and spent several minutes trying to by-pass a one-way street that got in our way, but eventually I found the major artery that took us to Lacombe Restuarante'.

When we drove into the parking lot, we were met by an interesting old building that had probably begun its life as someone's home once upon a time. Though it had been enlarged at least a time or two over the years, the majority of it had been around for at least a century.

"I hope we don't need reservations." I said, noticing the nearly full parking lot.

"I'm sure." Kelly responded with a smirk.

I hadn't seen the need to wear a suit, opting instead for a sport coat and a mock turtleneck. As we stepped through the busy front door, I realized I had opted wrong. I was somewhat underdressed. Kelly's exquisite reddish dress, on the other hand, fit right in and helped elevate my attire somewhat.

Inside the vestibule slash waiting area, people waiting in groups of two or more were gathered together enjoying small talk. I followed the guy ahead of me to the maitre d' to put my name in. He was quickly informed that the night was completely booked and that no one would be seated that didn't have a reservation from weeks in advance.

When the gentleman turned to leave, the maitre d' scowled as he looked at me and asked. "Do "you" have a reservation, Sir?"

I waited nervously after answering, "Yes, under Jared Maxwell, I believe."

As he looked over his list, his face grew sterner by the second.

"I'm sorry Sir. I don't see that name on our list anywhere." He stated in an almost arrogant tone.

Out of nowhere, Kelly spoke up. "Excuse me, perhaps I made the reservation under my name instead. Try Sims, Kelly Sims."

Chapter Forty Two

As I squirmed inside my skin, Kelly looked calmly at Charles the maître d' as he took another questioning look at his reservation book.

After only a few seconds, his facial expressions quickly softened as did his tone. "Ah yes, Ms. Sims, we have you right here. Yes. Your table is waiting. William, here, will take you to our finest table. Please, enjoy your dinner."

He snapped his fingers for Willie and whispered something into his ear, before motioning for us to follow him. Billy, Willie William, or whatever he preferred to be called, eyed us inquisitively as Charles spoke in his ear before leading us to an exquisite table near the central fountain where I believe at one time a fireplace had been.

Kelly, as usual, listened intently as I told her about the room around us. The ceilings were high in the tradition of the old home as it had begun. Our particular setting wasn't within the mainframe of the original house, near as my limited architectural skills could tell. The wood throughout was dark maple. The lighting was tastefully inserted into the ceiling using dropped panels that reflected the light upwards. The result was a soft glow that surrounded the room comfortably. Tapestries adorned the walls depicting various olden day European characters.

The seating was accomplished using solid wood pedestal tables covered with off-white linen table clothes. The chairs were floral patterned cushioned heavy wood pieces that went along with the theme of the house.

Because of the atmosphere, you felt as though you needed to whisper so as not to disturb those next to you. With that in mind, I sat next to Kelly so I could read the menu to her, quietly.

With help from our wine waiter, we ordered a modestly priced bottle of red Bordeaux from the wine list. For the main entrée, Kelly decided on the Tilapia, while I opted for the prime rib done medium-rare. Even though we both realized we were probably here for a purpose, the night before proved that not every directive necessarily meant something sinister was about to happen. With only a hint of reservation, we enjoyed our dinners and each other's company.

After we finished our main courses, we ordered coffees and shared a decadent chocolate dessert as we watched, waited and wondered. Neither of us dared to actually ask the question, what next?

Our dining pleasure lasted for well over an hour without incident. Finally, the bill came, which I playfully gave to Kelly who jokingly suggested where I could place it. Pulling out a credit card, I placed it on the table for our waiter to see. Once I signed the receipt, we walked out of the place a bit perplexed but glad that nothing had yet happened.

At the van, I opened the door and helped Kelly into her seat before going around to my side. When I opened the door, I was met by an interesting sight. The ark was sitting in my seat.

"Place it inside the Infinity." A voice whispered in my ear.

So much for being perplexed. Now I was horrified.

Parked next to us was a dark blue Infinity M35. Picking up the Ark, I did as I was told and took a step towards the car and reached for the passenger side door handle. I wasn't all that surprised to find it unlocked when I pulled on it. What I did find interesting was that after placing the Ark on the black leather seat, I heard the doors lock when I closed it again since I hadn't pressed any buttons.

When I finally climbed into the van, Kelly asked the obvious. "Where did you go?"

"Er...ah...well, I had an errand to run."

"You're kidding."

"Riiiight."

As I backed out of the parking spot, I told Kelly about the box and the voice. A wry smile was about the only reaction my story evoked from her.

"At least, we know why we were supposed to dine here," she said, nonchalantly.

As I headed out of the parking lot, I snickered at her remark before noticing someone in the rearview walking up to the M35.

"This could get interesting. It looks like someone is getting into the Infinity."

"Really?" Kelly said with a hint of curiosity.

Pausing at the end of the row, I continued watching in the mirror as a man opened the door and climbed in. The parking lot was only moderately lit so it was a little difficult to see so I began to turn around in my seat to get a better look.

Before I could do so, the same little voice whispered in my ear. "Don't turn around Jared."

"Why's that?" I asked.

"Why's what?" Kelly asked.

"Nothing, I thought I heard you say something."

"No, I didn't say anything." She assured me.

I knew she hadn't. My eyes quickly moved to look at the scene through the rearview mirror. But when my gaze got there, I found the luminous presence of Derry staring back at me. As our eyes met, a ghostly arm and hand reached past me and turned the mirror downward.

"Drive and don't look back." He whispered in my ear.

"Okay. "I said in submission.

"Okay what?" Kelly asked.

"I'll tell you in a minute."

My foot left the brake and I began rolling to the right towards the exit. Before the van had rolled ten feet, a blood curdling scream penetrated our closed windows sending chills up both our spines.

"What was that?" Kelly shouted.

Around us the darkness of the parking lot was suddenly replaced by a luminous glow that reminded me of the light I'd seen emanating from a certain room only a few days ago back in Niagara Falls. I'd hoped to never see anything like that again.

In another moment, the heavens in front of and above us seemed to open up to accept the great rush of white swirling streaks that raced towards it from down here on earth. As they passed through the opening, the darkness swallowed it and closed back unto itself.

"What the heck was that?" Kelly shouted again.

"Holy crap! I think God just made a long distance call to whoever just got into that Infinity!" I shouted.

Mashing the gas pedal, I drove out of the parking lot wanting to put as much distance as I could between this incident and us as quickly as possible.

Neither of us had any interest in seeing what had really happened to whoever it had been. And we didn't need to be answering any more questions about being around another happening.

Chapter Forty Three

The questions that bombarded us on our trip back to the hotel certainly didn't have any answers. And unlike the Niagara Falls Hotel incident, we were both up close and personal to this one. Though we didn't know who the victim was for sure, we obviously had a pretty good idea.

As I drove, I told Kelly all about Derry's haunting words in my ear and how his whispery hand had reached out to move the mirror so that I couldn't see behind us.

Kelly's almost hysterical laugh as I finished the story was not because she thought any part of it funny. It was simply an attempt to keep her sanity.

When we arrived back at our hotel, we sat and had a long heart to heart about everything that had happened thus far on our journey that no longer seemed to be a vacation in any stretch of the imagination. After a very lengthy discussion, we decided that if we allowed this situation to become ours personally, it would likely destroy us. This mission, or whatever it was, was our calling and until we were freed of it, we had to proceed. It was a bold decision that Kelly herself proposed and to which I could only concur.

Wired as we were, we walked into the room and talked on into the night concerning our fears about what might be to come. During that time, Kelly finally opened up about how she'd felt initially about me, my visions and the Ark.

She explained that she'd been extremely worried about my sanity during those first few episodes, from the lottery numbers to buying the van and all, but that now she finally understood why I did and acted like I had. She even apologized for having doubted me.

I only laughed as I accepted her apology. "Heck! I'd have thought you were nuts if you hadn't wondered about me." I teased.

By the time we doused the lights, I felt pretty sure that we were now finally on the same page, whatever the heck that meant. Though sleep was slow in coming, it at last overtook us allowing our minds to relax, if only for a while. It was barely dawn when the alarm, that was again never set, went off again.

"You do realize this is beginning to annoy me, don't you Jared?"

"You think? The question is, what are we supposed to do now, pack or what?"

"Perhaps the morning paper, the mirror or that little voice in your head will give us a clue." Kelly said rolling her unseeing eyes.

"Let's skip showers and see what happens at breakfast. Maybe the van is waiting to take us home." I suggested.

"We can hope." Kelly said, rolling out of bed. "I'll brush my teeth and throw on some jeans."

"I'll watch."

"Not without x-ray vision you won't." Kelly chuckled, as she closed the bathroom door behind her.

I donned my jeans while waiting for my turn at the bathroom. During that time, no unusual notes appeared on the walls, mirrors or ceiling and no little voices spoke in my ear.

Within ten minutes of the alarm sounding, we walked out of the room to our awaiting van. Still, there was nothing to suggest where we were headed. There was, however, something waiting for us in the van. There on the center console sat the Ark.

I noticed it sitting there when I opened the door for Kelly. Before I closed her door, I let her know about it. By the time I climbed in, Kelly had it in her hands examining it carefully with her fingertips.

"It doesn't seem any worse for wear." She exclaimed.

Placing the Ark back where she found it, she said quite sarcastically, "Maybe we should just drive around until the turn signal comes on."

With everything that had happened so far, how could I argue with that logic? Moments later her prophetic words came to fruition.

At the hotel exit as I reached to turn the right signal on to go to a Cowboy Rogers Restaurant I'd seen the night before, the left turn signal came on. Evidently, we were turning left. I didn't bother testing the lever. By now, it seemed a fruitless waste of time and energy. Patiently, I waited for the traffic to clear so I could turn left.

"A lot of traffic, Jared?"

"Not too much, I'm just waiting to turn left."

"There's nothing to our right?"

"There's a lot of stuff to our right, but that's not where we're headed, it seems."

"Already?" She asked with an exasperating shake of her head.

"Already."

Kelly's mouth formed a taught smirk, but she didn't utter another word as she waited to see where this newest adventure would lead.

A few more followed signals led us to a small local eatery that had a fair amount of vehicles parked in the lot outside. The sign above the tan vinyl sided building said the place was called Kelly Sue's. As we joined the cars parked there, the signal didn't seem to direct us to any particular parking spot so I just found one that suited me and backed into it.

Tossing a couple of quarters into the newspaper machine outside the place, I grabbed a newspaper before heading inside. When we were greeted by the hostess, I asked for a non-smoking table for two.

She smiled, realizing that we were tourists. "All of Maryland is non-smoking, except the bars."

"That's good to know. Thank you."

She then escorted us to a table by the window and handed us a menu. We obviously didn't need two.

"Is there anything you're hungry for or would you like me to read it all to you?" I asked.

"Do you suppose they have cheesy scrambled eggs?"

Browsing the menu quickly, I spotted them. "Yep, here they are."

"Good, that's what I want with bacon and wheat toast, extra dark."

"Dark? You mean dark like my French toast?" I asked with a laugh.

Chapter Forty Four

She grinned and pretended to think about it for a second before finally answering. "Maybe not quite that dark," She said with a smirk.

When the waitress arrived with the coffee pot, we ordered and worked on the coffee till our food arrived. After a few minutes of idle conversation, Kelly whispered so as not to offend someone in case she was overheard. "This isn't some unsavory place is it?"

I laughed. "No. It's actually very nice. It's a family owned place according to the sign on the wall. It probably seats about seventy five people and it's nearly full."

Since I'd already started, I finished telling her about the place before opening the newspaper. When I finally did, there on the front page was a picture of the Infinity from the night before. The caption read, "Godfrey's last attempt at a meal turns curiously deadly."

I leaned over and whispered the headline in Kelly's ear. She barely grimaced as she remembered the paper that had foretold our coming.

As I read the account, I found it interesting that there was no mention of anyone in or around the restaurant having seen any sort of eerie light racing into the heavens. The report did state that there were those who had heard Godfrey's haunting death screech and ran out to investigate, but not seeing anything had gone back inside. It wasn't until later when the people who had parked directly in front of Godfrey's Infinity turned on their headlights that anyone realized something had actually happened.

By their account, Godfrey's corpse was an interesting sight and at first they didn't even think it was real. It wasn't until someone actually took a closer look that they realized it was not someone's early attempt at a Halloween gag. His corpse not only looked scared to death, but looked as if he'd been dead for years, not minutes.

The article also reported that the maitre 'd had reported turning Godfrey away for not having a reservation moments before whatever the ruckus had been outside earlier in the evening.

I whispered the revelation in Kelly's ear. She winced and shook her head but otherwise didn't respond.

Before long, the food arrived and we ate. Our total dining experience barely lasted twenty minutes. As we contently enjoyed a third cup of coffee, I noticed several people's attention being directed towards something outside. Following their glances to see what they were looking at. I smiled at the sight of our van's lights alternately flashing similar to the way police car lights do when they're on a run.

"Drink up. We need to hit the road."

"Please."

"The van is calling. It's winking at us." I said softly.

That got her laughing hysterically. She did so all the way out the front door. Fortunately, she waited until we got outside before asking what I meant. She only slowed slightly when I explained it to her.

The left turn signal was already on when I started the engine, so I followed it to the entrance we'd come in from. At the exit, the signal still directed us to turn left.

Kelly chuckled nervously as we drove along. I'm sure her blindness was torturing her even more than usual. She remained a trooper, though.

The route the signals led us on took us back the way we'd come; back towards the hotel. As a matter of fact, the hotel sign was in sight when all hell broke loose. As I slowed for a red light, either the van took control literally or something took control of me. The gas pedal surged downward, the brake pedal refused to respond and the steering wheel suddenly had a mind of its own. I tried moving my right foot from the accelerator to the brake. I tried steering the wheel in the other direction. I tried putting both feet on the brake, but I can't say with any certainty that I did any of it.

All I know is that I watched through eyes that didn't seem to be mine as a car started into the intersection from our right. I wanted to warn them by honking the horn, but the horn wouldn't blow if my hand ever pushed the button.

"Damn it!"

"What's wrong, Jared?"

"We're going to T-bone someone. I can't stop the van. Hang on!" I shouted.

When the other driver saw what was happening and tried taking evasive actions, the hands at the ends of my arms jerked the wheel to compensate. Unable to control my hands, they maneuvered the van like a guided missile. The brakes didn't seem to respond even though I was sure I had both feet on the pedal, pushing as hard as I could. In another second we smashed into the driver's side front fender and door. The violent collision lifted both cars off the ground before they returned to earth with a thud.

Then there was silence.

Chapter Forty Five

Looking to my right, I called out from behind the air bag that pinned me to my seat, "Kelly, are you okay? Talk to me!"

I could see she was shaken, but trying to catch her breath and figure out what the heck had just happened from behind her deployed air bag. The seat belts and air bags had done their jobs effectively keeping both of us safe. Slowly, she shook her head yes to let me know she was alright. "I think I'm okay." She said breathlessly.

"I'll be right back. I'm going to check on whoever's in the car. Stay in the van, I'll come back to get you."

I didn't wait for a response. There was no way she would protest. She was always more concerned about everyone else. That was her nature.

As soon as I jumped out of the van and got a good look at the car I'd hit, I knew it was going to be bad. I'd seen a few accidents in my lifetime and this was the kind where people usually died. The size of our vehicle compared to theirs would only increase that likelihood.

I ran around to the passenger side to try to get to the unconscious person inside. The door was locked so I tried kicking the glass in, but was unable too. I yelled for someone to bring something to break the window. There were several people already running towards us to assist. The first one to get there was a big burly man. He grabbed me and threw me to the ground.

"You ran the red light, you son of a bitch!"

"My brakes failed." I shouted. "Help me get the door open."

"You keep your ass on the ground." He yelled, pointing a finger the size of my arm at me. I then watched as he braced himself before putting his big right foot through the window.

"I had some medical training in the service." I yelled from my position on the ground, not wanting to add to his already hostile feelings towards me.

"Get over here then." He snapped, stepping back from the now opened door.

I did as he said, but when I got close to the bloodied driver hunched over the wheel, I knew there wasn't any helping him. I checked for a pulse anyhow. There wasn't any. I was about to tell the hulk that when someone yelled from behind the car. "Hey! There's a child in the trunk! My God there's a child in the trunk!"

I'd seen that the collision had jarred the trunk open, but never in a million years thought it could happen again.

"There's no helping him." I told the big man. "Let's see about the child."

Someone was already starting to attend to the child by the time we got to the trunk. The big man told the guy to back off and let me in. As I had done, that person did as directed by the big guy.

I stuck my head in the trunk and found it was a little boy of about six or so. He'd been wrapped up in several blankets to conceal him. Fortunately, they had also protected him during the ensuing crash. Getting thrown around during the wreck had moved the blankets away so that he could be seen.

Gingerly, I removed the tape from his little mouth and listened to his chest. He was breathing. That was good. There was no way of telling whether or not the accident had knocked him unconscious, but it didn't appear as though he had suffered any severe cuts or bruises.

In the background, I heard sirens drawing close. Hopefully, someone had called for an ambulance, as well.

As I checked the boy over for lacerations and broken bones, someone yelled the words you never want to hear in an accident. "The engine compartment is on fire! Get out of there!"

My thoughts shot to Kelly in the van and back to the little boy. I could not let anything happen to her. Snatching the boy out of the trunk, I gave him to the big man.

"Take the boy! I think he's okay. I need to get my friend out of the van. She's blind!"

He didn't argument or hesitate. He took the boy and started running for safety while I ran to get Kelly.

"Kelly, unlock the door, quick!" I shouted as I neared the van.

Kelly opened the door and I grabbed her up in my arms out of her seat and began running away from both vehicles.

"What are you doing?" She demanded.

"The car is on fire! It's going to blow!" I answered as I continued running with her in my arms.

"Put me down, Jared. I can run, just lead me."

I did as she asked and we both high tailed it over behind the same truck where the big man had stopped with the little boy. He was just finishing removing the plastic restraints that had the boy handcuffed when we got there and crouched down next to them.

"Do you think we're safe here?" I asked.
He didn't have time to answer.
Boom!

Chapter Forty Six

The reply was immediate. The car's gas tank exploded and we all dropped to the ground. The big man covered the little guy with his body while I shielded Kelly with mine. Pieces of cars started dropping from the sky. Fortunately, none of them hit us. After a couple of seconds of quiet, the big man and I poked our heads over the top of the truck to look at the burning vehicles on the other side before looking at one another.

"You're still in deep shit mister. That's my truck over there all dented up by the debris."

I started to laugh, then stopped when his frown started to turn to anger. I really didn't want to piss him off. "Tell you what. I'll buy you a new one as long as that little guy's all right."

A smile started replacing the scowl on his face. He seemed to like the sound of that. He then nodded with his head for me to look down at the little fella. When I did, I saw his blue eyes were open and he was looking around, not at all in a panic. He'd already figured out he was in good hands.

"What's your name, little guy?" I asked.

"Tommie Moore, Sir." He said all prim and proper like.

Dressed as he was in some sort of school uniform, I figured the boy must have come from money.

"Well Tommie Moore, do you know your parents phone number? I'll call them so they can come and get you. How would that be?"

A broad smile that was missing a couple of front teeth lit up his round little face as I showed him the cell phone I was holding, ready to key in his numbers.

"301-555-1627, Sir."

As I pecked away at the numbers, I said, "My name is Jared, okay?"

He smiled and said, "Okay."

The call was answered on the first ring by a very shaky female voice. I couldn't even begin to imagine what she'd been going through, even with everything we'd been through.

"This is the Moore residence." Her unsteady voice answered, afraid of what she might hear next.

The true enormity of the moment had escaped me till I heard her speak. The sudden lump in my throat caused me to stammer as I struggled to speak. "I...ah...I have some great news for you Ma'am. We've found a little guy named Tommie. Is he your son?"

"Is he all right? Tell me he's all right!" The woman cried.

"He's fine and wants to talk to you. Just a second, here he is."

Before I could get the phone away from my ear, I heard her explode in screams and tears to those around her at the news.

"Mommy, it's me Tommie." He said.

It took a moment for his mother to stop crying from the joy in her heart. Tears instantly filled my eyes and when I looked at the Hulk next to me, he was wiping the tears off his cheeks too.

"I'm fine Mommy, really I am." He said. "These men saved me, Mommy."

I let them talk for a minute before I said. "Let me talk to her, Son."

"Where are you Mrs. Moore?"

"At home in Hagerstown, where did you find our Tommie?"

"We're in Frederick. The Police are just arriving so let me find one of them to talk to you. They can tell you where to come to get your son."

"God bless you. What's your name?"

"That's not important, Ma'am. Wait a sec while I find an officer."

The closest one to us was looking over the still burning wreckage, scratching his chin. I walked a few steps in his direction and motioned for him to come over to where we were.

When he arrived I said, "This is going to sound a little crazy, but you need to tell the woman at the other end of this call where to come to pick up her little boy over there. Whoever the dead person was in that car had evidently kidnapped him. He was in the trunk. That's all I know for sure."

By now, the big man had set the little boy in Kelly's nurturing arms. She tended to him like any woman would have. He put his arms around her feeling extremely safe. By now, she'd figured out what had happened and why we were here. Maybe, just maybe, she was thinking this assignment wasn't so bad, after all.

The officer's eyes showed the same puzzlement that we all shared as he spoke to Tommie's mother. I walked back over to the big man who'd thrown me to the ground earlier. Stretching my hand out to him, I introduced myself. "My name's Jared, Jared Maxwell."

A smile as large as the man himself greeted me with an outstretched hand of his own. "I'm George Wright. Sorry about roughing you up earlier."

"I wouldn't have wanted it any other way, George. You did the right thing. I guess Tommie there, is why my brakes failed. What do you think?"

He looked at me, over at little Tommie and back to me again before working up an answer. "That's one hell of a story, Mister, but it's probably the best one there is. Are you still offering to buy me a new truck?"

"I am if you promise not to tell anyone."

"That's a deal, Mr. Maxwell." He said, reaching out to shake my hand again.

"It's just Jared to my friends, George."

Although, I couldn't see how his smile could get any bigger, it did.

Chapter Forty Seven

The fire department, in their efforts to put out the fire, compounded the damage to our van by using hammers to open the locked side and rear doors. As nasty as it was, the van was the least of my worries right then. I could always buy another one of them.

My next hurdle would be the police and how they would react to my story. They'd be a lot less inclined to believe in divine intervention than George. The problem being of course, it was the truth.

After their on-site questioning, they drug me down to the precinct to have another go at it, obviously not liking my initial version. Kelly sat in the hallway while I repeated my tale, again and again.

I began to wonder if my story was too simple for them or something. My brakes and steering failed. That was it. Someone saw the little guy in the trunk as we tended to the dead driver, so I turned my attention to him. When someone yelled the cars were on fire, we got everyone out of the way, except the dead man.

Unfortunately, the story hit a brick wall when some Geek recalled a recent incident in New York State involving another child found in a truck. His computer and the internet finished me off. As far as they were concerned, no one could be that lucky, no one.

"How do you explain this?" The interrogating officer, Officer Smalls demanded.

I soon found myself repeating my answers to deaf ears. "The brakes failed. Check out the van."

I figured the fire and subsequent explosions would have messed with the front of the van enough to leave a positive conclusion unachievable. Regardless, it would have bought me time. Besides, I had to wonder why they'd even want to charge a man who'd saved two kids' lives in less than a week. On the other hand, I knew the newspaper would have a field day with it. There certainly wasn't any way of connecting me with these scourges of the earth, whoever this last joker was.

As I continued answering his invasive questions, I saw someone take Kelly into another room. That really upset me, but I knew Kelly was a smart cookie and a good poker player. She'd tell them what she wanted and nothing else. Even if she slipped up, what could she say? We had breakfast and God told us to run into a car several miles away? Give me a break.

After more than an hour, I decided I'd had enough. Getting up from the table, I told Smalls. "Arrest me or I'm walking out of here. And just so you know, if you do decide to arrest me my first call will be to the local TV station. It'll make one hell of a story, don't you think? Former vet arrested for saving child from certain death, because police can't do their job."

That seemingly got his attention. Five minutes later, Kelly and I walked out of the station where a news crew had already assembled waiting for us. There was no getting around it this time. Our faces were going to make TV, probably even nationally.

The questions flew at us at an alarming rate with multiple questions being fired simultaneously. After trying to answer several minutes of questions, I finally raised my hand to stop the turmoil and decided to make a statement and not answer any more.

"Thank you all very much for inquiring about our good or bad fortune, as you may see it. When Kelly and I started our vacation less than a week ago, we had no idea that we were going to impact anyone's lives. How could we have known that two young children would be alive today because we just happened to be in the right place at the right time? The heroes here are the children, not us. We thank God that we were able to help them. Thank you, but that's all we have to say. Good day."

In the background, I'd spotted Big George waiving his huge hand to us during the interview. Once I finished my little spiel, I took Kelly's hand. Together, we walked over to him with an entourage of reporters following us, still shouting questions at us.

"We could use a lift." I said.

He smiled that big grin of his. "Thought you might. Follow me." He said, turning to lead us to his slightly abused truck. I helped Kelly up into the cab before climbing in myself. Soon the reporters were dust in the wind, thanks to our new friend.

"Where too?" He asked.

"Wherever your new truck is waiting!" I said.

"You aren't kidding, are you?"

"If nothing else George, I'm true to my word. Besides, it looks like we need a new ride too. Maybe I can get a better deal buying in pairs."

His smile drove us all the way to a Chrysler/Dodge dealership.

"Got one already picked out, do you George?"

"That big ass black one over there caught my eye a few weeks ago. I keep driving by looking at it, but I know I can't afford it, so I never stop."

"Do me a favor. Drive through the lot once so I can see if anything catches my eye."

Kelly elbowed me at my choice of words and grinned.

"Whatever you say." George responded.

No signs flashed at us this time. I didn't necessarily want another van, but we needed room for the massive amount of luggage waiting back at our hotel room.

After we finished our circuit of the lot, we ended up back at the big black dually hemi one ton four by four. What a hunk of metal? Parked next to it to one side was a bronze colored SRT-8 Charger. Except for the luggage problem, that would have been my choice. On the other side of the massive truck was a maroon colored four liter Pacifica. All decked out with chrome wheels, sun roof, leather and all the other bells and whistles, it had an alluring quality about it. As much as I wanted the Charger, the Pacifica was obviously more like what we needed.

Before getting out, I asked George to let me do the talking. As I looked at him, I realized it wouldn't make any difference. The grin on his face was a dead giveaway.

A salesman came strolling up the second we slid out of his truck. "Can I help you folks?" He asked.

"My friend here would like to test drive this truck." I said, pointing at the big black beast.

He looked at George and the truck we rode in on and frowned. "Certainly, would you care to step into our show room so we can gather some information first?"

"No, not really, He wants to drive the truck. If he likes it, I'm going to buy it for him. I'm not spending half the day while you gather information about us that doesn't mean anything."

"I'm sorry Sir, but we have to at least gather insurance information."

Reaching into my hip pocket, I pulled out my billfold. "Here's my insurance card and driver's license. Check with your boss. If that's not good enough, have him come out here."

After the hour plus interrogation and dealing with the press, I wasn't in the mood to deal with car salesmen for the rest of the day. George was going to get his truck. Anything else depended on what kind of service we received.

The salesman reappeared a few minutes later with someone in tow, presumably the manager.

"Hello, my name is Peter Johnson. How can we help you?"

Since the name of the dealership was Johnson Chrysler Dodge, I had to assume I was talking to the main man.

"My name is Jared Maxwell and I want to buy this truck for my friend. He'd like to take a test drive in it first. It's not all that difficult. I've had a trying day and don't want to spend hours screwing around with unnecessary paperwork. I hope there's no problem with any of that."

"Not at all, Sir. Don, here, is just trying to comply with our guidelines to gather information for our files."

"I'm not from around here, so I doubt if I'll be back to buy another vehicle. Can he drive the truck while we talk price?"

"Certainly! Don, get the keys and a plate for Mr. Maxwell's friend. Would you care to follow me inside? We have free soft drinks and coffee."

"Sounds good. Come on Kelly. Let's go have something cold to drink while George, here, takes this monstrosity for a spin."

As we walked away, I turned and winked at George who was looking like a Cheshire cat with his toothy grin stretching from ear to ear. He realized he really was going to get his truck.

Chapter Forty Eight

"I'll have a cola, how about you, Kelly?"

She nodded that a cola would be fine. Soon we were drinking soft drinks and discussing price. The sticker on the truck was thirty nine something. He took six off the top and allowed another five grand for George's truck, mess and all.

I half expected him to say the window sticker was the price since I'd already told him that I was going to buy it. Now that I felt like we were dealing with reasonable people, I pushed the envelope a little further.

"What kind of package deal will you give me on the truck and the Pacifica that's parked next to it?" I said stopping to point out to where the truck had been parked. Following my finger's point outside, I realized the truck was long gone. "Or at least where it was parked?" I finished.

I chuckled and so did Mr. Johnson.

"Let me see what we have on that. I'll be back in a minute."

"Are we going to buy another vehicle?" Kelly asked.

"I'm afraid the van is down for the count, Kiddo. Even if they can fix it, which is questionable, it'll be down for at least two or three weeks. And there's no telling how soon someone can get the parts or get it in to work on."

Mr. Johnson came in seconds later and started talking before he sat down. "The Pacifica lists out at thirty six five. Because you're considering buying two vehicles today, we could let it go for,..." he paused to think or make me believe he was, "say thirty one."

"After George gets back, we'll take care of him. Then Kelly and I will take the Pacifica for a spin. How's that?"

"Sounds like a plan, Mr. Maxwell. Just so you know, these are special prices that I wouldn't give to just anyone. I know about your incident this morning and about the little girl in New York. If I could do more, believe me I would."

Now I felt a little embarrassed. "Your prices seem more than fair, Sir. How do you know about it, already?"

He smiled one of those grins that said I got-cha as he picked up the remote to a nearby TV and turned it on. Changing stations a couple of times; he found one with our faces plastered across the screen. "It's the news. What can I say?"

Wonderful, this wasn't even the local news. Fleeting thoughts passed through my mind about the two deaths and our close proximity to both. Close, hell, we were there! Like the Geek back at the police station, it wouldn't take someone very long to put it all together after seeing our faces broadcast across the air waves.

Saving the kids' lives was one thing. Being that close to three deaths was quite another. I figured my goose was cooked for sure. The law was going to get involved sooner or later. Maybe, I should just wait for the van and rent a car, after all. They sure as heck weren't going to let me leave town any time soon.

Nervously I smiled at Mr. Johnson, Peter, as he asked to be called.

"Kelly, we're on the news, nationally."

I couldn't see Kelly's eyes through her dark sunglasses, but I could tell by the way her eyebrows moved what she was thinking. She leaned over to whisper in my ear. "Maybe we should fly home...right now!" She knew all too well, we couldn't.

I looked up at Peter with a smile that eluded him. In order to cover up my own thoughts, I said. "Kelly said she wants to take the Pacifica for a ride while George is taking his."

"Of course! Let me have someone bring it around for you."

After he left the office, Kelly snickered. "That was pretty slick. Remind me not to play poker with you." It was an obvious rebuttal at one of my earlier jabs.

"Yeah, right!" I said.

Five minutes later, we rolled out of the dealership. A block down the street, we passed George who was returning to the car-lot. I'd told Peter to start on the paperwork when he got back and that I would write a check for the total, whatever that ended up being, when we got back.

George didn't see us as he drove past. His smile was probably blocking his own view. The sight of it filling the cab, made me smile too. I told Kelly about it. She just giggled.

Five blocks down, we turned onto a bumpy side street to check out the ride on not so smooth main streets. Next, we found a ramp to the interstate where I could push on the big Jeep transplant under the hood. It rode marvelously, firm but not harsh, much like a sports car.

"What do you think, Kelly? Do you like it?"

"Does it have a sun roof?"

With a grin, I reached for and pushed the power button that slid the roof back. The fresh air quickly filled the cabin to answer her question.

"It's got a CD player?"

"6 disc in dash, heated leather seats, navigational system and who knows what else is back there."

"I'll take it." She giggled. Though not quite as big, mind you as George's, her smile was radiant, none the less.

"Okay, but try to control your exuberance." I teased.

"Why? The price is already set."

"That's true. All right, you got me."

When we returned to the dealership, George was sitting at a desk signing away on the necessary paperwork. His grin hadn't shrunk any that I could tell.

Peter met us as we entered the showroom. Kelly's smile was still giving away her satisfaction. Out of sheer orneriness, I said. "Mind if I take that SRT-8 out for a spin before we commit?"

Peter didn't seem all that surprised, but I could tell by the finger nails cutting into my left arm that Kelly was.

"Certainly, I'll get the keys." Peter said.

"What's that all about?" Kelly demanded, after he'd gone.

"I just have this sudden urge. Why don't you just sit and listen to the TV and I'll take Peter for a ride. I want to see what that thing will do."

"Boys! Do they ever grow up?"

"We hope not." I laughed.

Accepting the situation for what it was, she said. "Fine! Find me a seat and the remote so you can go have your fun. Don't be leaving me here all afternoon though, if you know what's good for you."

"Trust me, Kel."

"Oh brother!" She replied, sporting a grin.

As requested, I found her a seat and the remote. Peter returned a few minutes later with the keys to the Charger that was already parked at the front door.

As he handed them to me, I said. "Want to take a ride?"

He looked out at the car, then at me and smiled. "Sure, why not."

After cinching up the seat belts, I turned the key and sat and listened to the supercharged hemi as it rumbled under the hood letting us know it was ready. Unlike the muscle cars of old, this one was a lion with the mannerisms of a lamb. At least it was until you unleashed all 520 horses that were pent up under the hood, waiting to run wild.

As we left the lot, Peter had me turn west. At the Cowboy Rodger's Restaurant, he had me turn south. A little over a mile up the road, we came to a t-road.

"Turn right. About a mile ahead there's a half mile stretch of pretty straight road." He said with a wry smile.

My answer was in my eyes. The car's eager anticipation was released moments later by my foot.

Chapter Forty Nine

When Kelly and I finally returned to the hotel that afternoon, there were, as half expected, people waiting for us. Fortunately, Kelly and I had stopped at a fast food joint to eat something after leaving the dealership. She was also still playfully badgering me about my ride in the Charger.

As we pulled in, I could tell right away these weren't police vehicles that awaited our return. Nor did they belong to any sort of news crew. These two large darkly tinted black vehicles belonged to the Feds.

Before coming to a stop, I gave Kelly a quick heads up. We had talked about the eventuality of this happening during our late lunch sitting at a plastic table inside the home of the arches, so it didn't come as a complete surprise that they were already here. Our talk also gave us some much needed time to decide on a game plan and a story. Our choices were simple. We could tell them about our divine expedition or play dumb. Obviously we opted for the latter.

Four black suits emerged from the two ominous vehicles before we even got stopped. Two remained next to their vehicles. The other two were quick to greet us as we climbed out of ours.

"Jared Maxwell?" The more elder, slightly balding agent asked.

I smiled. "You know I am."

Flashing his badge, he continued. "I'm Special Agent Higgins from the FBI. This is Special Agent Jacks. Could we speak with you and Ms. Sims?"

"Sure, I don't see why not. See our new wheels, thanks to our latest fiasco?"

Neither agent smiled. Both were wearing their game faces.

"Where would you like to talk?" I asked.

"We've borrowed a conference room inside the hotel. Would you follow us?" Higgins half order, half answered.

"Sure."

Taking Kelly by the hand, we followed Higgins lead while Jacks followed closely behind us. I thought it a bit surprising that they didn't separate the two of us once we entered the hotel. One of their own was already inside, standing guard outside the room that they led us to. Once inside the conference slash interrogation room, they asked us to take a seat at a large round table across from which they already had paperwork strewn. They then proceeded to ask their poignant questions. As expected, they'd managed to place us at the restaurant the night before where Godfrey was found.

That was a no brainer. After all, we did have reservations and I paid with a credit card. That was a tough one to figure out. When they asked about our dinner, I went ahead and told them what we'd ordered.

Their questions, though on track, made little sense, unless of course you believed in the supernatural, which of course we did and doubted if they did. Whatever their goal, we walked through their questions one by one, tip toeing very carefully around sensitive issues.

After quite a few carefully asked questions designed to trip us up or at least tie us to all the incidents of the past several days, I laughed out loud in the middle of their questioning concerning our collision this morning. Before I did, I squeezed Kelly's hand to prepare her for what I was about to say.

"You know," I hesitated in order to get their full attention, "I think you boys have us dead to rights. The real truth is God has been leading us on a divine mission. This morning, he took control of the van, caused the brakes to fail and then drove us smack dab into that car to free that young child."

Kelly started giggling as it came ripping out of my mouth.

"I believe that just as I believe he led us to that little girl up in New York State. So if you need to question someone, maybe you should put a call into God for answers. You're about as likely to get to the bottom of this situation that way as you are here questioning us."

"We're just trying to tie up loose ends, Mr. Maxwell." Higgins snarled, not caring much for my interruption or my humor.

"The loose ends as I see them are;

"One, I knew when reservations were made a week earlier that a little girl would be locked inside someone's trunk in New York State twenty some miles off the beaten path, at a place I've never been before.

"Two, I stumbled onto the wrong floor at what 3 or 5 in the morning when I went to get a book out of the van for Kelly at the same hotel where someone was, as I heard it, scared to death. From what I was told, screams weren't heard until hours after I returned to my floor.

"Three, Another goon is turned into a scared stiff last night and I'm supposed to know when I left Niagara Falls, to get away from publicity there, that he would be eating at the same restaurant, at the same time as us. By the way, exactly how does one scare someone to death, anyhow? Besides, you do know we'd made reservations there, as well, don't you?

"And number 4, I'm supposed to know that when we left breakfast this morning that a kidnapper would be at a particular intersection with a little boy in his truck so I could ram my van into his car in order to save the child's life.

"I have to ask, Agent Higgins, did you find my crystal ball in the van because I can't find it anywhere? I must have misplaced it. And, for the life of me, I can't remember where we are supposed to go next?"

Higgins and Jacks looked at one another then back at Kelly and me. She was laughing hysterically by now and I was snickering heartily myself. By now, even they were wearing broken smiles.

"It's pretty hard to find fault in your story when you put it that way." Higgins remarked.

"How else would you care to put it? I take it you didn't find my crystal ball?" I asked mockingly.

"No, and we can't make any sense of any of it. But the question remains, how could anyone be involved in this many incidents, in such a short period of time and not be involved somehow?"

"As I'm sure you know, Kelly's husband Derek was killed by scum who is still roaming the earth a free man."

They nodded that they were aware of the facts.

"There might come a day when I'll be under your scrutiny for his demise. Sometimes, though, you just can't make sense out of everything. This apparently is one of those times."

"For now, that's how we'll log this, unless new facts come to light." Higgins said, still shaking his head.

"When did that creep kidnap the little boy, anyhow? We hadn't even heard anything about it on the radio and we haven't turned the TV on since we got here yesterday afternoon. And who was the bum, anyhow?" I asked.

Jacks responded first with the facts. "Young Mr. Moore was abducted on his way home from school yesterday. A suspected sex offender named Chris Harmon was the dead man behind the wheel. The boy and his parents have asked that you and Ms. Sims stop by the hospital here in Frederick to see them, if possible."

"We'd be delighted. It's not every day you get to save a child's life."

Kelly instantly started snickering again, which got everyone doing the same.

Just that quickly, the interrogation that I would have expected to last for hours was over. Paper work got shuffled back inside their briefcase as we finished up with a few minutes of lighter conversation about our vacation thus far, which got us all laughing, again.

When we got up to leave, Special Agent Higgins opened the door for us. As I shook hands with him, he grinned before making the remark he'd created in his mind for that very moment. "Let us know where we need to go from here in case you have any further happenings." In his other hand was a business card.

I just smiled, as did Kelly. Maybe he had a feeling that there really was more to this story than he could imagine. With any luck, this was our last calling. I wasn't ready to go out on a limb and make a prediction either way at that point. It was quite possible that we would see him again, maybe even soon. Who knew? If so, the next time would be even harder to explain.

During our small talk, they had given us directions to the hospital where little Tommie was. That would be the first thing on our agenda, right after we took a nap and had a real dinner.

As we walked to our room, Kelly slugged me.

"What was that for?" I asked.

"What in the world were you thinking, telling them the truth?"

"It's the only thing that made any sense. Besides, isn't that what our parents taught us to do?"

"Oh brother! When did you ever listen to either of our parents?"

"Now that really hurts. How can you say such a thing to your bestest friend and partner?"

"Oh, come on before we get into any more trouble."

Naturally, I laughed, which of course got me clobbered again.

Chapter Fifty

Two things grabbed my attention as we entered the hotel room. One; the phone light was blinking. We had a message. The second was the Ark, in all its glory, was sitting on my bed. It was, as before, all in one piece, with no hint of having ever been blown to pieces or burned in any way. Obviously, we weren't quite finished yet.

Rolling my eyes, I sighed and decided not to tell Kelly about it just now. I was just too tired to go into another question and answer period. It could wait until after our naps. Instead I said, walking to the phone, still eyeing the box. "We have a message. I'll see who called."

Pressing the button, the speakerphone replayed our message aloud. It was the Moore's, leaving their cell number and asking us to call. I jotted the number down on the pad that was sitting there.

Kelly barely offered any acknowledgement. She was beat, too. We'd done enough for two days already. I flopped onto the bed after taking off my jeans and draping them over the nearby chair.

Kelly didn't even bother going into the bathroom to drop hers. The sight of her in her little pink bikini underwear was delightful. I fought off the urge to say something smart. Instead, I threw a pillow up over my head to block the view as well as the sun that the curtains couldn't contain. A few minutes later, I was out. More than likely, Kelly was too.

This time, no unset alarm clock sounded to rock us out of our naps. I was the first to awaken nearly an hour later. Using the slits of light protruding through the curtains, I looked over to see Kelly in the next bed, still asleep.

She was such a cutie. Thoughts of her in her panties made me smile and feel a bit ashamed to be thinking of her like that. The more I was around her, though, the more those thoughts seemed to prevail.

I knew if anything was to come of them, she would have to be the initiator. I wouldn't know how to and didn't want to jeopardize our lifelong friendship. As a man, I couldn't even think of how to ask her how she felt. Like most men, I suppose, I'm just a twit when it comes to affairs of the heart and talking about them in general.

Ten minutes went by before her breathing changed, announcing that she was beginning to awaken. Moments later, she opened her eyes. Though she couldn't see, what she heard told her more than I could understand.

"How long have you been watching me sleep?" She asked.

"How could you possibly know that?"

"If I told you, I'd have to kill you." She said with a grin.

"Funny girl. Just a couple of minutes, is all."

"Jared, would you lie next to me and hold me?"

Unsure of what to say or how to respond, I slowly got out of my bed, walked to hers and lay on top of the covers next to her. Putting my arm around her neck, she moved her head to rest atop my chest as her arm reached across me. The warmth of her body that close to me felt wonderfully good. Minutes passed as we inhaled each others spent air and relaxed in the silence.

I should have seen it coming, I suppose, but I didn't. At least I don't think I did. Kelly's head turned towards me and soon our lips met. Fire flew through me as I fought to get away, but I couldn't find the strength or the desire to do so. The kiss was everything I'd never thought a kiss could be. I couldn't have dreamed anything so absorbing or pure.

When the kiss ended, I didn't know what to say or do. As for her, she simply laid her head back on my chest as if she'd done it a million times.

"Did you like that, Jared?"

After a moment to clear my throat, I said. "I'd be lying if I said I didn't."

"I should be mad at you. You know that, don't you?"

Talk about confused! Why should she be mad at me, I thought? She was the one who kissed me. Instead of trying to figure it out, I gave up and said. "I confess. I don't have a clue."

"That's the problem, Jared Maxwell. You never had a clue that I've wanted to kiss you and be held in your arms like this for, well since we were kids. You've always been so clueless. Then you brought Derek home and I had to love both of you. He always knew how I felt. Why were you always so darned blind?"

I started to tear up at hearing the confessions of this wonderful person who I was too blind to see, when she was the one without her sight and could see everything. She was right. I really was a fool.

"Derry knew?"

"Yes, you big oaf. He knew I loved him, but he always knew how I felt about you, too. He used to tease me, because of how you lit up my life whenever you came around as much as he did."

"I'm sorry, Kelly."

"Don't be Jared. In a way, you did me a great favor. You allowed me the honor of loving two men in my life. Perhaps the best is yet to come."

Now I really was a mess. A few tears ran down my face and fell into her hair. Naturally, Kelly, who never missed anything, felt them and raised her head to look at me with eyes that actually looked at me even though I knew it didn't register in her brain, for some unknown reason. With her thumb, she wiped away the tears from my cheeks and kissed me again.

"I love you, Jared Maxwell. For a hundred years, I've waited to say those words."

"I've loved you forever too."

"Why didn't you ever tell me before? Was it because you're white and I'm not?"

"What? You're kidding me right?"

"Well then, why?" She asked as she put her head back on my chest.

"Because I'm an idiot, I suppose, but I've always held myself to blame for you losing your sight. If I hadn't been giving you such a rough time that morning for running late, you wouldn't have fallen. I've hated myself for years. I still do."

As if I wasn't already a mess, I started trembling at hearing the words I'd never had the courage to say out loud, even to myself.

Raising up and clutching my face with both hands, she looked at me with those all-knowing unseeing eyes and said. "Oh, Jared! Dear Jared. It wasn't your fault. You know darned well it was me who left those shoes on the top step of the staircase. I'd forgotten they were there. That's why I fell. It wasn't because of you."

"But if I hadn't been yelling at you, you would have remembered they were there and you wouldn't have fallen."

"Silly Boy. I've never held you to blame. I accepted it as the life God had written for me. I've learned so much about myself and people in general that I never would have discovered if I hadn't lost my sight."

"You really are incredible." I whispered.

"Yes I am and don't you ever forget it!" She said with a snicker.

"You're right. We'll have a great rest of our lives together." I said pulling her close.

More than anything, I just wanted to hold her. Knowing how much time we'd wasted already, I was afraid that I might awaken to find that I was only dreaming the entire thing. But this was no dream. I could feel her heart beating against my chest and through my soul.

Chapter Fifty One

As I held her close, a car door closed outside our window. Normally, it wouldn't have been a big deal, but for some reason I knew this time was different. There was something ominous about the sound that reverberated around in my brain. Rolling Kelly off to the side, I slid off the bed and walked to the window and slid open the drapes to see why. No one was there, but I knew who it was.

"What is it?" Kelly asked.

"We're about to have visitors. Better get dressed." I said, as I walked over to my jeans and slipped them on before going to open the door for our guests.

"Who is it?" She asked, grabbing her jeans and slipping into the bathroom.

I answered her question with my greeting.

"Good evening Agent Higgins, Agent Jacks. Didn't expect to see you quite so soon."

Seeing the surprised looks on their faces from being met before they ever knocked made me grin.

"See us roll in?" Higgins asked.

"No. I was lying in bed."

Behind me, I heard Kelly slide out of the bathroom and take a seat on her bed.

"Then how...?" Jacks started then stopped, realizing he didn't really want to know.

"So what do we owe the pleasure of your visit this time? You find another loose end or did you find my crystal ball?"

Jacks almost smiled, but Higgins remained stoic.

"You may find this humorous, Mr. Maxwell, but the truth is...," he stammered, trying to choose the correct words, but settling on the ones that made sense. "We came to ask a favor of you and Ms. Sims. Do you mind if we come in?"

"A favor? For the FBI? This I gotta hear." I said as I stepped aside to allow them in. I wanted to know what this truck could be hauling.

They walked past me and over to our little table for two, but not before noticing the Ark that was sitting on the bed. Jacks studied it for a moment with his eyes before commenting. "That's quite an interesting box. What kind of inscriptions are those?"

I shot a quick glance at Kelly, because I hadn't told her about it yet. She grimaced, but not enough to raise any suspicions from our guests.

"It's a gift from the Loriman's, Molly's parents from up in New York." I said as I took a seat on the bed. "Mostly Arabic, I think."

It was a lie, but it appeased him. Neither of them wasted any further time with niceties as Jacks took the reins for whatever this meeting was about.

"This is going to sound a bit odd..." He said stopping short, seemingly unsure how to proceed.

I interrupted his pause. "I like it already, I think."

"AHHHMMM." He tried clearing his throat. "We have a case we've been working for several years and were hoping you'd take a look at it for us. Perhaps you can shed some light on it."

You could have knocked me over with a feather. I'm not sure who was more stupefied at this point, Kelly, them or me. The immediate question streaking through my mind was, "Were they trying to trick me into implicating myself in something or what?"

'Good luck with that.' I thought.

Closing my eyes and shaking my head trying to rattle some sense into what I'd just heard just put off the inevitable. After several seconds of silence, I drummed up enough courage to ask the obvious.

"What in the world makes you think we could possibly help you? I'm a brand new lucky ass millionaire, a veteran turned machinist who bowls pretty well. Kelly is blind and has the knack of being able to see what others can't. How could any of that possibly help the FBI?"

The two agents looked at one another before looking back at me.

"When you put it that way, it sounds even more preposterous than it did when we discussed the idea ourselves. Still, we'd like you to listen to what we have to say with an open mind." Higgins said.

"Well, let the dog hunt!" I said.

"What?" Jacks asked.

"Just spit it out. What do you want?"

From the briefcase that had been hanging from his shoulder, Jacks produced a folder. He handed it to Higgins who flopped it open on the table in front of me like I was supposed to make sense of it or something.

Though I glanced at it, it might just as well been in Greek. "Yeah? So?"

"Can we trust you not to repeat any of this?" Jacks asked.

"As long as it doesn't get me in any trouble." I said, nodding my head yes.

Higgins took charge of the conversation this time. "As Agent Jacks said, this is a case we've been working for some time. There's a serial killer out there who kidnaps young boys in the northeastern part of the country and kills them after four days. He doesn't strike very often so we've been unable to learn much about him. He abducted a little boy two days ago outside of Boston."

To say I stopped to gulp would be a gross understatement. What were they asking of us, to help find this boy before it was too late? I closed my eyes again, trying to sort out the questions from the facts. They patiently waited as my synapses misfired thoughts around in my brain.

Finally, I said. "If I knew how I could possibly help you, believe me when I say I'd be glad to, but you're barking up the wrong tree here. What makes you think we could possibly help?"

Higgins reached over and flipped the page to the next one.

Tears welled up in my eyes and rage grew in my gut at what the pictures revealed.

After several seconds, I pushed the pictures away and tried clearing the lump that had hold of my throat. "Aaaahhhem! I didn't say you didn't have my attention. I just don't know how in the hell we can possibly help."

Recognizing the sudden strain and anger in my voice, Kelly quickly came around the bed to sit next to me. I reached out to direct her as she came near. When I did so, my hand was shaking.

"What is it, Jared?"

Choking back tears, I fought to answer her. "They're showing me pictures of four little boys who've been taken by this animal. Three of them are dead and you don't even want to know what else he's done to them."

Even with Kelly next to me, I was fighting implosion. Much like back in the court room months ago, everything I saw was tinged in red. I'd have no compunctions about killing anyone who had done these things to a child. I'd done it decades before and this time was even worse. And I hadn't thought it even possible.

"How do you know these cases are related?" She asked.

"Each time the perp kidnaps a victim; he leaves a good bye note for the parents and makes the boy sign it." Higgins answered.

"God, how insane!" Kelly said, totally appalled.

'You don't even know the half of it.' I thought to myself, looking back at the pictures one last time.

Squeezing my hand, she asked Higgins. "So what is it you want us to do? We still have no idea why you're here."

"We're pushing the envelope to the max, hoping you have some kind of connection that..., well, what can I say, is unexplainable, I guess. This little guy is about out of time and we have no frigging leads." He said.

I fought off the rage that boiled inside by focusing on the empathy I felt for the boys' families. The memories that tried erupting, I knew would control me like they once had if I couldn't keep them at bay.

Looking over at Kelly, she was frowning at the agents, still waiting for a proper response. Not getting what she wanted, she asked the question again. "I repeat, what is it you want from us?"

"Well,...we don't know, exactly. To tell the truth, we received an email from someone in our Boston field office suggesting that we should talk to the two of you about this case. The problem is, we can't verify or even figure out who actually sent us the message."

"Why's that?" I asked.

"They say none of them sent the message and furthermore there is no agent stationed with that name. All we know for sure is that whoever sent it signed his name as Derek."

Chapter Fifty Two

"My God!" Kelly gasped. Her free hand flew up to cover her mouth, realizing what she'd just heard.

I wasn't short on being caught off guard myself. Her other hand gripped mine as we fought the emotions that suddenly gripped us both.

The agents' faces were as stunned as we were at our reactions.

"I take it that means something to you?" They both asked, obviously not connecting their Derek to ours.

It would seem as though we were going to be involved, after all. Now, the problem was figuring out how much information to divulge. Anything was more than likely too much.

"Could the two of you wait outside? Kelly and I need to talk."

"But..." Higgins started.

"Outside now!" My request turned into an order.

The two agents slowly got up and went to the door to let themselves out. I followed and asked them to wait down the hall. I didn't want them snooping around outside our door, listening to our upcoming conversation. Once I was sure they were gone, I closed the door and walked over to where Kelly sat trembling.

"You need to go back to Toledo to your parent's. I'll have them fly you home, while I go with them."

Kelly jumped to her feet. Poking her finger in my chest as she spoke, she said, "You will not be sending me home like some little school girl, Jared Maxwell. I am here with you and I intend to stay here with you. So don't even go there."

Before I could even start to say it, she read my heart and put her finger against my lips. "No buts."

"Alright then, you're agreed we need to go, right?"

"We must."

"Okay then, that's settled, but before we go any further there's something you need to know. This case is different than the others."

"How so?" Kelly asked.

"I can't really say. It just is." The horrific pictures had cracked open a part of my past I remembered far too well, but never wanted to see again. Trouble was, there was no way I could begin to tell Kelly about either.

"That's not an answer Jared."

"That's the best one I have right now. You'll have to trust me on this. So what kind of story should we come up with?" I asked.

"Why do we need to come up any story? They asked for our help, so we will. Have them fly us to wherever the boy was taken and give us a car. They can follow us and we can communicate with them by radio. How much simpler could it be?"

"You're amazing." I said, turning to head for the door.

Kelly grabbed my arm. "Wait Jared. Don't be closing me out. Why didn't you tell me about the box?"

"The Ark was here when we got back to the room. We needed a nap, so I decided to tell you about it afterward. They arrived before I got the chance."

"Why do you think Derek contacted the FBI on this and not just lead us like he has before?" Kelly asked.

"I've kind of wondered about that too. Several answers come to mind. Since we can't be in two places at once, this Godfrey fellow must have required our immediate attention for some reason. There's also the possibility that wherever this is going might be too dangerous for just the two of us to deal with alone."

"You're probably right. Just remember that I love you Jared. Don't hold out on me. I can help if you let me, okay?"

"I know and I'll try." I said, giving her a kiss on the forehead.

Turning around, I headed for the door to call the agents back from their hallway perch. As I walked, I surmised another reason why Derry had brought in the FBI. He'd know that if I got my hands on this piece of dung, his own mother wouldn't recognize him when I was finished with him."

As the two re-entered the room, I pointed to the two chairs they had earlier been in. "Please have seat."

After allowing them time to get situated, I continued. "We'll help, but there are a couple of conditions."

Without waiting for a such as or what kind of, I continued. "Fly us to Boston and take us to wherever the boy was kidnapped. Give us a car with a radio so we can keep in contact with you. You'll have to follow us, but, and this is a big one, no one will be allowed to ride with us after that. That's it and there are no questions that I can answer. Does that about cover everything, Kelly?"

She nodded her confirmation.

The agent's faces were filled with questions, maybe even a little shock as to what had just happened. Before they could muster a question, I added. "Get it Okayed and call us when you're ready to pick us up. We need to throw a few things together. Also, you need to take care of our lodging and make suitable arrangements for our vehicle. I don't want our new car stolen while we're gone. Is there anything else we need to discuss?"

Surprisingly, Higgins had an answer this time. "Can you be ready in twenty minutes?"

"Give us five." Kelly responded.

"Good! We'll wait in the hallway." Higgins said.

At least we didn't have to wait on any red tape. It was a go. In less than thirty minutes we boarded a small jet outside of Frederick. By nine o'clock we arrived in Boston. We had packed lightly. Other than a few bathroom necessities, the Ark was the only thing we took in the butt bag.

There was no time to waste, because we were under the time frame set by the pervert. Even with escort, it took almost another hour to arrive at the abduction site.

During the plane ride, Higgins and Jacks briefed us on what to expect and how to operate the radio. We were totally shocked that they didn't give us any static about our conditions. They did however set a few guide lines of their own that we needed to follow.

Five minutes after arriving at the sight, we sat alone in a black government vehicle awaiting directions. The Ark sat on the console between us. Higgins and Jacks had both looked at it inquisitively when I took it out of the bag and placed it between Kelly and me, but neither offered any comment. They must have correctly assumed it was one of those questions that I would not answer and it had not been a gift from the Loriman's. Kelly and I weren't 100% sure we needed it, but we also knew we couldn't just press On Star to ask for directions.

Our trailing agents were impatient and called several times as we waited for our sign from above. Kelly took charge of the radio and told them, "Keep off the air. We'll roll when we're ready."

Suddenly, the left turn signal blinked. I slipped the gear shifter into drive and the caravan started rolling with no one down here, especially the leader knowing where we were headed. One thing was for sure, the chase was on.

Chapter Fifty Three

Within minutes, our procession was on I-93 headed north out of Boston. The black convoy was like a pack of blood hounds contently following a trail that couldn't be seen. Those behind us likely hoped the trail didn't run cold. As for Kelly and me, we hoped we didn't run out of time. If the low-life kept to the same timetable as before, we should have a chance. Besides, we hadn't been late yet.

Agent Higgins had ordered me not to exceed 80 mph. Our navigator evidently had higher expectations or needs. Every time I set the cruise at 80 mph, the car ran up to 85. After trying several times to comply with Higgins' orders, I finally gave up and let the car determine the speed we were supposed to go. Though I fully expected a reprimand from Higgins to slow down, none came. For close to three hours we raced northward, waiting for our next directive.

After blowing through New Hampshire and shortly after crossing the border into Vermont, we finally received another heading. With daylight looming on the horizon, the turn signal came on directing us to leave the interstate near St. Johnsbury. Because our gas tank needed fuel, I pulled into a Marathon convenience station at the exit. The three black vehicles that followed all pulled up to open pumps as well. From each, someone jumped out and started filling there tanks. From one of them, someone scurried over to take care of ours.

As the fuel situation was being dealt with, everyone took the opportunity to stretch their legs and empty their bladders. I walked Kelly inside and got something for the two of us to drink while Kelly visited the bathroom with assistance from a female agent.

As I collected two bottles of water, Higgins paid all our bills and asked, "How much further?"

"Your guess is as good as mine. This is the way. That's all I can tell you." I answered with a shrug of my shoulders.

I could tell he wanted to know how I knew in the worst way, but decided against asking. Instead he said, "The roads ahead will be winding, so keep it at a safe speed."

"Gotcha."

As we pulled back out onto the highway, I realized we were on US 2, which is the same road that runs through Toledo and almost past my home. Following it, we headed west on into Vermont. It soon turned into one of those winding roads that took an hour to travel twenty miles the way the crow flies.

Trees and dark shadows lined the road, keeping the turns ahead a secret until we were almost upon them. Another hour passed before the sun actually rose high enough in the sky to be our ally. During that time we'd made several more turns, but the general direction remained the same; west and slightly north. If we'd have been five hundred miles farther south, we'd have looked like a caravan of revenuers with our black government vehicles running through the countryside with quiet resolve.

At ten after eight, we reached our destination. As I followed the signal's instruction to turn right onto a dirt road, the car's engine suddenly died and we rolled quietly to a stop. We weren't out of gas and it wouldn't start up again, so the only logical conclusion was that we were as close as we were supposed to go. Logical would, however, seem to be a bit speculative. Either way, it was up to the pros now.

No more had we stopped than everyone emptied out of their vehicles ready for action. Higgins and Jacks came running up to see what was going on.

I told them what I knew, such as it was. "The best I can tell you is you'd better have your agents scour the area ahead cautiously so you don't spook whoever it is that has the boy."

His looks weren't any more perplexed than they'd been back at the hotel, only more fatigued after our long drive. They'd been awake for over twenty four hours. Adrenaline would have to get them over this last hurdle. Though I could see the questions and skepticism surfacing, he went about his job without voicing them.

"Stay here and for God's sake, don't follow us." Higgins ordered.

"Do you have a backup piece in case he gets past you somehow, for our protection?"

Higgins gave me a stern look, before reaching down to his left leg to produce his Smith and Wesson J Frame back-up piece. "Do you know how to use this?"

I nodded my head in assurance. "I have one just like it at home."

"Okay, well don't follow us." He repeated as he handed it to me.

We watched as twelve agents headed up the dirt road; all carrying their government issued Sig P229's in hand ready for action. We suddenly felt terribly helpless as we leaned against the car, not knowing what they would find. Since we were here at Derek's bequest, we had to expect the best. Whether gun shots would erupt was quite another matter.

While we waited, I flipped open the swing out cylinder of the .38 that Higgins had given me to see where the full chamber was and what kind of ammo it held. I didn't want any surprises if it was needed. Instead of .38's, I noticed it held 357 slugs. That's getting more bang for your buck, I thought. Seeing all five chambers were full and ready for action, I slapped the cylinder closed and stuffed it in my belt.

After nearly ten long minutes of silence, the FBI car radio cracked with static. They had a building and a possible suspect spotted. They were moving in to check it out.

Several seconds later, the radio cackled with shouts that the suspect had spotted them and was on the run. In my ears I heard orders to fire up the car and head back east. That order didn't come from the radio.

"Get in the car." I shouted at Kelly.

"Why?" She asked.

"Just do it." I said a bit sharply as I opened her door before scurrying around the car to jump in the driver's seat. As soon as I was half way in, I reached for and gave the key a twist. The previously dead engine snapped to life with a hearty roar. Throwing the gear selector into drive, I pegged the accelerator. Stones flew out the rear as the cruiser spun around and raced away in the other direction. From the urgent orders echoing in my ears, there was no time to do a modest turn around. By now, orders were filling my head in stereo, only some came from the radio.

"What are you doing?" Kelly demanded.

"I've got orders." I said as I pulled my seat belt into place across my lap.

"I didn't hear anything about us."

"Probably not, but I did." I answered.

"What can I do?" She asked excitedly, finally grasping the situation for what it was.

"Hang on tight! And make sure you're seat belt is fastened tight." I yelled over the scream of the police interceptor engine as it strained to put out the horsepower my foot demanded of it.

After traveling about a quarter mile down the road, I caught a glimpse of a dirt bike and its rider racing through the trees off to our left.

Derry's voice shouted in my ears. "Whatever you do, don't let him cross the road, Jared."

Surveying the road ahead and remembering what I had just been down, I realized the biker's problem was land or rather the lack of it. A large stream was closing in on him quickly. If he got across the road to the other side, no one would ever catch him. My job was to not let that happen.

Over the radio, we heard the words from the agents that we so much wanted to hear. The boy was found and he was still alive. In just a few seconds, I hoped to have news for them too. I knew I'd probably get in trouble for this. But even if I killed the sonofabitch, who'd really care?

The cycle streaked through the woods like a scared cat carrying a wild banshee on its back. Its screaming engine filled the air with eerie echoes that could have come from hell itself. If the wild eyed rider had worn spurs, he'd have likely been kicking the flanks of the beast to make it go faster. As it was, fear and rage drove the two as one.

Our car was obviously quicker on the road than the demon duo running through the trees. In that, I knew I had the tactical advantage. Ahead in the distance, I saw where he needed to cross. I watched the biker as he tried to figure out if he could make it. I slowed the car a little to let him think he could. Once he committed to making a run for the opening he thought he had, I'd have to slam the door closed.

I yelled at Kelly. "Get ready."

"For what?"

"He's going to get a face full of our car."

"Oh God!" She gasped.

Once the biker took the bait and headed for the ditch in an attempt to fly the roadway, I mashed the pedal to the floor. Demanding everything that the super-charged cruiser had, the car obliged and rocketed ahead like a stallion in full gallop pushed maybe even faster by God's own hand.

The cyclist's head flashed back and forth between the car and the trail that he was now committed to. When his head disappeared below the roadway on his run through the ditch, he had to know it was going to be close. When he topped the ditch again, he had to know he didn't have a chance.

Seeing our car sliding to a stop right where he needed to land, hate and anguish filled the face of the beast as the two flew through the air as one. Seeing me smile at him had to really piss him off.

His rear tire almost made it to earth before hitting our car. The front one never did. It smashed against the cruiser's front fender; stopping the bike immediately. As the rider flew through the air, I leapt out of the car grabbing Higgins' back-up piece in my right hand. As I ran, I slipped the safety to off.

Chapter Fifty Four

The rider landed in the ditch beyond the cruiser with a thud. As he struggled to get to his feet, I took a running dive at him from the roadway above. His hand started for something under his jacket. Before he could get to it, I caught him with a full body block that would have made a defensive linebacker proud. My shoulder buried itself into his chest, sending him deep into the soft bank behind him. The heavy impact blew any remaining air out of his lungs like a burst balloon.

My days in the service were a long time past, but my training must have been pretty good. Instinctively, I knew what to do. My knee pounced on his chest and my hand fished for whatever he was trying to grab. A .38 revolver much like Higgins' piece slid out from its resting place, only it was in my hand, not his. Backing away quickly out of reach of any sort of retaliatory action, I checked the safety on his gun before sheathing it in my belt, all the while keeping Higgins' weapon aimed at the little bastard.

As I stood there, the pictures the Agents had shown me back at the hotel began playing in my mind. Those pictures quickly reminded me of a time in Nam when similar rage had overtaken Derry and me. As I slipped off the safety and prepared to pull the trigger, a voice whispered in my ear.

"Don't do it, Jerry! Let it go."

"I don't think I can, Bro." I said, not bothering to look at where he might be.

"Look, if he was supposed to be dead, he would be already. This scourge of the earth needs to go to prison where he can bend over for the big boys there for the rest of his miserable life."

I couldn't deny his logic. Say what you want about men in prison, at least they have a code of ethics that the mealy mouthed wimps who dole out punishment could learn from. Even so, all I could see was a time nearly forty years ago when Derry and I hadn't let it go nor had we looked the other way.

"This isn't any different, Bro. You know it isn't, not really!"

"This is different. That was Nam, Jared. We didn't have a choice back then. We were the choice. Here you have people coming to deal with the situation. All you have to do is to wait for them."

"I don't know if I can." My hand started shaking and tears began to roll down my cheek. "I really don't think I can Derry." As I said it, I slipped the safety off and my finger slid towards the trigger.

"Sure you can, Jared. It's time to let it go. Let it all go." As I listened to his words, I felt a hand touch my right shoulder and another take my gun hand and force the gun barrel down. I turned to see Derry's ghostly figure standing next to me, smiling at me.

"It's time to let it go. Kelly loves you and so do I. Let me take this burden from you so you can enjoy the rest of your life. You've dealt with it long enough."

A sudden calmness came over me as if a bolder had been removed from my back. I looked at the gun in my hand and at the vermin lying in the ditch. My hand quit shaking and I removed my finger from the trigger and reset the safety.

"Okay, Bro. You win this time." As I said it, I realized he was already gone. Taking a moment to take a quick look around, I gathered my thoughts.

"Kelly! Call Higgins and tell him that we have the dirt bag detained about a mile east on the road we came in on." I shouted.

"Are you okay?" She called back.

"I am now." I answered. After I said it, I realized it was the first time in my adult life that I really meant it. "I am now." I repeated softly for my own sake.

The bastard opened his eyes and gasped for breath only to see me standing there looking down at him. He quickly went for his gun again, which obviously wasn't there. He then made a move like he was going to try to make a run for it.

I slipped the safety off Higgins' gun and let a round go that splashed dirt about six inches from his head.

"Don't even think about running or I'll blow a hole in your knee cap, ass hole."

"What was that?" Kelly screamed.

"It's alright, Kelly. The idiot thought about trying to outrun a bullet. I had to change his mind."

"Screw you!" He shouted.

"Oh, it's not me who's gonna get screwed, you Douche-bag." I assured him.

Keeping him in front of me and Higgins gun, I carefully backed up the ditch bank and sat down, hanging both feet over the edge. The 30ish long haired grease-ball offered up several more choice comments that I chose to ignore while we waited for his rescuers to save him. I say rescuers because I knew if it would have been just him and me, it would have already been just me, Derry or no Derry. Obviously that was why he had gotten the FBI involved.

The sound of roaring V-8's soon filled the otherwise peaceful country air. Seconds later, two cars came sliding to a halt next to me, spewing loose stones everywhere. Before anyone could get out of their cars, I laid both guns down on the ground beside me. I half expected someone to yell for me to lie on my belly and put my hands on my head, but no one did.

Higgins was the first one to make it to me while Jacks hurried down into the ditch to get the suspect. Higgins quickly looked the situation over, before turning his attention to me and the two guns lying next to me.

"Sorry about the big dent in your car. I couldn't let him get away."

"I told you to stay put." He barked as he grabbed his own piece off the ground before carefully picking up the extra gun using a rubber glove to protect the prints.

"Actually, you said not to follow you." I replied with a smirk.

"It's not funny." He added.

"If you say so, but letting him get away wouldn't have been very funny either."

"I suppose not. I heard a shot, what was that all about?" He asked, stopping to smell the two gun barrels.

"Your guy down there had ideas of running. I gave him incentive not to."

Higgins looked at me, at the perp, then back at me. "I'm glad you didn't plug him. The paperwork would have been a frigging nightmare."

I laughed before saying. "I couldn't deprive him of all that fun he's gonna have in prison now could I? Those guys really hate child killers. Want to take dibs on how long he lasts before he offs himself or someone does it for him?"

Higgins rolled his eyes, realizing that any further attempt of reprimanding me was going to fall on deaf ears. "Go tend to your girl friend before I change my mind." He snapped.

"How's the little boy back there?"

"My people are taking care of him. It looks like he's going to be okay, thanks to you."

I smiled as I got up and walked over to Kelly who had been standing outside the car door listening to everything. Behind me, Higgins headed down into the ditch where Jacks already had the jerk rolled over onto his stomach in cuffs and reading him his rights.

My footsteps foretold my coming long before I got there. "Are you alright?" she asked.

"I couldn't be better." I assured her as I took her in my arms. It was true too. I hadn't been better in years, probably close to forty.

Chapter Fifty Five

We arrived back in Frederick around 4 PM. Both Higgins and Jacks had accompanied us on the plane. They'd left several of their people behind to wrap up the situation. After identifying the perp from the ditch as his abductor, the boy was taken to the local hospital where he was checked out. He appeared shaken, but otherwise unhurt. He was indeed one lucky little guy.

The FBI had flown the boys' parents to nearby Littleton, New Hampshire in a smallish twin engine plane to be with him. We had boarded the same plane to fly back to Frederick. The Feds had made no mention of our involvement to the parents or the press. For all they knew, this had been purely an FBI operation. The FBI jackets that Higgins had given Kelly and me helped solidify that facade. That was fine by us. Seeing the relieved looks on the parents' faces was more satisfaction than we deserved anyhow.

During our flight across Pennsylvania on the twelve seat plane, Jacks finally asked the question that was killing him. "How did you...?" Was enough to accomplish the question.

How to answer his half question was just as tenuous. I'd spent days, and I guess I could say weeks, trying to come up with an answer that I could actually put to words. None really made any since.

"I don't know. Sometimes I hear voices no one else hears. Sometimes I see things that no one else sees. I can't explain it."

"How about the guys at the hotel and restaurant?" He asked.

A little voice suddenly spoke to me. As I had so many times recently, I felt obliged to do its calling.

"Kelly, give me the box."

She didn't hesitate. I think she even approved of the idea before I knew what it was. Pulling it out of her yellow bag, she handed it to me.

"This is for you." I said, giving the Ark to Agent Jacks. "Maybe you can do more good with this than we can."

He winced at seeing the box from our room again, but reached out to take it without hesitation.

In my ear, a little voice told me to hold the box tightly.

When Jacks hands touched the box too, it was like we were joined as one by it. Immediately, tingling heat flowed through my hands and arms followed by a sharp and sudden release of energy. His body shook at the transfer of power.

For a moment, we looked at each other through the brightness that suddenly surrounded us both. Then, just as quickly, it was gone, as was the heat and tingling from my hands.

"Wow! I think I understand." He whispered as he sat the box on his lap.

"That would make one of us, Agent Jacks, because I certainly do not."

"What do you mean by that?" Higgins quizzed Jacks.

"Didn't you see the light?" Jacks asked.

"Light? There wasn't any light."

Jacks looked at me and grinned. "I see what you mean."

"No, I don't think you do. Not yet anyhow."

Jacks winced, but didn't respond.

When I looked at Kelly, she was smiling, which made me wonder whether she'd seen it all somehow. Though Higgins pressed Jacks for an explanation, it was not forthcoming, at least not in our presence.

When we got to the hotel, our Pacifica was parked in a different spot than when we'd left. Perhaps someone had searched it to find that elusive crystal ball I'd mentioned earlier. Or maybe, just maybe, they'd just been diligent in watching over our possessions.

As we said our farewells to our new, for the lack of a better term, associates, Agent Jacks pulled me aside out of earshot of Higgins.

"So if I have this right, if we get another message from Derek to call you, it'll be all right?"

"I don't foresee that happening, you have the Ark now. But if it does, you'll know what to do. I hope you can put it to good use."

"This Ark, it didn't come from the Loriman's, did it?" He asked.

"No. Only God knows where it really came from." I said.

I could tell by his look that he didn't have a clue what I meant, but I also knew he would. For some reason he felt the urge to hug me as if we were old friends who had just been reunited. Or quite possibly, he realized that we might never see one another again. There was also the possibility that it was Derry's spirit in him wanting to hug me one last time.

Before the two left, I received a solid right hands from both agents in thanks and a reminder to call the Moore's.

"I'm sure they'd love to thank you for getting their little boy back. Your car keys are in the room." Higgins said, as they climbed in their cruiser.

It was a little sad watching them drive away, because it felt like a part of me left with them. Maybe they did carry away more than just the Ark.

"You did good Jared Maxwell." Kelly assured me.

I squeezed her hand as we headed for our room. "No kiddo. We did good. What do you say we find the Moore's number and grab a bite to eat before heading to the hospital? Tomorrow, we'll go shopping for a diamond. We'll treat the rest of our vacation as a pre-wedding honeymoon. What do you say?"

"Oh Jared! Are you sure?"

"I've never been more sure."

Suddenly, my arms were full of this wonderful loving person, who had loved me all her life, and I her. I wasn't about to let anymore life pass by that way.

Everything in our room was like we'd left it, except for the car keys on the dresser. I picked up the paper with the Moore's number on it and we retraced our steps out to the car.

As we walked, I pecked out their number on my cell phone. After two rings, I was talking to Ed Moore, Tommie's father. Tommie was fine and they were delighted that we were stopping by.

Dinner consisted of a quiet stop at a local pizzeria that was on our way. The place was pretty busy, but our little place in the corner was cozy enough for us. As we sat there eating, we were almost like the giddy teenagers we were a lifetime ago when I used to walk her to school and back. In many ways, nothing much had changed after all these years of being together.

I wondered how I'd missed seeing that I'd lit up her life. Silly me. Heaven knows she'd always lit up mine.

After putting away the best part of a large supreme with extra cheese, we paid the bill and went to see Tommie. It was fun introducing Kelly as my long time friend and fiancée. Somehow, the only thing that would sound any more natural would be when I could call her my wife.

We only spent a few minutes with the family. Their true-life horror story was over. What they really needed was time to heal, especially for the little guy. I couldn't imagine the terror he must have felt. Kelly on the other hand, knew only too well, because of her own ordeal with Clinton Hess.

Fortunately, most kids are resilient. I felt Tommie would be no exception. During our short stay, he seemed pretty chipper, considering. His family was well to do, so in that regard there wasn't much we could offer them. We exchanged phone numbers and wished them well before leaving so they could start putting this ordeal behind them.

On our way back to the hotel, I asked Kelly. "Are you going to call your mother and let her in on the news?"

"Oh, she already knows. You probably ought to call your parents though."

"When did you call home?"

"Silly boy. I told her before we left home. As far as that goes, she's probably already called your parents, too. By the time we get home, they'll have the decorations picked out and the church booked."

"You are kidding me, aren't you?"

"Oh Jared, you really are without a clue. Aren't you?"

"I guess I really am. So what is it that you would like to do next? Go home? Go back to the Falls? Or stay here for a few more days?"

"Why don't we check into a classy hotel suite and save Niagara Falls for our real honeymoon? Maybe we can still enjoy some of this vacation that we haven't actually seen much of yet."

"That's true. You really are a special lady."

"And don't you ever forget it!" She teased.

"I won't."

"I know and just so you know, Molly said Derek wants us to be happy together and he loved us both dearly. That's what she whispered to me."

Just like that I knew the first thing I needed to do when we got back to the hotel was tell Kelly about the one thing I had never told anyone. Only Derry ever knew about it, because he was there.

Chapter Fifty Six

As soon as we walked into the room, I said, "Kelly, take a seat. There's something that I need to tell you."

"What is it Jared." Her eyebrows tilting as if she already knew this was going to be painful.

"Remember when Higgins and Jacks asked for our help?"

"Yes."

"I told you this case was different, but that I couldn't tell you how."

"Go on."

"Besides the time limitations there was another reason Derry needed the FBI to be involved this time."

"And what would that be."

"Because he knew I'd go berserk and kill that piece of crap if no one was around to stop me."

"But no one was around when he landed in the ditch and you took his gun away."

"That's where you're wrong. I wasn't alone. Not really. The agents were coming and Derry was there. He talked me out of hurting or killing that man."

"Why would you want to do that?"

"The pictures the agents showed me of what he had done to those other boys took me back to a time when Bro and I were half way around the world in the middle of what we thought was hell. But there came a day when we really did see hell for what it truly was. We'd fought to forget that day the rest of our lives. I know I never have and I doubt if Derry ever really did."

Tears rolled out of my eyes as the scenes from that day played over one more time in my mind, knowing that I needed Kelly to hear the story if I was ever going to really get beyond it.

Kelly took my hand. "I'm here for you, Jared. No matter what happened back then, I'll still love you."

I grimaced at her through my tear laden eyes. "We'll see."

Taking a deep breath, I started telling the story that had played in my mind a million times since it happened and became the nightmare that plagued my life.

"Like a lot of days, Derry and I had been sent out to scout ahead of our patrol that day. While we were out there, we came across signs that some of our own troops had recently passed that way in front of us for some reason. You got good fast at reading sign if you wanted to stay alive over there. We could tell the trail was barely an hour old. That didn't happen very often because patrols were usually sent to designated coordinates for a reason and they were seldom piggy backed by other units.

Because they had cleared the way of booby traps and such, we were able to cover more ground quicker than usual. We were kind of eager to team up with them because there was always safety in numbers. Believe me, over there, you never knew when you might encounter an enemy patrol and need extra help."

I stopped to take a breath and remember.

"Go on."

"We made our way along as quickly as was safe for another half hour or so when all of a sudden there was an explosion ahead of us. Near as we could tell, it was about a click in front of us. That's a little over half a mile. Anyway, seconds later, gunfire erupted. We couldn't decide whether to go back for our own guys or go see if we could help our guys ahead of us. We quickly decided not to wait. Our guys could have been in real trouble. We would have expected them to help us if at all possible.

"When we came to the edge of a small clearing, we saw a small mud hut village standing just inside the tree line on the other side. That's about all you saw over there. Those people had less than nothing. Families pooled their resources just to survive.

"For the most part, the machine gun fire had ceased, but we heard continual screams and an occasional short burst from what sounded like US made BAR's. We made our way around the clearing to come in from behind the little village using the trees as cover. We sure as heck didn't want to walk into an ambush.

"As Derry and I snuck up to the row of huts from the other side, we didn't know what to expect. We thought we were ready for anything, but we sure as hell weren't ready for what we found.

"We watched in horror. What was left of a squad was systematically..."

The sound of the screaming children suddenly echoed in my head and I had to stop.

Kelly squeezed my hand to give me strength to continue.

I pulled my hand from hers, stood and walked over to the sink to wash my face. Looking in the mirror, I wasn't sure if I could do this or not.

A moment later, she was standing behind me with her hand on my shoulder. It's oaky, you can tell me.

It took another minute, but with her help, I composed myself enough to continue.

"They were dragging kids out of their huts or wherever they'd found to hide and shooting them in the dirt paths that ran from shack to shack. From the looks of those already dead, it didn't seem to make any difference how old or what sex they were. Nearly a half dozen kids were already dead, lying on the ground where they'd been shot. Almost twenty adults had already been killed and lying everywhere.

"We watched in horror as one of the wild eyed kids in the unit drug a little four or five year old kid out from under a hut kicking and screaming. He put the kid down and as the kid tried to run away, he let his BAR rip the kid in half then turned to start looking for another victim.

"I looked at Derry. He was looking at me and asking, 'What do we do?'

"Well, I whispered, we sure as hell aren't going to let them keep doing this. I don't give a shit what happened before we got here.

"Before he could say anything I motioned for him to stay put while I circled around to the other side of the hut we were huddled next to. When I got there, I signaled to him that I was going in and to watch my six. We both didn't need to show ourselves. When I stood up, I shouted at our guys and gave them the call sign for the day so they'd know I was an American.

'Get out of here. We have things under control.' The sergeant shouted dragging a terrified little girl out from her hiding place from under some brush.

'Those are just kids. I can't do that.'

'One of the little bastards was booby trapped and killed three of my men. They won't be killing anymore of our guys. He shouted back.'

'Stand down, Sergeant. That's an order!' I told him,

'The hell with your orders!' He shouted. As he did so he pulled the trigger on his machine gun and ripped the little girl to pieces.

"I don't really know what happened next, because the next thing I knew I was standing over him and three other American soldiers who had piled out of nearby shanties where they had been searching for kids. My machine gun was spewing smoke and my clip was empty. When I looked around, Derry was standing next to me. I never looked at his gun so I never knew if he'd ever opened fire or not. As far as I knew, it had been just me.

"When I looked him in the face, he looked at me. He didn't say a word, but with a movement of his head he let me know we needed to head back to our unit. We never spoke of the incident again. For years I saw the faces of those guys every day. Except for the sergeant, they were only nineteen and had probably never even shaved. They should have never been to or seen a place like that."

Kelly face was dripping tears when she took my face in her hands and made me look at her. "You were barely twenty, yourself. You're right, they shouldn't have been there, but they were. A lot of young guys had to grow up fast over there and didn't go off killing kids and families like they did. You and Derek did the right thing."

"There's more. Before we left the village, we collected one dog tag from each of our dead guys. We figured we'd better do that in case the Cong came in and did something to their bodies before we could get a chopper in to remove them. When I got to the kids who'd been blown up by the booby trapped kid, I realized one of them was Bobby Long, a kid I grew up with here in Toledo."

"Oh Jared."

"Who's to say? If I'd been there to see what they 'd seen, maybe I'd have lost it and done the same thing."

"You know darned well you wouldn't have, Jared Maxwell."

"I've asked myself that question nearly everyday since and I'm just not so sure. We did a lot of things during interrogation of captured Vietcong back then that would turn your stomach. Even now, about the time I talk myself into believing I did the right thing, I see Bobby's parents at the grocery store or drive by their old house. It's then that I see us playing ball in their back yard and I have to wonder about it all over again. Just as quickly, I see those other kids' scared faces who just wanted to get back home alive. And they didn't get to because of me."

"Darn it Jared! It's time to quit torturing yourself. Do you really think Derek wouldn't have told me something about it? He had your back. You hadn't been alone over there and you aren't alone now. You have me to lean on now."

"You don't hate me?" I asked with tears streaming down my face.

"Hate you? Hate you? How could I hate you? I love you! No one could hate you for doing the right thing and taking a stand."

Before I could protest, she wrapped her arms around me. "I love you Jared!" She cried with her head buried against chest. "I love you."

Held in her protective arms, I cried too. Nearly fifty years of anguish came pouring out of me till I couldn't cry anymore.

Chapter Fifty Seven

In the morning, a new man emerged from our hotel our room; the old one hopefully gone forever. Between Derry's intervention and my confession to Kelly, the weight of the world seemed to have been lifted from my shoulders. What had happened hadn't changed. Just knowing that someone else knew and didn't condemn me for it seemed to make all the difference. I realized I would probably always see those kids' faces, but now I could accept that what had happened had been forced upon us all. Maybe I'd even quit having those torturous nightmares that had plagued me for as long as I could remember.

After breakfast, we went rock shopping. We also moved our stuff out of the Maryland Vacation Inn and found a lovely suite at the Hampton to occupy, just outside the city in Ft. Detrick. Then for the next several days, we became true tourists without the fear of another mission to be hurried off to. Visiting historic and other notable sights in and around Frederick, we thoroughly enjoyed each other's company.

During our little stay, we even got to go Duckpin bowling. Both of us had a great time doing that and for me it was a blast watching Kelly listen to see if her ball fell in the gutter or knocked any pins over. She even got pretty good at telling me how many pins she had knocked over. I found it even more amazing to be around her all the time now that I realized her true feelings and mine.

Four days later, we headed home. We'd only been on vacation for ten days, but they were the most consuming ten days of our lives. At seven in the morning, after a short stop for breakfast on our way out of town, we hit I-70 and headed west. This time, no unexplained blinkers interrupted our eight hour plus trip back to Ohio.

Kelly, of course, had been right. When I called home, Mom assured me they already knew. She just needed to know what the date was. Which begged the question, why are men always the last to know? As far as the date? It depended on what the church had open. The earliest one available would be our first choice. Not that we were rushing anything, we'd already waited plenty long enough.

Before anything happened, though, we wanted time to speak with Derek's parents, together. We were sure they wouldn't be unhappy with us, but we wanted them to be part of our new lives, almost as if Derek was still there. In many ways, he always would be.

After a long day of driving with only a short stop for a potty break and gas, we pulled into her parent's driveway a little after five. Of course Helen and John were quick to come out to greet us.

As Helen came scurrying up to the car, I greeted her differently than ever before, then braced for my ear pinching.

"Hi Mom."

She reached for my ear, but pulled up short. Tears welled up in her eyes at my new greeting. Instead of pinching my ear, she reached out and put a big bear hug on me like she hadn't seen me in years. John just waited in line behind her to shake my hand and congratulate me. The wink he shot me while he waited his turn, said it was about time.

I'd expected to leave Kelly there while I visited my folks, but Kelly and Helen had already taken care of that situation without my knowledge. Fifteen minutes after we arrived, my parents drove in. Mom got out of the car carrying two pies to go with the food Helen had cooked.

"It's a good thing we didn't take any side trips." I said. "Or you guys would have had a lot of food to eat."

"Just keep it up, Jared, and you'll get that ear pinching yet." Helen said, sporting a smile.

We all laughed, because everyone knew about the running joke that had gone on forever. I knew I'd actually miss it if she ever quit doing it all together.

The family get together wasn't the last surprise of the day. As we ate, some of our closest friends started rolling in. You'd have thought it was a Greek wedding getting started the way it was going.

Fortunately, the entourage of guests stopped arriving after only ten or so. I'm sure the neighbors were happy about that. If it had been a Friday instead of a Wednesday, I'd have hated to be them. We'd have put a serious bottleneck in the addition for several days.

The reality of most people having to work in the morning set in and people showed respect for their need of sleep. By eleven, the guests were gone. My parents had headed home and I helped Helen and John finish cleaning up the place. Kelly sat in the kitchen throwing little quips in as Helen and I sparred with words while we put stuff away.

It wasn't like I'd ever missed out on much of this. We'd always badgered one another all the while Kelly and I grew up. Even when Kelly could see, I helped Helen and Kelly clean up. We'd always had a great time.

At closing time, I felt a bit uncomfortable leaving with Kelly, probably due to my spiritual upbringing I suppose. Neither John nor Helen said anything to make me feel that way. I just felt guilty taking their daughter home from their house even at our age. Wondering where we were actually going was probably as much to blame as anything, since we hadn't discussed it, as yet. Once in the car, Kelly took care of that situation first thing.

"You know, Jared," she said sliding her hand up my leg as I backed the Pacifica out of the driveway. "When we get up tomorrow, we need to decide where we'd like to live, your house, my house or a new house that's all ours. Till then, me casa su casa."

I'd never taken Spanish in high school, but even I knew how that got translated.

Chapter Fifty Eight

As we walked up the steps to Kelly's house, the slight squeeze of her hand in mine sent blood rushing to my brain. I stopped and pulled her close and gave her a warm wet passionate kiss. Running my fingers through her spiky black hair, I looked into those eyes that I knew saw more than I did.

"I really do love you, Kelly."

"I know. Isn't it great?" She whispered in that soft sensual voice that could drive any man crazy.

I picked her up in my arms and carried her up the steps to the front door. It took her a few seconds to unlock the door from this unusual position, but soon we were inside. After she locked the door behind us, I carried her to her bedroom using the city light that penetrated the shears to illuminate my way. When we got to the bedroom, I gently pushed the slightly closed door open with my left foot and carried Kelly to her bed.

As I leaned over to sit her down, something powerful hit me from behind. A sudden searing pain shot through my head and I dropped her. She landed on the bed with a surprised whimper. The driving force of the impact drove my head into Kelly's with a heavy thud. Just as quickly, my knees buckled, forcing me to collapse to the floor.

My first question was, "What the hell was that?" Unfortunately, I knew right away it was the wrong question.

We'd grown complacent during our trip. I'd neglected to check the house out before entering. My biggest surprise of the day was here and it was going to be a bad one.

I didn't know for sure what had hit me, but I sure had a pretty good idea. Whatever Hess had hit me with had done something to my equilibrium. I found myself on the floor on my hands and knees fighting to stay there. It was all I could do to keep from falling flat on my face. I was totally powerless. There were no stars to look through; no black, no gray, just nothing.

Kelly screamed! But as much as I tried, I couldn't move. Every time I went to raise a hand, I started to collapse.

"Please God, don't let this happen to her again." I prayed.

Then there was his voice and a crash as he threw Kelly against the far wall. I heard her hit the pictures that hung there and heard them fall down on top of her.

"Wait there Bitch while I finish up your second man here. Then I'll do you like I did before, only better this time."

Not that I had any doubt, but I was right. It was Clinton Hess. He must have been stalking her parents' home and found out we were back. The fact that I knew what was happening, didn't help any. With no balance or sight, I was helpless. When he hit me, he must have broken my ear drum or something, like he had done to Derry.

From behind, Hess grabbed me by the shirt and threw me across the room. My head hit the wall and I ended up on my back. Screaming and hollering as he did so, he started kicking me in the ribs. I raised my hands in defense, but I still couldn't see him. He grabbed me again and my face hit the floor or his foot several more times. I was so dazed I couldn't tell which.

The pain kept coming and I had no way of stopping it. Muscular control was still non-existent even though panic had long since set in.

A moment later, I felt myself land against what I perceived was the wall. Probably away from where Kelly was, but I couldn't be sure. It could have been the floor next to her for all I knew. I couldn't tell up from down. Then he kicked me in the gut. Now, not only could I not see, I couldn't breathe.

"This must be what happened to Derry." I thought as I fought the fear and waited for control of any kind to return. After a couple of seconds, my eyes cleared, at least partially. Whether seeing could be of any use, was yet to be seen. As my lungs burned and fought for air, I saw Hess standing there in the light of the dimly lit room. He was staring down at me, holding an aluminum ball bat in his right hand and tapping it against his left hand in a show of force, just to let me know how much he was enjoying this.

I still couldn't see Kelly. I was on the floor, half sitting against the wall where Hess had thrown me the last time, still too dazed to even think about getting up.

As I looked up at my soon to be executioner, air started to fill my otherwise burning lungs. I thought I could probably raise my hands to defend against another attack from his foot or the bat, but I knew that would end up being only a token gesture. More than likely that move would only result in my arms being broken. Then, I would be screwed.

Using those few seconds, I tried to compile a plan. What could I possibly do till I had enough strength to fight back? If something didn't happen soon, I knew I would die like Derry had. And then, who knew what kind of torture he'd put Kelly through this time. Her death would probably be even more torturous than mine.

"God help me." I pleaded. In the back of my mind, I wished Derry's spirit was here. Certainly, he'd be able to help.

As Hess moved closer to start using the bat on me, he stepped on the throw rug that protected the wooden floors in Kelly's bedroom. It wasn't much in the way of a plan, but it was something.

With as much strength as I could possibly muster plus a little from above, I reached out and jerked the rug out from under Hess's feet sending him flying backward onto the floor with a thud. It didn't knock him out, but it bought me a few seconds. With time, came the possibility of other ideas or outside intervention. Maybe a neighbor heard Kelly's screams and called the cops. Maybe help was on the way. Maybe it wasn't.

If we could just hold out till sirens filled the night air, Hess would have to flee. If I could just gain more control of my body, I could stand and fight. The common denominator to survival was more time. Ifs were rattling around in my brain, but ideas weren't and neither were the things I needed, strength and balance. At least, they weren't coming nearly as quick as I needed them too.

Chapter Fifty Nine

By now, Hess was back on his feet and if he wasn't ready to kill us before, now he really was really pissed. I thought again of how Bro must have been in this same predicament over a year earlier. If he wasn't able to get the job done, why did I think I could? That said, I certainly wasn't about to give up yet.

As Hess started at me again, I knew I had to protect my hands and arms at all costs. Near me was a small nightstand. I grabbed the drawer handle and pulled it out, spewing its contents across the floor at Hess. At least I had a shield, such as it was. Though it wasn't much, it was buying time. If I could buy enough, I knew I could win.

Hess laughed at my pittance of a shield. I couldn't deny the feebleness of the act and my eyes searched for something better as Hess started whaling away at the drawer with the bat. It took four good blows to blast the drawer into smithereens, but again it had bought me another few seconds. Along with that, came a little more strength. It was also four times that he didn't hit me with that damn bat.

As he raised the bat to finish me off, I realized he'd gotten careless in his battering of the drawer and had gotten too close to me. I lunged at his legs. Using my arms, I tied them together forcing him off balance. My unexpected move knocked the bat from his hands. It went bouncing around on the wooden floor. Its metallic twangs echoed off the walls on the room.

At this point, we both knew that if I got him down to my level, he'd be a dead man. I was bigger than him. Even in my weakened condition, I could break his neck if I could just get to it.

He caught himself somehow, using the bed post or something. I couldn't see what because I had my head buried against his legs where my arms were fighting to bring him down with every fiber of my being. Somehow his lower center of gravity must have helped him stave off my every attempt to get him to the floor, because I just couldn't get the job done.

Still I was alive. I just needed more time, more strength.

I held on for dear life as his fists repeatedly slammed into the back of my head. I knew I couldn't let go. If I did, I'd be dead for sure. Again and again he hit me.

I felt like I could deal with the pain as long as he didn't get hold of that damn bat. As long as that didn't happen, we still had a chance. Over and over he hit me as hard as he could muster, cursing me with every blow.

After nearly a two more minutes of his continual beating of my head and back, I started having trouble keeping his legs together. My grip was loosening and I was being drug across the wooden floor. He must have been trying to get to that danged bat. I knew my fate was in not letting that happen, but I was failing.

We were both fighting for our lives now. My problem was he wasn't hurt. Still, if I could last just a little longer, there was hope no matter how faint. Two minutes ago we were both sure I'd be dead by now.

"Another minute." I prayed. "Another minute is all I need, Lord."

I didn't care where help came from. Maybe Kelly could help bring him down. We could do it together. That's what I needed. That's what I was waiting for.

"Kelly! Help me! I need your help!" I shouted. "Follow my voice! Help me!"

As I said it, I realized there was no way for her to know how she could help. But as I watched and called out, a shadowy figure started to rise up the far wall where Hess had thrown her.

"This way Kelly! Run at my voice! Jump on Hess! Kick, scratch, bite, do anything! Together we can beat him!" I pleaded.

But Kelly didn't come at us. She just stood there. She acted dazed. More than likely she was, but we needed to work together and now while I could still help her.

Hess must have hit her really hard before throwing her against the wall. She probably had a concussion, but that wasn't our problem right now. Hess was.

"Please Kelly!" I begged. "Run at my voice! Help me before it's too late for us both!"

I knew I was losing the fight and fast. With every blow from his fists, my hold loosened a little more. My strength was failing, not building as I had hoped. Without help soon, I would lose the slight grip that I did have. And who knew where that frigging bat was or how close he was to getting it back.

Still, Kelly stood there against the wall, unable or too afraid to move. Without her help, I knew neither one of us would win. Then, all of a sudden, he found something else to hit me with. It must have been the metal lamp that Derry had kept on his night stand. When Hess took a wild swing at my back with it, whatever strength I had left was suddenly gone. In a spasm, my body jerked backward and I landed on my back looking up at my soon to be executioner holding the lamp and leaning over to get the bat back in his hands.

"Last chance Jared." I told myself as I waited for the crushing blow that would send me into the next world to see Derry again, not so much in person. I prepared for the last ditch effort of trying to grab the bat out of his hands when he swung it at me. It would have been nearly impossible if I wasn't hurt. In the state I was in, chances were in the stratosphere.

He tossed the lamp aside as he came nearer with a firm grip on the bat. I listened, but hope like time itself had run out. There were no sirens racing down the street to rescue us. No shouts outside from neighbors coming to our aid. I resigned myself to the fact that life as I knew it was just about to end.

Chapter Sixty

I lay there on the floor, preparing for my last ditch effort to reclaim the life that had only minutes before been so full of hope. My life expectancy now seemed more like that of a male fly after mating, maybe less.

Hess stood above me, poised to wield the bat one last time. Before he took his swing, he had to run off at the mouth one last time. "You don't look so smug down there on the floor do you, Mr. High-and-mighty from the courtroom?"

"No matter what happens to me Hess, you're still a piss ant that needs to be stepped on and sooner or later someone will."

"Maybe so, but it won't be you doing it. Once I'm through with you, I'm going to mess up the bitch you've been banging real bad. Don't feel bad though. I'll give it to her really good one last time before I send her to be with you in hell."

As he lifted the bat to deliver the final blow, another voice called out from out of the nearby darkness. This one was feminine and strong. It was Kelly.

"It won't be him going to hell, Clinton Hess. You're a no good piece of shit." She shouted. "Look at me. I want you to see something."

"What do you want, Bitch?" He shouted, as he turned to find her standing in the faint light emanating through the shear covered window. "I'll get to you in a minute. I'm about done with him."

"That's what you think, ass hole." She sternly replied. "Just so you know; you're the first person I've seen in nearly forty years and I'm the last one you'll ever see. Rot in hell with all the other maggots. And don't forget to tell them who sent you there."

The dim light from over Kelly's shoulder faintly lit up his face and I could see fear well up in Hess's eyes. In the next moment, a small white flash followed by the sound of a small caliber gun echoed throughout the room. Once, then twice, then a third, and a fourth followed. Each time the percussion of the blast moved Hess a little farther away from my position and Kelly's.

Then a fifth and final report rang out from the little .22 that Kelly carried in her purse. The last one hit Hess square in the face. After that, the gun went click..., click..., click... And each time Hess flinched as if he'd been shot yet again. But he'd been shot enough times already. He was dead. It was just a matter of how long he'd stand before death finally brought him to the floor.

His heart was pumping blood out of his body through several extra orifices that normally aren't there. The wooden floor was being covered by the gushing spews.

For several more seconds, Hess stood there trying to make sense out of what had already happened, flinching with each continuing click of her gun. Whether or not he ever figured it out? Who really cares? He finally dropped to the floor in the middle of his own puddle of blood, dead.

Not pulling the trigger any longer after Hess hit the floor, Kelly called out to me from where she stood. "Jared, are you alright?"

"I will be. Are you?"

"Give me a minute. I'll be there to help you."

"Wait there. I'll come to you." I said.

Working my way up the side of the bed, I fought the weakness in my legs to stand. In the distance, sirens finally filled the night air. Figures. The impending necessity was over.

Kelly still stood with her gun pointing at Hess in case he tried rising up. He wasn't going anywhere under his own power. Using the bed as a make-shift crutch, I made my way around it. When I reached her, I took the gun from her hand and tossed it on the bed.

"We're okay now, Kiddo. You did good. He won't hurt anybody ever again."

Her eyes moved from being fixed on him to looking at me. I was amazed. She could really see. It was a miracle delivered by the devil himself.

"It's good to see you again, Jared. You haven't changed a bit."

"Ah jeez. I thought you could see. You're still blind." I snickered.

She started to slug me in the arm, but then thought better of it. I was glad. I hurt too much already. Instead, we laughed and melted into each other's arms as sirens died just outside.

Cars and people flooded the driveway. I suppose I could have let go of her and opened the front door for them, but they knew the combination. Besides, we had insurance to take care of the damage. Right now, holding Kelly was a lot more important.

In the mirror to my left, a shadowy figure caught my attention. It didn't startle me as I would have expected. As I watched, Derry waived a two finger salute to me over his right brow. Evidently, he'd had my back even now. I realized that for Kelly to see again, he couldn't intercede on our behalf. For Kelly's sake, I was glad he hadn't. A tear ran down my cheek as I watched him fade away. I wondered if I would ever see him again. My lips said goodbye as he disappeared.

Kelly helped me onto the bed where we took a seat on its edge to wait for our tardy rescuers to finally deluge the place. After crashing through the front door, they followed my voice back to the bedroom. With flashlight beams breaking the darkness, blue uniforms quickly followed.

"Close your eyes Kelly. The light is gonna hurt."

"Thanks Jared."

"Yeah." I chuckled with a shake of my head. It was I who was thankful.

Before they entered, someone rapped a gun butt against the door and called out. "Who's in there?"

"Jared Maxwell and Kelly Sims. There's a dead man on the floor, but we're okay. There's a light switch just inside the door to the left."

Seconds later, the room swarmed with police. I tried to help shield Kelly's eyes with my hand. The man in charge stood in front of us and asked, "Are you two alright?"

We replied in unison. "We couldn't be better."

Keeping her eyes closed, she grinned and put her head against my shoulder.

Together we had endured and together we would prosper. We'd been given time to make up for what was lost. Sometime, I knew I'd have to tell her about our last visit from Derry.

Thinking of him, my gaze drifted back to the mirror where I had seen him only moments earlier. In the light that now lit up the room, my attention shot to something that was hidden by the darkness. There, sitting on the dresser, was the Ark.

"What the heck! Why isn't that with Agent Jacks?" I silently asked myself.

But as I studied the box from where we sat, I noticed something different about it. Then I realized that it wasn't the box that had accompanied us eastward. For a moment, I sat puzzled. Suddenly, I remembered the rest of my dream from weeks earlier. We hadn't built one Ark. Together, we had built two.

A chill ran down my spine.

Maybe I would see Bro again and sooner than I might have wished.

Coming Soon to Paperback

Made in the USA
Charleston, SC
12 December 2013